henry's end

BESTSELLING AUTHOR
julie a. richman

Julie A. Richman
Text copyright © 2015 Julie A. Richman

This book is a work of fiction. All names, characters, locations and incidents are products of the author's imagination. Any resemblance to actual persons, living or dead, locales or events is entirely coincidental.

Henry's End
Photograph: Scott Hoover/Scott Hoover Photography
Model: David Filipiak
Cover Design: Robin Harper/Wicked by Design
Interior Design/Layout: Deena Rae / E-BookBuilders

other works by julie

For Oliver John,
Because Love is Love
And I have loved you forever
1976 –>

JaP

henry

prologue

Now...

RUNNING THROUGH THE CROWDED TERMINAL, weaving between the clusters of people, Henry Clark quickly glanced down at his watch, "Shit." This was the closest he'd ever cut it to boarding a flight.

Silently, he cursed himself for not leaving Montauk earlier. He knew the ride back to JFK was a long one, and that like southern California, New York City traffic could be unpredictable. He'd just found it so hard to leave everyone, after one of the most amazing weekends of his life, that he'd delayed it to the last possible second, and now he was paying the price.

Clipping the arm of a burly tattooed guy in cargo shorts that were falling off his ass, he looked back over his shoulder and yelled, "Sorry, man," without breaking his stride. *Why did slow people always get in your path when you were rushing?*

He could see his gate. Finally. And the door to the jetway was still open with two people waiting in line. *Yes!*

As he reached the gate, the attendant was scanning the boarding pass of the last passenger. Out of breath, he dug into his pocket and handed the pretty brunette his cellphone so that she could scan his barcode.

"You just made it, Mr. Clark." She handed him back his

phone, smiling.

Jogging down the jetway, he got to the door of the plane. There were two seats still empty in first class. His and the one next to him.

Thank you, Travel Gods.

Henry Clark did an internal high five with himself and breathed a sigh of relief as the flight attendant secured that useless looking little strap across the now closed cabin door and announced that all cellphones needed to be turned off.

No seatmate on his cross-country journey back to southern California was the best thing that had happened to him all day, well, besides not missing the flight. The worst thing that had happened was leaving everyone out in Montauk, and feeling so alone, and lonely, on the nearly three hour drive back to the airport.

The long weekend in New York had been one of the most memorable weekends of his life. It was fast and furious – every second packed with a memory that had his emotions in overdrive. Henry had not felt this connected in a very long time.

Reuniting with old friends, meeting new ones, and the wedding of two people who should have been celebrating their twenty-fifth anniversary and not their wedding day, made for an incredible weekend. And now that it was over, he was exhausted and could feel the blues starting to creep in.

Looking out the window, yet seeing nothing, Henry tried to process the events of the past few days, but his fatigue was preventing his logical left brain from functioning properly. His emotional right brain, which usually stayed put in its snug fitting box, was running rampant like an over-stimulated toddler, stirring feelings far out of his comfort range. *What is it with all these feelings?* He couldn't quite put his finger on it.

Once airborne, the flight attendant placed a Gin & Tonic on the armrest between Henry and the empty seat and provided a steaming wet towel. Unfolding the white square, Henry pressed his face into the scratchy terrycloth and closed his eyes, wondering what it would feel like to be pressing his cheek into the hands of a lover, wanting to feel his face cradled by strong, adoring hands.

What do his hands feel like? he wondered.

Depositing the now cooled towel onto the armrest, Henry picked up his drink, almost immediately feeling the alcohol hit his bloodstream as it burned down the back of his throat.

As he reclined his seat, a snippet of a conversation from the weekend began to gnaw at him, poking him incessantly in the gut and not letting up. Henry finally realized that this was it. This was what was at the core of why he was feeling so out of sorts. It was this.

"I want to sit in a café on Sunday mornings in the West Village, reading the New York Times for hours, with my lover sitting across from me, spend hours planning vacations to places like Bali or the Seychelles, have Schooner and Mia over for a gourmet dinner that we've cooked for them." Mia's friend and business partner, Seth Shapiro, had been passionate in his delivery, speaking from deep in his heart to him, Henry Clark, a virtual stranger, *"That's what I want."*

He had so wanted to confess to Seth, this snarky New York fashion-queen, that he had just eloquently verbalized a dream that was buried deep within his own soul. That he, Henry Ethan Clark, in fact, wanted the exact same thing – although his fantasy probably resided in San Diego and not the West Village. But before he had a chance to articulate his feelings and make a full confession, Seth flitted away, leaving Henry with an ache he never expected to feel. Nah, it wasn't even an ache. He was gutted. Surprisingly eviscerated.

Damn you, Seth Shapiro. I didn't even know I wanted those things anymore.

But seeing his old friends, Schooner and Mia, who'd been apart for twenty-four years, joined together, finally; watching them attain a dream that was born in their hearts when they were just teens made Henry realize that he wanted it, too. He wanted the dream. Where was his fairytale ending? He snickered at his pun.

And damn you, Seth. Just damn you for perfectly verbalizing my dream. That was my dream. How did you know it? You just freaking met me. How did you know my dream? How did you know a dream that even I didn't know was there anymore? At least not until you said it. I thought it was gone long ago. And how did you know it down to the minutest of details? Bali? The Seychelles? How could you possibly know that?

And now I don't know how I'm going to live without it.

Henry slowly let out a lungful of air and shook his head. At least he had the new job in which he could bury himself. There was still so much to learn. So much to come up to speed on – and fast. A month ago, his friend Schooner had handed him a lot of responsibility. Carte blanche. And he was going to sink his teeth in and make it work like a well-oiled machine. He'd make sure that his old buddy always felt confident that he was the right choice to head up the west coast operations of his fitness empire.

And the rest, well, he was just going to try to bury that. That should be easy enough. It wasn't like he had never done it before.

But now that it was out there in the universe, he wondered if he really could bury it. How was he going to live without the dream?

And he had this odd, sneaking suspicion that he didn't know how he was going to live without him.

Then...

ENRY CLARK LIKED MEN IN uniform. He never spent too much time analyzing why, he just did. A good looking cop or firefighter was an open invitation to have to rearrange his twitching junk. Kick that up a notch to military, and it was an instant hard-on. If said military was brass, his cock literally wept. Strong, in charge, cocky men were always Henry's weakness.

On more than one occasion, Henry actually sped up when he drove past a cop and it became a personal challenge to see how often he could "talk" his way out of a ticket. Well, he wasn't quite talking, but he was using his mouth. His close rate, as he liked to refer to it, was in excess of forty-five percent.

Repping heart drugs to cardiologists for one of the big Pharma companies was his first job out of college. It didn't take long to start enjoying the freedom of being on the road and being in different places, meeting new people, every day.

Tall, lean and ginger-haired with a strong, square jaw and eyes that appeared violet in the right light, the receptionists in the doctors' offices loved Henry's visits. His slow, sweet smile and laid back demeanor made him an instant favorite with office staffs and, in turn, a top performer for his company.

With his first commission checks deposited in his newly

established savings account, Henry made his way to Nordstrom and was quickly schooled by an openly gay, and marginally hot, salesman on the fine art of dressing for success. He finished off his look with a few days of auburn stubble against his fair complexion, making the blue in his eyes pop, and that was the pièce de résistance that had both men and women alike turning their heads when Henry Clark entered a room. A jeans and tee-shirt guy at heart, he was not used to the attention, either from men or women, and it initially took him out of his comfort zone.

It wasn't long before he discovered that a wink and a shoulder squeeze to the receptionist or office manager got him the closed door meeting he sought with even the most elusive of cardiac surgeons. Henry was quick to learn that hot doctors kind of did it for him, with their cocky confidence and overt God complexes. Surgical scrubs and white lab coats were quasi uniform-like, and he soon realized that arrogant cardiac surgeons were almost impossible to resist. And they weren't used to being resisted. Their professions demanded they be the ultimate control freak, which provided the perfect top to Henry's preferred bottom. Like military officers, cardiac surgeons invariably made Henry Clark's cock literally moist with desire.

An outgoing child, he was only nine when his first sexual encounter occurred. His mother's cousin, Iris, had come to live with them and babysat for Henry and his little sister, Emmy, while his mother, a single mom working two and often three jobs, was at work.

Cousin Iris was a sensual bottle-blonde with a perfect round ass and nipples that always stood at attention. Her weaknesses included tight, low-cut dresses, come-fuck-me heels in bright colors, bikers and cocaine. Bikers with cocaine were the ultimate catch.

Jimmy Blauvelt fit the bill. Big, burly, and tatted, he could disarm anyone with his blue-eyed gaze and surprisingly dimpled smile. Unlike the others, he stuck around for a few months and Iris was sure he was 'the one'. What Henry's older cousin wasn't aware of was the nightly ritual that began when Jimmy volunteered to help Henry with his homework and put him to bed, while Iris tended to Emmy.

Book smarts was not Jimmy's forte, but he was a fucking brain surgeon when it came to street smarts and survival. The only thing Jimmy was schooling young Henry in was the fine art of the blow job, both giving and getting, and eventually penetration.

"I think we have something in common," he'd made Henry feel like he was taking him into his confidence. "I like boys and I think you do, too."

Years later Henry admitted, for the first time, to his college friends Schooner, Mia and Rosie, what had occurred. While his friends were devastated hearing of the molestation, Henry tried to make them understand that it was OK. That he'd actually liked it.

He loved when men more powerful than he took control of his body. Men using him for their pleasure was actually a turn-on for Henry Clark. He knew that not everyone would understand that, but that was just how he was wired.

When Jimmy finally left Iris, a depressed Henry spent months daydreaming that the biker would show up late one night, come through his bedroom window and take him – both physically and far away. He wanted Jimmy to tell him that he would be his forever and together they'd explore the country, meeting up with other bikers and he'd be Jimmy's or whoever Jimmy wanted him to be with. The thought of doing whatever Jimmy wanted to make him happy was all young Henry could dream about.

Now, thirteen years later, and fresh out of college, Henry loved being pursued by powerful men. Or at least he did in the moment. Sex behind locked doors with men that could never be his was the ultimate aphrodisiac. It was hot, forbidden and furious. Feeling a surgeon come up behind him and stand too close, while nonchalantly asking Henry to come into his office, was the consummate thrill. It was always the same for Henry. He'd feel his breath shallow and his balls tighten at the thought of what was going to come next.

Each doctor was different. Henry's favorite was in his late forties with a very reserved personality; multiple pictures of his perfect blonde wife and athletic children graced his bookshelves. Their encounters were always the same. He'd silently push Henry over his immaculate desk. He was there for the doctor's pleasure and even as his bottom, Henry felt powerful.

I T WAS A TUESDAY MORNING when Henry was called into the regional Vice President's office for an unscheduled, closed-door chat. The request made him curious, but not concerned.

Still a top producer after four years, Henry was loved by senior management and his female coworkers, but generally snubbed by his male counterparts. He was never quite sure if it was because he kicked their asses in sales, or if it was because he was gay, but ventured it was most likely a combination of the two.

Sitting down across the desk from Rick Powell, Henry couldn't help but notice Rick's affected air of success, right down to the Cole-Haan loafers. *He looks like a mannequin,* Henry mused. To the untrained eye, he looked really put together, but to the queer eye, his dress was akin to Garanimals, where you match up the numbers to create a complete coordinated outfit. Henry wanted to coach him on breaking up his head-to-toe uni-designer look with pieces that gave him personality, but that was assuming he actually had one. It was at that moment he realized he wanted to zuzh him up a bit and had to stifle a laugh at the thought of Rick actually allowing him to zuzh him. The guy was the definition of straight – pure vanilla straight.

"Another great month," Rick was nodding at Henry.

"Not complaining." Henry met his gaze.

"You've done an amazing job of building Orange County and

maintaining it as a top five territory nationally," Rick paused. "This isn't common knowledge yet, but Monica's told me that she's not coming back after the baby's born."

"Really?" Henry was genuinely surprised. Monica had her territory rocking and was making a boatload of money.

"I was surprised, too." Sitting back in his chair, Rick stretched, his hands going to the back of his head. "So, the decision I'm left with is do I replace her or not?"

"Would you carve up the San Diego territory if you don't bring on someone new?" Henry was now sitting forward in his chair, a panther ready to spring.

"Well, if you don't want the whole territory…" Rick's voice trailed off as a sly smile appeared.

"No," Henry was shaking his head, his strawberry blonde hair cascading down his forehead, "I want every last inch." His smile was now as sly as Rick's.

"I thought you might," Rick was openly smirking. "It's always been a great producing territory, but I have the feeling 'We ain't seen nothin' yet'."

"I'll try working my magic." Henry's brain was already spinning off; Navy, Marines, Coast Guard, Camp Pendleton's Naval Hospital, Naval Air Command, Point Loma. His semi was hardening with each military facility his mind clicked off. San Diego, for a gay man who loved men in uniform, was paradise by the sea.

"Although this is a very lucrative territory, I think you could increase revenues by at least sixty percent. We know the amount of time you're going to have to invest to yield that growth, so the last thing we want to see is your time being eaten up commuting and sitting in traffic. So work with our relocation staff in HR to find a furnished apartment. I've gotten a budget of $750/month approved, and this way it will make splitting your time more productive."

Henry nodded, "Sounds great, Rick. Thank you for this opportunity." He hoped he didn't seem less than enthusiastic, but the blood from his brain had long sojourned south and he was no longer sporting merely a semi.

Henry was thankful for his suit jacket.

As he headed down to HR, he knew exactly where he was going to tell them to look for a place for him. Hillcrest. San Diego's gay mecca was the neighborhood of his dreams, just as San Diego, with its proliferation of military bases and hot military men, was the city of his dreams.

Thank you, Monica. Enjoy being a mommy. Maybe now I'll meet the man of my dreams.

Sailors and Airmen and Marines… Oh my!

S AN DIEGO'S GAY NIGHTLIFE IN the mid-90's was legendary and thriving. It was also hot, nasty and absolutely perfect. Henry had to walk mere blocks from his apartment to be writhing shirtless under a disco ball, feeling anonymous bulges pressed against his ass crack on a packed dance floor regularly raided by the Fire Marshalls for being over-capacity. Tall and handsome with his strawberry-blonde hair, Henry was not lacking for dance partners or dates.

Bears and cubs and aunties, Chapstick and diesel dykes were all living openly and harmoniously in Hillcrest. AIDS had ripped the community apart and glued it back together with a renewed mission and purpose. Dancing and drinking were the escape from the still harsh reality, as friends and lovers fell by the wayside. A single purplish-black skin lesion became a signed death warrant, and even the most prolific of debaters couldn't talk their way out of its verdict. And so they fell, from waiters to lawyers, 20-somethings to 60-somethings. This plague did not discriminate, as it washed through the streets, with its tsunami-like voracity, smoking out victims living under bridges, in stucco'ed mid-centuries, renovated Craftsman cottages, and the stateliest of Victorian homes.

As a culture was torn apart by this common foe, a solidarity formed right alongside it. Strangers helping their new, unfortunate brethren, lawyers and laymen waging battles against everyone from local politicians to big Pharma, in an attempt to stem the toxic tide. Amid the relentless torrent, a voice was found, loud and proud, in what once was skirted in hushed hallways. And in death's wake, a true community arose, fueled by loss and the resolve not only to survive, but to live grandly.

Henry met him in a dark club. Leaning seductively against the bar, his long, tanned frame relaxed as he blew wisps of white smoke into the air with the finesse of a Forties matinee idol. Supposing he was close to fifty, Henry was amused at how openly the old queen was checking him out.

His smile was slow and more than slightly predatory as he bared overly white, straight teeth. "You have one fine ass," he drawled with a prevalent southern accent.

"So I've been told," Henry matched back his audacity.

The approaching bartender laughed, "This one is not going to be so easy, Edwin." Turning to Henry, "What can I get you?"

"Gin & Tonic."

"I haven't seen you here before. Are you visiting?" Edwin was now shoulder to shoulder with Henry at the bar.

"No, but I just moved to the area a few months ago."

The bartender set down Henry's glass, "Five-fifty."

As he went to reach for the twenty dollar bill he'd shoved with his ID into his back pocket, Henry felt a hand just above his wrist.

"I've got this," Edwin shook his head, laying a ten on the bar. "Keep the change, Sean."

"Thanks, Edwin." Sean smiled brightly at the older man.

"Thank you," Henry offered, pleased to get a free drink, but wondering how he was going to get out of it. Old guys were not his deal. Airmen, SEALS, Sailors, Marines – that was his weakness and San Diego had no shortage of them. "So, how long have you been in the area?" Henry attempted to make polite conversation over the din of the music.

Edwin leaned in, putting a hand on his shoulder. "Twenty-six years."

"Wow, that's as long as I've been alive."

Edwin smiled and there was nothing lascivious or leering, "I've seen it all in this town."

He was definitely aging movie star handsome, and Henry imagined he must've had a wild time when he was young with his leading man looks.

"I'll bet you've got stories." Henry smiled and took a sip of his drink.

"Sweetheart, I could bury half the politicians in this state and identify their dicks in a line-up!" he ended with a flourish, brushing away a lock of dyed black hair, the cuffs on his white silk shirt flowing open.

There was something so likable about him. *He's everything I'm not*, Henry thought, *over-the-top, flamboyant, outspoken, fearless.* "I want to hear your stories," Henry confessed. And suddenly the excitement was no longer on the dance floor for Henry, it was with this man, this treasure trove of local lore and wanton tales.

More than a little drunk after several hours of Edwin's generosity as he regaled Henry with local legend, he was not upset to be leaving the club without a conquest, for he knew he'd found a friend in the most unlikely of characters, and that Edwin would be around a lot longer than his usual Friday night companions.

With plans to meet for pancakes Sunday morning, Henry felt closer to the scene around him than he did when he'd walked into the club. Oddly, tonight's meeting had left him feeling like a true Hillcrest resident. As he reached his apartment, he was finally able to put his finger on what it was – he belonged. After being different his entire life, he was no longer different. He fit in. He blended in. No one was judging anything but his damn fine ass.

Locking up his bicycle, the cool breeze off the ocean chilled his skin and caused it to tingle as a slightly sweaty Henry removed his helmet and gloves. Taking in a deep breath of sea air, he stretched his muscles and made his way into The Menu Restaurant.

Walking in from the bright morning sunshine, Henry immediately swiped his Ray-Bans off his face, momentarily blinded as his eyes adjusted to the dark hues of wide planked wood paneled walls and terracotta tile floor. As soon as he regained his focus, his attention was drawn to the curved planked wood ceiling that made the space feel like an airplane hangar.

Waving from a table at the back, Henry made his way toward where Edwin sat, admiring the framed photos of San Diego sunsets and surfers decorating the walls.

"Good morning," Henry greeted, happy to see the older man again.

"You rode a bicycle here? I would've picked you up if I'd known you didn't have a car."

Laughing, "I have a car and I spend way too much time in it during the week. I really don't get to ride my bike enough and the weather was perfect for it this morning. It's just really good for my head and my legs and my ass, too," Henry added as an afterthought, knowing Edwin would appreciate it.

"But it's far." Edwin was shaking his head in disbelief.

Picking up a menu, "No, not too bad, seven or eight miles and the Ocean Beach Bike Path by Sea World brought me right here. I need to get out and ride more."

After giving their orders to the waitress, Edwin looked seriously at Henry, "How would you like to ride your bike every night?"

"I'd love to. It would be like when I was back in college. My friend Schooner and I ran the track every night. I have never felt so good, both body and mind."

"I can trump that," Edwin bragged. "How about body, mind

and heart."

"I'm intrigued. Go on." Edwin had piqued his curiosity.

"One of the things I do for the community is work for Auntie Helen's Fluff and Fold laundry service." Edwin locked eyes with Henry.

"I've heard of it. That's the place in North Park that Gary Cheatham runs. I saw him on the news. What a great thing it is to take care of the laundry for people no longer well enough to do their own. That is really cool." Cutting into his granola crusted French toast, Henry looked back up at Edwin. "So, you work with them?"

Nodding, "I've been helping Gary since it was operating out of his little one-car garage."

With a smile, Henry shook his head, "Edwin, I have the feeling you will always continue to amaze me. So, what is it I can do to help?"

"Get on your bicycle and do pick-ups and drop-offs to clients." Edwin was very matter of fact.

"I can absolutely do that. Actually, I would love to do that." Just the thought made Henry feel as if he were a part of things, a member of San Diego's gay community and doing his part. "When can I start?" Henry was eager to meet the people who needed his help.

"I'll talk to Gary today and we'll see if we can get you scheduled this week." Edwin paused, his perfectly tweezed brows coming together to form an almost perfectly straight line. Cocking his head slightly, he looked up at Henry as he reached for the bright blue pack of Galoises sitting on the table, extracting a cigarette, and lighting it with dramatic flourish, "Did you say your friend's name was Schooner? Is that like some Biff, Buff, Skippy type nickname?"

Laughing, Henry shook his head. "No, that is actually his real name."

"What the hell were those parents thinking? They should be

shot."

Henry's smile remained bright as he spoke of his good friend, "Believe it or not, it is the perfect name for him."

"A large sailboat? Does he have a big mast?" Edwin laughed at his own joke, blowing a plume of white smoke toward the arched wooden ceiling.

"It's ummm, sizable. He's a big guy."

"Tell me more. Were you two ..."

"No," Henry waved his hand. "He's straight. And actually married with two kids, his wife just had their second baby."

"So, you are friends with a married, straight guy?" Stubbing out the French cigarette, Edwin leaned into the table and looked Henry straight in the eye. "Why?"

Henry shook his head, laughing. "We're an unlikely pair, but he's like a brother to me. He's never judged me or looked down on me for being gay. He didn't care what other people thought about our friendship – and he lived in the all-guys jock dorm when we were in school. But he's kind of a larger than life character, so no one was going to bust on him about it."

"He'd have to be larger than life with a name like that."

Smiling at his new friend, Henry laughed, "It actually fits him."

Biking southbound on the Ocean Beach Bike Path, Henry made the split second decision not to go directly home. Meeting Edwin and now about to become part of Auntie Helen's laundry crew, he realized that this weekend was the turning point. He was no longer just a commuter, he was now a resident of San Diego and a proud member of San Diego's gay community. Up until this point, getting Monica's old sales territory producing had been his singular focus, and he'd made good headway, enough to start exploring expanding the social areas of his life.

It was that decision that propelled Henry's muscular legs to cycle down Nimitz Blvd. and hang a left onto Chatsworth Blvd., cycling with fervor toward Portal Loma, home of The Hole, a legendary gay dive bar famously known for its popularity with hot military men and sun-bleached surfers. Located across from the Naval Recruitment Center, Henry had, up until now, avoided The Hole, knowing it could easily become an addiction. The bars and clubs in his Hillcrest neighborhood were generally frequented by the 'pose and be seen' crowd, and although he might find a hook-up for the night, those men were not his Achilles' heel. The military men of The Hole were another story and he knew it.

With his heart racing nearly as fast as his feet pounded the pedals, Henry locked up his bike and descended the staircase down into The Hole. Literally laughing out loud at the sign, "Only Sailors Get Blown Off Shore," his smile was bright as he emerged onto the patio packed with gorgeous guys and everyday Joe's. Peeling off his cycling gloves, he made his way to the bar where a bare-chested hunk of a bartender met him with a heart-stopping smile.

"Great day for cycling," he acknowledged. "What can I get for you?"

Henry noticed everyone was drinking out of mini-pitchers. "What are you known for?" he yelled across the bar.

"Well, Sunday is our barbeque and beer day. Is this your first time here?"

Henry nodded at the tanned cutie. "It is."

"OK, well I'm going to make you something special then." He turned toward the bottle lined shelves, then over his shoulder called, "On the house."

Vodka. Rum. Gin. Tequila. Triple Sec. Midori. Stabbing a pink straw into the pitcher, he slid it across the bar to Henry with a sex-on-a-stick smile. "Welcome to The Hole."

"Wow. Thank you. What is this?" Henry took his first sip

through the pink straw, immediately feeling the concoction of liquor coursing through his blood stream with a bang.

"It's a Tokyo Tea. You should head out to the patio, that's where all the action is."

Leaving a healthy tip for his new favorite bartender, Henry negotiated his way through the crowd to the strains of Gloria Estefan's *Everlasting Love* and out onto the circular tropical patio packed to the gills with bears and cubs and Marines. Oh my.

Sunglasses back firmly in place shading his eyes from the bright sun and inquiring eyes, Henry wished he had a wingman with him.

"Nice ass," a bear, with a warm smile, commented.

"Thanks," Henry looked down at his butt and realized he was wearing his second skin black bike shorts, leaving very little to the imaginations of the throngs of men surrounding him on the palm-lined patio. *Well, if I'm going to make a splash into San Diego gay life, this is the way to do it,* he smiled to himself.

As he made his way over to a wooden railing to set down his mini-pitcher of Tokyo 'kick-ass' Tea, he saw a guy across the patio leaning against the bar, beer in hand. Tall and muscled, from both his regal bearing and short hair, as well as his observant eagle eyes scanning the crowd, Henry surmised that the guy was military. If he were to define his guess a little more, he'd venture to say he was a bona fide Marine. The man was hot, yet aloof, making him even hotter. He took no part in the conversations, laughter or dancing that was taking place all around him. Henry could feel his balls tighten just looking at the guy and had to turn away before he was sporting a semi in bike shorts and embarrassing himself publicly.

"New here?" a voice beside him asked.

Turning to see who was talking to him, Henry nodded at the guy. He appeared to be young, early twenties, maybe. Again, the short hair was a dead giveaway. Military. Yes! The place was crawling with them.

"Just moved here recently on business," Henry offered as he took another sip of his now half-empty mini-pitcher.

"Oh, a pink straw," the guy commented on his drink. "Someone behind the bar thought you were a hottie."

Laughing, "Seriously, color-coded straws?" It was then that Henry began to observe the patterns in the straw colors and their respective sippers. "Hottie, I'll take that." He smiled to himself.

"Come dance with me." The guy grabbed his hand and pulled him to the center of the patio, "I'm David."

"Henry," he yelled over the music, immediately taken away by the beat, as the undeniably masculine scent of sweat and alcohol, and of the men dancing irresistibly too close on the packed dance floor, transported him somewhere, nowhere, just where the music was, as the warm San Diego sun beat down on his face.

With eyes semi-closed, his too tight from cycling shoulders loosened as he rhythmically stretched them with the lithe grace of a cat. *I belong,* he thought. *I totally and thoroughly belong.* And he wondered if he'd ever had that actual thought pattern before – that his belonging and acceptance was so total. Only once before in his life, during a magical month freshman year in college, when he'd worked day and night on a project with three friends, was this feeling approximated. They'd lived and breathed in their own cocoon for those four weeks, baring their souls, and irrevocably becoming one, even though missing members were later nowhere to be found.

Lost in the perfect memory and the déjà vu of finding Moksha again, he enjoyed the contact of the hot, sweaty bodies strafing him from every direction. Free and relaxed, with more than a slight Tokyo Tea buzz, the bright San Diego sun warmed his fair skin, and Henry knew that he was exactly where he was supposed to be. Everything had led to this moment in time. His moment.

Prying open his eyes, as if willed by some inexplicable dominant force, and ripping him violently from his reverie, the assault was completed as Henry locked eyes with the aloof Marine. The man's pale blue Husky-like eyes were trained unwaveringly on Henry, taking a slow, leisurely stroll all over his body, leaving him feeling both assaulted and aroused. Even halfway across the patio, the man sucked the oxygen away, leaving Henry gasping for air. His look was confusing, appearing almost angry, angry that Henry was dancing amongst a throng of boys.

Holding eye contact with the man, meeting the challenge head on, Henry didn't flinch. He wanted him to know that he was aware that he was being watched. The energy between the two was sharp and direct. There was no mistaking that contact had been made, and Henry could feel his stomach cramping with excitement, and his balls tightening with desire. This was a man he had dreamed about his whole life. He exuded absolute power. Envisioning him in uniform made Henry inexplicably ache even more.

Definitely a Marine, he thought. *A lieutenant? A captain? This man gave orders and expected them to be followed. He commanded. Demanded. And received.*

Turning away, Henry made his way through the crowd in search of the bathroom. Mostly he needed his air back and a moment to process what had transpired. He knew that wasn't all in his head.

The man hadn't just cruised him.

He'd claimed him.

Heading into the bathroom, the site of an open stall door felt like an immediate godsend and he needed to get behind it, alone. Quickly.

It happened so fast, he wasn't quite sure how it occurred. Entering the stall, he turned to close the door but was propelled against the metal stall wall to his right, knocking the air out of him. He heard the muffled sound of the stall door latch being locked. The larger man pinned him with his body, his muscular chest pressing Henry flush against the cold metal. The cool smooth surface felt good against his hot, sunburned cheek. Henry could feel the man's cock pressed against his ass crack on the outside of his bike shorts and wondered if the guy's cock was still in his pants or not. It wasn't until that moment that he realized the man had him in a loose choke hold. He didn't feel fear, and somehow instinctually knew this guy wasn't going to hurt him. He was establishing his control and position.

With lips next to Henry's ear, his voice was little more than a growl. "Is that what you want? Little boys? Little boys that will never satisfy you? Is that what you want?" His sizable cock pressed harder against Henry's ass. With his free hand, the man reached around to the front of Henry's bike shorts and found exactly what he was looking for – a hard, excited cock. Giving it a squeeze through the slippery material of his bike shorts, Henry hardened immediately to the man's touch. Continuing to fondle him through the thin fabric, while simultaneously pressing him from behind, the Marine hissed into Henry's ear, "I asked you a question."

Brain cells blown away by the physical assault both front and rear, for the life of him, Henry could not remember the man's question and answered by pressing his junk harder into the guy's hand, needing to feel possessed by his grasp. He did not disappoint Henry as he squeezed his balls tighter.

"You still want little boys?" he growled, his arm tightening around Henry's neck.

The moment Henry felt the crook of his arm squeeze his neck, he began to pump himself into the man's hand, "No. I don't want little boys."

"Then what is it you want?" The man had Henry by his cock and was pressing him firmly against his own hard-on, grinding harshly against his ass.

"I want you."

"Good. And I don't want you dancing with those boys. Do you understand that?"

Henry nodded his head, yes.

With his hand firmly encasing Henry's privates, the Marine pressed the smaller man against him and continued to let Henry feel the pressure of his cock against his ass.

Henry leaned his weight back into him, eyes closed. There was nothing in the world except the guy's hand kneading and pressing his balls. He wanted to stay in the moment forever. Submit to whatever the man wanted from him.

And then he was gone. Leaving Henry against the wall with a raging hard-on and a need to feel the Marine's hands and cock again, hear his voice, low and raspy, in his ear. Without removing an article of clothing or coming, he had never had a sexual experience that excited him as much, and he knew, beyond a shadow of a doubt, that he would always remember the sublime feeling of being restrained by this man.

He wanted more.

When he exited the bathroom, the Husky-eyed Marine was nowhere to be found, and a breathless Henry staggered into the daylight and embarked on a stunned bike ride home.

chapter
four

"IT WAS THE HOTTEST THING ever," he confessed to Edwin, in a hushed tone, three nights later at the laundry. Helping to fold before going out on his nightly delivery run, "He had me immobilized and I could feel every inch of his big, beautiful cock."

"You don't know if it's beautiful. The damn thing could be covered with warts," Edwin snarked, with a dismissive wave.

"Or sores," a nearby worker piped in and was met with a chorus of "ewwww".

"I had warts," Edwin confessed, as if he were letting the world in on an Earth-shattering secret. "I did," he looked at them all seriously. "I had to be circumcised at forty-three. I'm serious. It was the most painful thing in the world. And no one threw me a Bris. I didn't get any presents. Not a single one. But let me tell you, those bandages made me look like I had the hugest package. I've never gotten cruised so much in my life. It was fabulous," he reminisced.

"So why did it take you three days to tell me this?" Edwin finally asked, as he loaded sheets and towels into a plastic bag and labeled them.

"I don't know," Henry shrugged his shoulders, "I've been processing what happened. Trying to make sense of it."

"Sister, lust never makes sense," the older man advised.

"Ain't that the truth," another worker chimed in.

With his laundry parcels in panniers on either side of his bike, Henry cycled off for his evening's deliveries.

His last delivery of the night was Stephen, a former fabric designer. "They misdiagnosed me for nine months," he confided in Henry, "telling me that it was an ingrown hair, then a mole with an ingrown hair, and then would you believe it, an infected spider bite." The black lesion on his leg had grown to the size of a half dollar and his once handsome face was marred by at least a half dozen of the irregularly-shaped black spots.

"Is there anything more that I can do for you? Pick up groceries?" Henry realized that Stephen and the other clients were probably venturing into public less and less, when in fact, they needed the interaction and support of community more than ever. "Please tell me what can I do?"

"I was just going to sit down and watch *Beverly Hills 90210*, my secret guilty pleasure." He smiled with a shrug.

Stephen had been his last drop off of the night, "I'd love to join you." Henry sat down on the couch next to him and settled in for the hour, watching Dylan and Brandon and Brenda and Kelly and a handful of other characters he didn't know. As the hour progressed, Stephen explained the doomed love affairs and other trials and tribulations of the teens in a zip code to their north. *Beverly Hills 90210* would become a weekly ritual and a favorite show with Henry and Stephen, always at odds over who was the hotter character, Dylan or Brandon.

Thursday night was the first night that week since "Marine Sunday", as it was now officially known, that Henry wasn't on the schedule for the laundry. Arriving home from work, he showered and changed out of his suit into khakis and a tight V-necked black tee.

Every cell in his body was on high alert as he descended the stairs into The Hole. Immediately taking a seat at the bar, he ordered a beer and struck up a conversation with Ryan, the shirtless bartender he had met on Sunday. Henry longed to ask him about the Marine – Did he know who he was? Was he a regular? Did he always come alone? And more importantly, did he leave alone? Henry was dying to see him again. Feel him again.

His concentration was shit at work, picturing the Marine around every corner. He'd been jacking off twice a day in the shower, just thinking about their encounter and what the Marine's hand felt like massaging his cock through his bike shorts. At night, he'd grind himself into the sheets trying to remember the pressure with which he'd held him against the cold metal of the stall, metal as hard as the cock pressing against his ass had been. He knew his thoughts were becoming obsessive, but he couldn't get what had transpired out of his mind.

Nursing his second beer, there was no sight of the Marine and he kept his conversations brief with the men who approached him, knowing the Marine wouldn't want him talking to them. After his third beer, he called it a night.

The next day, after a branch sales meeting up in Orange County, Henry joined his colleagues for dinner and drinks. Laughing and hanging out with the people he'd known for the last five years was the best medicine for getting his mind off his obsessive thoughts of the man with the Husky-blue eyes. As he drove toward San Diego, he promised himself he'd go straight home, get a good night's sleep and get out early for a bike ride, but as he headed down I-5, he was powerless to stop himself from getting off and heading east toward Portal Loma instead of west toward his apartment.

Still in his suit and tie from work, the charcoal suit accentuated his long, lean stature and classic bone structure. With his wave of ginger hair and intense blue eyes, every head he passed turned to cruise him and he walked a little taller and with more swag than he usually did.

Ryan was at the bar and handed a smiling Henry a beer,

"Wow, you clean up really nice. I thought you looked damn hot when you came in Sunday in your bike shorts and gloves, hiding behind those sunglasses, but this – wow! You're getting me hard, bro."

Laughing, "Well, tonight might be the night to buy you a shot," Henry flirted back.

Setting up two glasses on the bar, "Buyer's choice."

Henry thought for a second, "Let's make it simple. Jack."

"Jack, it is." Ryan filled the two glasses.

With eyes meeting in a smile, the two clinked shot glasses and threw back the Jack.

Slamming them simultaneously on the bar with a laugh, Ryan picked up the bottle of Jack and refilled the shot glasses.

An hour and three beers later, still no Marine. Henry longed to venture out onto the center of the dance floor, tie loosened and just let it go. Let go of the work pressure, let go of the sadness in seeing members of the community devastated by HIV, let go of the sexual tension building in him, every single day, brought on by this elusive man who he was beginning to think was merely a fantasy he'd created, fueled by a mini-pitcher of Tokyo Tea and the hot sun.

Climbing the steps out of The Hole, Henry swore he would give it until Sunday and then stop his obsession cold turkey. He'd met him on a Sunday and maybe that was his day off, he reasoned. So Sunday was it. If the Marine no-showed on Sunday, that was it, he was going to dance with whomever the fuck he wanted, and he was going to pick the cutest military boy in the place and suck his cock. No more waiting for Mr. I-Don't-Want-You-To-Dance-With-Them.

Henry was deeply ensconced in his own head, making resolutions about moving on, not paying attention to his surroundings, or seeing the man, as he approached his car. He was leaning against the hood, his thick muscled arms folded across his chest. Calm, cool, collected, in charge and so damn freaking handsome.

"Your place?" was all he said.

Henry felt the sharp stab in his heart as his adrenal glands shot a release of hormones into his blood stream. Shaking his head no, he was shocked at how cool and calm his voice sounded, when he was anything but, "No. I don't think so. You haven't even bought me a drink yet."

Walking around the big Marine to the driver's side, Henry hit the remote, unlocking the door.

With a palm to the solar plexus to stop him, "Where are you going?" the Marine asked.

"Home," Henry was very matter-of-fact.

"I thought you wanted me to buy you a drink?"

Stepping around the Marine, Henry opened the door to his black BMW and got in. "I do…" and he closed the door and started the engine.

Rolling down the window, he added with a smile, "… on Sunday." Gunning the Beamer's engine, he left the Marine in the dusty parking lot with a smile on his handsome face.

Well played, Henry congratulated himself. *Let him ache for me as much as I've been aching for him.*

"You did what?" Edwin gasped over Sunday morning breakfast, fanning himself. "That was such a hot move. You are a man after my heart, my little protégé. That was just brilliant."

Henry chuckled and took another sip of his coffee, "I swear I don't know where it came from. It was like my alter ego took over. You know this man gets what he wants, when he wants it. And I just wanted to give him a run for his money."

"He's had a chub since Friday night thinking about what he wants to do to you. Are you nervous?" Edwin raised his brows.

Holding out a shaking hand, "I don't know how I'm going to drive down there. My knees are shaking. I knew I couldn't cycle it, but I kind of wish I had, just to get rid of this nervous energy."

Sitting back in his chair, Edwin pulled out his pack of Galoises and lit one, "Oh to be young again. Promise me details. I am living vicariously through your twenty-something year old cock."

Henry wasn't surprised the Marine was nowhere in sight when he descended the steep wooden staircase leading to The Hole's patio. With every cell in his body humming on an elevated frequency, he wanted to jump out of his skin, feel the Marine's hands on him, his body crushed up against his. Walking over to the bar, Ryan greeted him with a warm smile and a shot of Jack.

"I definitely need this," Henry was shaking his head knowingly.

"Hard day?" Ryan awaited his response.

"No, but I'm hoping it gets hard soon," and he gazed around the darkened inside space.

"Looking for someone to take on that task?" Ryan poured a second shot for Henry and a first one for himself.

Clinking glasses, they simultaneously threw back the shots, "We'll see if he shows." Henry's expression was dubious. Leaning across the bar and talking in a hushed tone, "I can't get this guy off my mind. I will be seriously bummed if he no-shows."

With his face just inches from Henry's, eyes locked, "Whoever he is, he'd be an ass to stand you up."

Henry laughed, "You are so good for my ego."

And out of nowhere, descending like an eagle whose position was being poached by foreign interlopers, the Marine was there, slinging an arm quickly and casually over Henry's shoulder, staking his claim. Except there was nothing casual in his smooth and swift assertion. He was letting Ryan know, in no uncertain terms, "Back off, dude." Henry was his.

Straightening up, Ryan didn't skip a beat as he slapped another shot glass on the bar and poured a drink for the three of them. Lifting his glass, he said to the Marine, "We haven't met yet, I'm Ryan."

"Cody," the Husky-eyed Marine clinked glasses with both men.

A name. I have a name. Cody, thought Henry. Feeling like he had the upper hand for the first time, as the guy didn't know his name.

His victory was short-lived.

Tightening his hold on Henry's shoulder and pulling him closer, "Henry, I didn't know if you were biking or taking the car today."

Henry stiffened against him. *How the fuck does he know my name?*

There was a smile in Cody's eyes, a dangerous smile, which made Henry feel as if his knees were going to buckle. The Marine was now asserting his dominance over Henry emotionally. Last week it had been physical dominance. The few brain cells that were still correctly synapsing screamed, "Run," but Henry just searched the man's mirth-filled eyes.

Cody signed his claim by leaning forward and placing a rough kiss on Henry's lips.

I'm so fucked. Literally. Henry knew he was so far over his head with the handsome Marine that he was rendered speechless. And powerless.

Clearly enjoying his effect, Cody grabbed Henry's hand, "Excuse us," he said to Ryan, "I still owe Henry a dance from last Sunday."

Pulling him over his stumbling feet out onto the patio, Cody insinuated them into the throbbing, tightly-packed, crowd-filling–every-inch small dance floor. Although not a slow dance, the Marine pulled Henry against his muscular frame, hands sliding around to Henry's ass, pressing their pelvises together. Cody's large hands roughly kneaded Henry's rear, pressing him firmly into his ever-hardening cock.

The soft, full lips against Henry's ear were the pièce de résistance. "I told you that you don't want to dance with little boys."

Speechless, Henry nodded.

"You only dance with me. Is that clear?"

Continuing to nod, Henry found both his voice and his smile. "Are you always this bossy?"

And for the first time, Henry heard Cody genuinely laugh, an irresistible dimple claiming his right cheek. "I guess I am."

"Tell me about you," Henry searched his impossibly blue eyes, marveling that they turned almost pure white around the pupil.

"What do you want to know?" Cody's hips were grinding into him, their cocks rubbing through their clothes.

"Everything. Where are you from?" Henry had detected a southern drawl.

Cody's eyes shone, "Calhoun, Georgia."

"Ah, a southern gentleman." It was hard to speak with a long, hard cock rubbing slowly against his own. "An officer and a gentleman?" Henry questioned.

Throwing his head back with laughter, "Don't ever expect me to be a gentle man with you."

Trying to hide the slight tremble in his hands as he inserted the key into the lock, Henry leaned his shoulder against the door to steady himself. Feeling Cody's heat so close behind him, he could not remember wanting someone so much since he was a little boy. Since Jimmy. The anticipation was reaching a fevered pitch and he could feel the fine hairs on the back of his neck standing at attention for the military man.

"How'd you know my name?" Turning to him, a perplexed look on his face, it had been on his mind since they were at The Hole.

With a cocky smile, he laughed. "DMV contacts."

Handing him a cold beer, they clinked bottles and each took a long swig. Setting his bottle on a coaster, Cody pulled Henry against him so that he could feel his hardness through his pants.

"I've been like this since you told me no the other night." He ground himself into Henry's hardening groin.

"You're not used to being told no, are you?" Henry was becoming amused.

Shaking his head, "No one tells me no. No one."

Sliding a hand between them so that he could run his fingers down Cody's impressive bulge, giving it a slight tug as he reached the down-facing head. "Don't like having your chain yanked?"

"You are very surprising," Cody laughed. "Most people I deal with would be afraid to do that. I'm used to people being afraid of me."

With a hand still caressing the head of Cody's cock through his worn jeans, "Should I be?"

Cody's eyes were locked onto his and the slight, barely imperceptible nod of his head made Henry gasp. Turned on by the reaction, he placed a hand behind Henry's head and pulled it to him, crushing his lips into Henry's and claiming his mouth with a greedy and adventurous tongue.

With a hand on either side of Henry's face, Cody continued to pillage his mouth and then suddenly pulled away, letting his lips graze Henry's cheek to his ear.

"Yes, you should be. Now get on your knees." He pushed Henry firmly from the shoulders downward toward the rug. They had already shared latest blood test results, the new gay ritual as prevalent as exchanging business cards at a networking lunch, and now Cody was done letting Henry have any power.

Obliging, Henry willingly sank to his knees. Cody unzipped with his right hand, holding Henry's head at bay with his left. Once free from his jeans, saluting in all his engorged glory, he pulled Henry by the hair to his expecting cock.

"I've waited all week for this," his voice was gruff as he pushed Henry's mouth onto its weeping head. "I don't wait for anyone, but I waited for you, Henry Clark."

Henry had imagined this exact scenario all week. The Marine's cock was exactly what he'd expected: thick, long and cut. He took him deep and fast.

He waited for me. If his lips hadn't been wrapped around the man, Henry knew he'd be smiling at the thought. This man had been as obsessed all week as he had. Whatever this crazy animal attraction was between them, it wasn't a one way street.

With the tip of his stiffened tongue, Henry swiped around the ridge of the domed head and then followed lightly with his front teeth.

"Oh yeah. Do me like that. Just like that."

I'm going to make you come undone. Your head won't be turning to look at any of those hot boys on the base when I'm done with you. You're going to crave my mouth, only my mouth. Henry was determined to make Cody want exactly what he wanted from Henry.

Lost in the sensation, his own cock grew stiffer every time the Marine pulled on his hair and groaned. Inching his hands up the back of Cody's thighs, Henry let his fingers stray to the hard, round muscles of his ass. With a hand on each cheek, he pressed forward, forcing the throbbing sensation to reach close to the back of his throat. He wanted to gag, but consciously told himself not to, determined to show Cody he could take everything he was giving, which Henry estimated to be close to seven, thick inches.

"God, you suck like a pro." Continuing to drive deep, "I could live with my cock in your mouth. You love this, don't you? Sucking my cock. I've been hard for you for a week. I wanted to ram my cock up your hot ass last Sunday in that bathroom stall."

Henry moaned at the last part of the Marine's monologue, remembering the pressure of what it felt like to have Cody pressed against him, restraining him.

"Yeah, you like that thought, huh? You can't wait to feel my cock buried in your ass. I know that's what you want. You don't just want to be on your knees, you want to be on all fours feeling me ram into you. I can't wait to feel you under me buried in your tight ass." Cody was driving relentlessly into Henry's mouth and he was lost to both the sensation and his own fantasy. "You are going to bottom for me and no one else." Pulling Henry's hair so that he'd look up at him. "You got that, my bottom only."

Attempting to stare intently into Henry's eyes, Cody appeared to be trying hard to remain focused. "You bottom only for me." He was looking for a response.

Henry nodded, sending him over the edge, thrusting to the back of Henry's throat, thick hot spurts lining Henry's mouth. "Suck it all down, fag. Take every drop, you dirty fag."

With red flags popping up left and right, Henry's throat closed. *Oh God, is he a gay hater? Is he going to kill me or something?* Henry started to choke as his fight or flight mechanism steamrolled into control.

With a final loud grunt-like moan and thrust, Cody shot the last of his load into Henry's mouth, holding him tight and close, forcing him to swallow.

A shiver of fear wracked through Henry's body, which Cody mistook for a shiver of pleasure. "That was freaking intense." And in one swift move he pulled Henry to his feet, surprising him as he pulled him close, in what appeared to be a tender bear hug.

"Damn you are good. That may be the best blow job I've ever had in my life. My legs are like jello, I need to sit." He led Henry toward the couch, playfully tugging him down next to him.

Overwhelmed by what had just transpired, Henry remained silent. *What is this guy's story?* he wondered. *Gay? Straight? Straight who can't admit he's gay? Gay hater?* Henry's head was spinning from a situation that was hot as all get out one minute, and the next had him fearing for his life. *People say weird shit in the throes of passion,* thought Henry, but seriously, Cody's homophobic declarations had made his blood run cold.

With his legs spread wide, the big Marine pulled Henry between his muscular thighs with Henry's back resting against his chest, stroking his hair tenderly as he brushed the soft ginger waves away from his forehead. Lying like that, in silence, Henry was struck by the polar essence of the situation. This was so soft and tender and loving. What had occurred earlier had been hot and frenzied and tinged with more than just an edge of danger.

Taking a deep breath, Henry allowed himself to relax against Cody.

"I wish I could stay the night, but I've got to be back on base."

Henry just nodded, not quite sure what to make of it.

Snaking his hands around into Henry's lap, Cody unbuttoned the top button of his jeans and tugged at his zipper. "I can be a pretty selfish guy, but you did such a great job getting me off tonight, I'd hate not to return the favor."

"It's ok," Henry stammered, not quite sure if his voice was hitching from excitement or fear, or some unhealthy combination of the two. Part of him just wanted to melt back into Cody, close his eyes and fall prey to the master's touch, yet a strong instinctual murmur sang a different tune, desperately wanting to be locking the door to his apartment behind the Marine.

"No, it's not. See, maybe you are making a gentleman out of me yet," he laughed, his hand gently stroking Henry to almost immediate hardness.

Freaking traitor. You little ho! Henry silently chastised his erection. It felt so damn good as Cody used both hands to slowly stroke him from base to tip, one hand after the next, slowly rubbing his thumb over the slit and then rubbing the slickness back down his throbbing shaft. With his face nestled in Henry's neck, Cody softly bit a trail from right below his ear to the nook at the top of his shoulder.

Henry heard himself moan, which elicited a sexy, guttural rumble from Cody, "Look how you react to my touch. Just like you did in that bathroom, hardening in my hands."

With a snake charmer's prowess, Henry's already erect cock stiffened even more within the mastery of Cody's hands. "Look what I can do to you. I'm going to make you shoot come all over yourself. You're going to do that for me, aren't you?"

Leaning his head back onto Cody's chest, Henry felt as if his eyes were going to roll back into his head. His moment of relaxation came to an abrupt halt as his head was jerked back by a savage tug on his hair.

"I asked you a question," Cody hissed into his ear. "You're going to come all over yourself for me, aren't you?"

"Yes," Henry nodded. His head still immobilized.

"You're so hot, letting me jerk you off all over yourself for me. I can't wait to see what else you'll do for me."

With both of Cody's hands now back working his cock, Henry let himself slide back to the other side where his consciousness' sole focus lay within another's grasp.

"I want you to do this for me," Cody whispered.

The build was quick, climbing rapidly toward release as Henry heard a grunting sound that seemed to be in the distance, but as the warm spurt hit his chest, he knew it had been him.

Cody's arms tightened around him, "You are so hot. You have no idea how hot you are. Every guy in that bar wanted you the day I first saw you, but I knew you were going to be mine."

Closing his eyes, suddenly exhausted after both the adrenaline rush and his orgasm, Henry knew that Cody's words were true. They both knew he'd be his. A slight stubble grazing his neck felt comforting as they sat there, wrapped up in one another.

Henry had not anticipated that the big Marine would be a snuggler. He'd pegged him as a "come and go" kind of guy and thought post-blow job the dude would be out the door. But he'd stayed. He'd stayed to make sure Henry came and to just hang out, with Henry snug in his tight embrace.

"You know I don't like sharing," Cody's tone was serious.

Turning in his arms, Henry locked onto his pale blue eyes, knowing his own were dancing with laughter as he broke into a hearty laugh, "No kidding. I never would've guessed that."

Breaking into a handsome smile of his own, the big Marine laughed at himself, "Yeah, I guess I made that clear the day we met. You'll bottom for me?" He was now asking permission, something that didn't seem very characteristic.

Afraid to admit that he'd never actually done anything but bottom, Henry nodded slightly, not breaking eye contact.

"I can't wait to be with you again. I'll get an overnight pass for next time so I don't have to leave. I don't want to leave," Cody's tone was sincere.

When he closed his apartment door behind him that night, Henry stood there for a long moment, motionless. Confused. The man was strong, passionate, hot, scary, beautiful, intense, cold, confusing and confounding.

What the hell happened here today, Henry wondered. Picking up a throw pillow off the couch, he brought it to his face, inhaling the clean, citrus scent of the handsome Marine. Never in his life, not even as a boy with Jimmy, had he felt such an incongruous combination of fear and lust. He wanted this man, like he'd never wanted another, but the red flags were everywhere, popping up to warn him, a swimmer caught in a dangerous riptide about to take on a massive, perilous wave for the ride of his life.

But it was easy to ignore the waving red sheaths when all he could see were ice-blue eyes in an exceedingly handsome face.

Both Edwin and Stephen would tell him to be careful, but chalk it off to people say crazy stuff when testosterone is flooding their systems.

"Oh please," Edwin waved his hand dramatically, "how many times have we all said the 'L' word to a one night stand when we're coming. Passion overload. People say weird shit when they're in the middle of it. That's all it probably was. He becomes the big, tough Marine when you have him at his most vulnerable. You said he was great the rest of the time."

Nodding, Henry agreed. "He was amazing. Warm, funny, fun. We had a really great afternoon hanging out together."

"Edwin's probably right," Stephen agreed, passing the bowl of popcorn. "Sounds like that is just his dirty talk. Everyone has their own brand of dirty talk."

And that was exactly what Henry wanted to hear.

H E HAD CALLED HENRY TO let him know that he'd be a little late. There was some Washington brass visiting the base and all officers were required to attend a cocktail function, but what Henry was not prepared for, was seeing Cody standing at his door in full dress blues, carrying a small overnight bag.

Weak at the knees, Henry was speechless looking at the handsome vision before him, his cock already at a full salute.

Holding up his bag with a smile, "I have a pass until tomorrow."

Welcoming him, Henry's feelings were mixed. Cody had not left his thoughts, not for one second. He wanted more than anything to taste his mouth again, feel his arms around him. But spending a night together. This guy just moved fast and took what he wanted. But damn, he was so beautiful and standing there in full dress uniform was making Henry's heart burst. This man just had so much power and presence.

"I missed you," Cody confessed, as if reading Henry's mind. "And I don't know why. I hardly know you."

"I missed you, too," Henry's admission was out of his mouth before he could stop it.

Like a large cat stalking its prey, Cody was on Henry, backing him with force into the wall, a hand quickly on either side of his face, before his mouth came down with an urgency neither man fought.

Wrapping his arms around Cody's waist, Henry pulled him close, needing to feel the Marine's hardness against his own. Running his hand down to his ass, he could feel how hard Cody was for him, how much he wanted him, and Henry felt powerful again, as he stood wrapped around this man in a uniform that screamed badass motherfucker. This man was a captain in the United States Marine Corps and he had a raging hard-on just for him. Damn.

Wanting him still in uniform when he went down on him, Henry began to undo Cody's belt under the blue dress uniform jacket.

"Let me take my coat off," Cody began.

Shaking his head, Henry succeeded unfastening the belt.

Laughing, Cody realized Henry was turned on by the uniform, "Hell, for your killer blow job, I will wear it every time," and he pulled Henry's mouth in for another consuming kiss, exploring and conquering every last inch.

With his hand inside Cody's dress trousers, Henry slowly stroked him until he was what he would describe as painfully hard. The man's cock was standing straight up, with his soft, velvety head already leaking pre-come. "Are you ready to be thanked for your service to this country?"

As he sank to his knees, Henry thought that Cody was also totally getting off that he was in uniform. The big, highly decorated Marine was getting his cock sucked. As it should be.

Tightly grabbing handfuls of Henry's hair, Cody was in no mood for anything but getting off, driving deep into Henry's mouth, his rhythm relentless. It wasn't long before he got what he wanted, finishing with the declaration that made Henry's throat and shoulders tighten, "Yes, suck me, fag." His knees quivered as he unloaded the last spurt, deep into Henry's throat.

They stayed there like that for a few minutes, his hands still holding Henry's head, before he gently began to run his fingers through the soft waves. Pulling Henry to his feet, Cody tipped Henry's head back, gently biting at his lips before consuming his mouth again.

"Henry Clark, you are a fine addiction," he whispered, his embrace tightening. "Now let me get out of uniform and I'll take you out for dinner. What are you in the mood for?"

"Anything but meat." Henry's smile was sly.

Breaking into a handsome grin, the irresistible dimple claiming his right cheek, and giving him an air of boyishness, Cody nodded, "Guess you're already up to the dessert course."

Two bottles of wine and dinner at the Crest Cafe had them staggering back into Henry's apartment a little past 1 A.M. As Henry tried to get the key into the lock, Cody pressed up behind him, flattening him against the door. Henry could feel his urgency pressing into him, reminding him of their initial meeting at The Hole.

"You know just what I want, don't you," his lips grazed Henry's ear.

"Think you still can after all that wine," Henry taunted.

"Get the key in the fucking door, Henry. Now," he demanded.

As the door opened, their combined weight pressing against it caused them to stumble in. In a drunken fit of laughter, they amused themselves, as they barely landed on their feet.

Looking at the handsome Marine, Henry thought how young he looked now that he was drunk and relaxed. His military bearing appeared softer, and when he looked back at Henry, there was that smile with the one dimple.

I could fall in love with that lone dimple, Henry thought to himself as he stood there staring at him.

Cody closed the space between them with two strides. Snaking his arms around Henry's waist, he let his hands drop to his ass, pulling him tight against his erection.

"It's about time I saw you without your clothes on." The dimple had reappeared. "I want to be deep in your ass right now."

Taking him by the hand, Henry led Cody into his bedroom for a slow dance of clothes falling by the wayside as they tasted one another's mouths and necks, felt fingers pressing deep into the flesh of each other's backs, and stood uncovering the nuances they'd yet to discover.

Gripping Henry's face in his large right hand, Cody's steely eyes turned hard and serious. "I wasn't kidding the day we met, you don't dance with another, you don't flirt with another, no one else fucks you."

Bringing up a hand to grasp Cody's wrist, "You're asking a lot for someone I've just met. Don't you think that might be a little soon?" Henry had no desire to be with anyone else, but was certainly not going to disclose that fact.

"A little soon?" And there was the dimple. "I'm about to fuck your ass and spend the night with my arms wrapped around you. Is that a little soon?"

"Yeah, it's a lot soon."

"Isn't that what you want?" Cody seemed surprised.

"It is what I want. It's just," Henry ran a hand through his thick hair, "confusing. It's really confusing. It's like here's this thing between us that is clearly just a physical thing and then you have these demands of me." *Give me something, anything. Something that this is more than just a throwaway fuck.*

As Cody's muscles tightened, his spine stiffened and straightened, making him appear even larger and more intimidating. "I'll be honest with you. I don't know what this is, Henry. It's not a one-night stand. You're not just some flighty guy I'm going to fuck and forget. I can't get you out of my freaking mind. But I don't know what this is. I want you. I want to dominate you, but then I want this other thing with you." He stopped, a pained look on his face. "Am I even making sense?"

"Sort of." Henry stared at his handsome face.

"Do you want me to go?"

They stood there naked, facing one another. The long moment of silence filled with words neither had the capacity to express.

"Not until morning," Henry's voice was soft.

The relaxation of Cody's muscles was visible and he began to shake out his shoulders. "Good. That's good." He looked down, as if trying to formulate a thought before verbalizing it. When he looked up, he locked eyes with Henry's. "Do you want me to do this to you?"

"I thought I did," he paused. "I think I do. But what I want right now is for us to get in bed and just get to know each other."

The dimple reappeared as Cody put a hand around the back of Henry's head. "I think you just topped from the bottom."

Laughing, "Maybe I did."

"Don't get used to it." Cody pulled him in for a kiss.

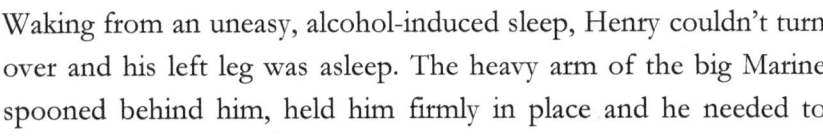

Waking from an uneasy, alcohol-induced sleep, Henry couldn't turn over and his left leg was asleep. The heavy arm of the big Marine spooned behind him, held him firmly in place and he needed to move.

A spooner. Never would have guessed that. And dead to the world, too.

Rubbing back into him, he could feel the tip of Cody's cock on the crack of his ass. Slowly he moved up and down, pressing himself firmly into the sleeping giant. Henry could feel himself growing hard just feeling Cody's cock on his ass. Still in a deep sleep, the big Marine began to harden and Henry kept up the motion until he felt Cody starting to grind into him.

"Mmmm," Cody's moan was filled with sleep as he thrust himself against Henry's crack. "What a perfect way to wake up," his morning voice was gravelly.

"Do you want a condom and some lube?"

"In a few minutes." Cody swung a leg over Henry's, pulling him even closer and moving his hand down to Henry's waiting cock. Wrapping his large fingers around Henry's girth, he slowly began to stroke him. "First, I want to feel how hard you get for me. Only me."

Henry began to move with the motion of Cody's hand, loving that this hot guy was jerking him off.

"You like that, don't you? You like me stroking your cock and jerking you off."

"Yes, I do." He pumped more voraciously into Cody's hand.

"Then come for me." He sank his teeth into Henry's shoulder.

"Oh God."

And Cody bit harder. "Come for me," he hissed.

"Yes," Henry cried, spasming and spurting into Cody's hand.

"Good boy," he whispered into Henry's ear. "I like when you listen to what I tell you to do. For that you get a reward."

Barely coming down off one sensation, Henry was immediately lost to another as he felt a wetness at his anus.

"Oh God," he moaned again, as Cody continued to massage his come into his ass.

With lips grazing Henry's neck, while his fingers continued to play. "I'm going to fuck you with your own come."

"Oh fuck, if I hadn't just come that would have made me come," Henry's voice was barely a low moan.

"Get me a condom and lube and then get on all fours." The Marine Captain commanded, totally in control and spitting out orders.

Henry did as he was told.

Cody's large hand came down in a stinging slap across Henry's ass. The unexpected assault had a delicious burn, Henry thought, his brain trying to keep pace with the onslaught of sensations. He heard the top of the lube bottle click open, followed by a wet stream of viscous solution slowly tunneling its way down his crack. When it reached the opening, Cody massaged it into the rim in a sensual, slow clockwise motion.

Pressing the tip of his finger in elicited a moan of "Oh God," from Henry.

"Mmm, you are sensitive," there was amusement in the Marine's voice, as he thrust his finger in deeper, "and so, so tight. God, my cock is going to love being inside you."

Henry felt more lube running down his ass just before Cody inserted a second finger and began a smooth languid motion of thrusting them in and twisting them to massage Henry's prostate, causing his spent cock to begin hardening almost immediately.

"Fuck, Cody. Fuck, fuck, fuck."

"Are you ready to be fucked by a real man and not some fag?" his voice was hoarse and deep.

Henry moaned and immediately felt a sharp tug on his hair.

"I asked you a question, fag," his tone serious and threatening.

"Yes."

"Yes, what?" He yanked Henry's hair sharply again, pulling his head back.

"Yes, I'm ready to be fucked by a real man," Henry choked out, wildly anticipating the painful burning of Cody's entry.

"And only I fuck you." Cody withdrew his fingers slowly and spread Henry's ass cheeks wide. "None of those fags anymore, got that?"

"Y-Y-Yes," Henry stuttered, "only you fuck me."

Holding his breath at the delicious feeling of pressure the head of Cody's thick cock created against his ass, Henry thought if he doesn't fuck me right now I will beg for it, I will literally beg this man to fuck me.

As he had flippantly warned, the big Marine was not a gentle man. He took what he wanted. Forcefully. Deriving extreme pleasure from his conquest, knowing his total sexual domination of Henry fully met both their needs perfectly.

Before returning to the base later that day, he would take Henry's ass another two times, once with Henry's legs over his shoulders so that he could watch his face as he deeply plowed down into him and the final time lying on his back, with Henry sitting on him facing away. "You've earned controlling the depth and rhythm this time," he told Henry. "You've given me what I needed."

Henry was glad to have pleased him, hoping he'd want to come back for more. Like Jimmy. Maybe they could actually build something, be more. Be something. Something real this time.

As Cody began to spend all his base leave at Henry's apartment, he let himself dream for the first time since he was nine, a dream he'd buried so deeply, he really wasn't sure he'd ever dreamed it.

He wanted that someone. That forever someone.

"**S**ERIOUSLY, ARE WE EVER GOING to meet him? I would like to meet him before I die." Stephen was the only one who could get away with saying that. Although he did so tongue-in-cheek, both Henry and Edwin inwardly winced, already feeling the deep pain in the knowledge that time with their special, new friend was rapidly drawing to a close.

"I'll ask him. He's kind of private. It's the whole military thing and being discreet."

The weeks had now passed into months and their routine was comforting to Henry. Nights at his apartment when Cody could get off base, dinners out, dinners in, the occasional drunk, wild night dancing. Cody taking him. Roughly. Sometimes almost savagely. Meeting both their needs perfectly.

This was their rhythm and Henry let himself believe that as much as he was Cody's, Cody was his. Letting himself believe that was a place he'd never ventured before, not with his college relationships or those that came after.

"I want you to meet my friends." Henry was almost timid in his request, not sure of the response.

Cody looked up from the cutting board where he was chopping carrots. "Which friends?"

"Just Edwin and Stephen."

Cody remained silent and Henry forged on, "We're going to

lose Stephen soon and he really wants to meet you."

Turning to face Henry, "What exactly do they know about me?" Cody stuck the tip of the knife into the butcher block cutting board.

"That your name is Cody and you're hot and you've done two tours in Baghdad and I'm insanely crazy about you." Henry smiled.

The one dimple appeared and the big Marine shook his head as he turned back to the task at hand, "Sure, I'll meet your friends."

Grabbing two plates from the cabinet to set the table, Henry felt his heart lighten. That had gone better than he'd anticipated. It was difficult to gauge how Cody would react.

Sitting down to eat, Henry filled their wine glasses. "To meeting my friends," he toasted with a smile.

Cody leveled a steely-eyed glance at Henry over the rim of his wine glass. "You understand I need to be discreet."

"I do, but I don't see how this is any more threatening to your privacy than walking into The Hole."

"No one knows a damn thing about me at The Hole. Not even people I went home with. You're my first actual relationship of anyone I've met there. I never saw any of the others again."

Henry looked down at the suddenly unappetizing food on his plate. They'd never discussed the past. It was one of the parts of Cody's world that was locked in a bunker. Henry knew a man this beautiful and charismatic had been around the block a few times, but thinking about him picking up other guys at The Hole made him sad and evoked both feelings of jealousy and insecurity. He could be gone tomorrow. Like Jimmy.

"Don't get like that, Henry. I can't deal with that shit. Who am I here with? All my leave is spent with you." It was clear Cody didn't have a lot of tolerance for sulking.

"I know. I'm just being a jealous bitch." Henry forced a smile.

Laughing, "Yeah, but you're my bitch. And I like that." Stabbing his fork into his food, "OK, so what do I need to know about them before we meet? Edwin's the old guy, right? What's his story?"

Stephen's death was upon them before that meeting ever had a date attached to it. As Henry left a client meeting, his pager buzzed and he recognized Edwin's number.

Heading directly to the Beamer for his car phone, "He went into cardiac arrest last night and he had a DNR," Edwin's voice was thick with emotion.

"Oh fuck." The pain stabbing acutely through Henry's heart riveted him to the seat. *Did I do enough? Did he know how much I cared about him? Was I there enough for him? Really there?* "His family is in Indiana. Are they flying his body back?"

Edwin was silent for a moment and Henry could feel the bile rising in his throat.

"They don't want to have anything to do with him. Apparently they disowned him when he was seventeen." Edwin could barely speak the words.

"So, who is taking care of this? Who is taking care of Stephen?" The air in the Beamer was starting to disappear.

"We're starting a fund…" Edwin began.

"No. No. No," Henry screamed. "Stephen is not getting stuck in some refrigerator for God knows how long, while we beg strangers for spare change. He's not," a distraught Henry continued to scream.

"Pull over, Henry. You shouldn't be driving," Edwin chastised. "I don't want to lose you, too."

"Where is he, Edwin? Did they take him to Mercy Hospital?" Henry pulled a U-turn.

"Yes."

"Ok, I'm headed there now."

"I'll meet you. I'm headed to his house first to gather his papers. Drive safely, Henry, I'm not kidding." Edwin warned.

Stabbing the numbers into his phone for Cody's pager, Henry left his number followed by a 911, their code for call me ASAP.

He didn't hear back.

A man takes care of his family. That is what Henry thought. It was what he aspired to do. When his father left his mother with two small children, he knew right then that if he ever had a family, he would never cause such sadness and stress by not owning up to his responsibilities. When Stephen's family didn't own up to theirs, and shirked the duty of burying their own, Henry was not going to let his friend's send-off be marred by prejudice and hate.

The money to bury Stephen with respect and dignity amounted to a month's worth of sales commissions for Henry. He never thought twice about what was the right thing to do. Stepping in to make sure everything was done properly and with the right amount of glitter and flourish to honor their friend, was Edwin, seeing to all the details and making the arrangements.

It had been three days and an innumerable amount of pages and still no word from Cody. Had he been shipped back to Baghdad on some middle of the night covert mission? Called on to help take out a high value target? Henry had no clue. With Stephen's loss tearing deeply into him, he ached for the big Marine, needing to find solace in his arms.

For three long nights, he laid in bed, imagining the feel of Cody's warm body spooned against his, giving him the strength to make it through the next few days until the burial.

Where are you? Please be safe. I can't lose you. I can't, were his last thoughts as he fell asleep at night and his first when he opened his eyes in the morning before grabbing his pager off the nightstand to see if he'd slept through a message from Cody.

But there were none.

"Dress is San Diego surfer dude casual," Edwin informed him.

"For a funeral?"

"No, for the celebration of the life of a brilliant Midwestern fabric designer who loved hot surfer boys. So we're all going as surfer boys. He's getting sent off by the hottest surfers in San Diego." There was pride in Edwin's voice at the event he was orchestrating in Stephen's memory.

"So, like board shorts and flip flops?" Henry couldn't quite wrap his mind around it, but just the thought of a beach themed send-off versus a heavy funeral lifted the dark anxiety that had been pressing down on him, choking him for days.

It felt more than a little weird entering a church in yellow board shorts, flip flops and a tank top with a funky drawing of a rainbow colored surfboard, a guitar and a VW bus that said, 'surf, jam, live in a van'. It was light and fun-hearted and Henry didn't comb his hair after his morning shower, so that he'd be sporting a tousled, just out of the ocean look.

"You look stunning and so gay in that," Edwin kissed both his cheeks and ran a hand through Henry's mussed-up hair. "Stephen is sporting a hard-on in Heaven for you right now."

Standing at the front of the church, they greeted guests that milled in. People who had known Stephen for years, volunteers from the Fluff and Fold, neighborhood shopkeepers, gays, lesbians, transsexuals – all looking like they were heading out for a day at the beach. Instead of the heavy perfumed fragrance of flowers that overwhelmed the senses at funerals, wafting through the air was the light scent of Coppertone and Hawaiian Tropic.

As the minister began his eulogy, Henry closed his eyes and breathed in deeply, picturing sitting on the beach next to a healthy Stephen, toes dug in the sand, rating the surfer boys as they approached the shore. *Yeah, he's hot. What do you think of that one? Eww, when was the last time he washed his hair! Look over there. Oh my God, he just gave me a semi. How about that one? He has worked hard for that six-pack. I want to lick those abs.*

"Henry, go up there." Edwin was elbowing him out of his reverie. "It's your turn to speak."

Disoriented, one minute he was on the beach with Stephen and now he was in a dark church, Henry stood to make his way to the altar, trying hard to regain his bearings after being ripped from his daydream.

"Hi everyone. Thanks for coming. I'm Henry Clark and I was a friend of Stephen's." He looked out at the packed church and thought Stephen, who was so isolated at the end, would have been blown away by the turnout. "I met Stephen Bennett a few months ago, yet I would swear that I've known him my whole life. That we'd gone to school together and gotten kicked out of Cub Scouts together and been each other's wingmen on Friday nights in bars. But none of that ever happened. The truth is, I met Stephen Bennett halfway through the final act. By the time we met, this insidious disease had already ravaged Stephen's body, leaving him weakened and unable to do the simple things that are a part of everyday living. As the months went on, the disease continued to take its toll, and Stephen required more and more assistance to get basic things done. It was hard to watch and not just because of what it was robbing from him, but because of what it wasn't. Stephen never let this disease define who he was or allow it to steal his spirit. Last Wednesday, he was still fighting with me over critical matters. Who was hotter – Brandon or Dylan? Was David really in the closet? If I were straight – Kelly or Brenda?" he paused as the audience erupted into laughter hearing about the TV show, *90210*. "Right until the end, he never lost his essence, never allowed it to be taken away and he taught me a lesson I am sure I will revisit for the rest of my life. I'm so proud and thankful that I got to call

Stephen Bennett a friend. I only have but one regret," Henry's voice cracked, "that we didn't have more time. I'll miss you Stephen. I already do."

When he reached the pew, Edwin was there with open arms as Henry cried openly into his shoulder. "Do not snot up this shirt. It's Versace," the older man bitched.

Laughing, Henry lifted his face from the white silk shirt. "I love you."

"I love you, too." Edwin squeezed his hand and held it tightly as they sat and listened to the other send-off speeches, before ending the service with a rousing sing-along of The Beach Boys' iconic classic, *Surfer Girl*.

"I've never been to this place," Henry said to Edwin as the crowd of about a dozen very gay surfer-boy-wannabe-dressed-funeral-goers entered the beachfront restaurant.

One of their party turned around, "It was always one of Stephen's favorite places to come for lunch on weekends. His favorite dish is called 'Man Pleasing Meatloaf'. How could you not love something with that name?"

They all laughed as they attempted to negotiate through the closely-positioned tables to a long reserved one set up for them by the window.

The glass wall looking out over the ocean, where the sun glinted on the waves, made Henry feel less overwhelmed than he'd been feeling. The ocean always had that effect on him, and it brought back the feeling of the daydream he'd seen in his head in the church. Stephen would have liked this, and he would've liked that they were all there together. People from different facets of his life, meeting for the first time, through him.

Still focused on the ocean, Henry was not watching what was

going on right in front of him, and didn't realize the line of people in their party had stopped, as they started to take their seats. Practically plowing into Edwin, he placed a hand on the back of the chair next to him to steady himself.

"So sorry," he said to the tow-headed little girl who looked up, startled by the jolt. As his gaze rose to take in her family, the shock and proximity caused the knee-jerk reaction as he stared into the cold eyes of his lover just a few feet across the table. His name just tumbled from Henry's mouth, the shock evident. "Cody?"

The woman whose back had been to him looked up and smiled. A pretty blonde with wide blue eyes, she reminded him, in looks, of his friend Schooner's wife, CJ. This woman had definitely been a sorority girl and prom queen.

"Well, hello," she greeted Henry with a bright smile and a thick southern accent.

Henry's eyes shot back to Cody's face. He was speechless. The Marine's eyes were flat and narrowed, his clenched jaw twitching.

"Daddy, Ashley won't give me the purple crayon."

Cody ignored the child, his eyes transfixed on Henry.

Looking back at the wife, "Hi," Henry managed.

"Cody, aren't you going to introduce us to your friend?" She was clearly intrigued as to why her Marine husband would be acquainted with this openly gay man.

Henry needed to fill the awkward silence immediately. "I'm Henry," he extended a hand to the woman. "My company works with the Marines and Cody's unit," was all he could think of quickly.

"Well, I'm Shelby and these are our girls, Ashley and Chloe."

Our girls? Stunned, he didn't immediately respond to her introduction of the children. He kept expecting her to say, "Bless your heart" with her thick southern drawl.

Finally, "Well, I'll let you get back to your dinner."

"You all look like you're coming from a fun day on the

beach," Shelby observed.

Looking at Cody and locking eyes with him, "No, actually we're coming from a funeral. I lost a very close friend this week."

"Oh, I am so sorry for your loss."

Her husband had still not uttered a word.

"Enjoy your meal. It was nice meeting you, Shelby." He nodded at Cody.

Numb. Shell shocked. Angry. Destroyed. Heartbroken.

He sat down next to Edwin, glad the only available seat had him with his back to Cody and his family. Married. He was married. He had a wife. Two little girls. He was freaking married. He wasn't his. He was married.

"Friends of yours?" Edwin asked.

Henry stared at him, blank-faced, sure his tattered heart was bleeding right through his surfer tee-shirt for all to see.

"That's Cody."

Edwin looked confused.

"That's Cody," Henry hissed through clenched teeth. "With his wife and kids."

"Wife and kids?" Edwin merely mouthed the words.

Nodding. "So while I've been worried about him for days, he's been with his family that I knew nothing about."

Grabbing a glass of water off the table, Henry downed the whole thing.

"He's fucking married, Edwin. He's a god-damn fucking straight guy. What the fuck has he been doing with me?" Henry searched Edwin's face for answers.

"I think you've had enough to deal with today. Let's get you out of here. Stephen would understand." Grabbing Henry by the hand, he pulled him out of his chair and quickly made their goodbyes to the other guests.

As they negotiated their way through the tables, Henry stared straight forward, his eyes trained on the exit. Edwin, however, turned to get a good look at Cody.

He was watching them leave.

"Asshole," Edwin mouthed, the anger on his face evident.

The Marine tried not to react, but the muscles on both sides of his jaw were singing their own tune.

What Edwin did not see, was Cody's wife turn around and watch him and Henry leave after witnessing the look on her husband's face.

It took all the strength he had on Monday morning to call in sick. Rolling back over in bed, he prayed for sleep, needing to escape the searing pain that was wracking his body. How could a heart cause so much pain?

Stephen and Cody.

The loss was devastating. One compounding the other.

Stephen and Cody.

Both gone.

The ringing of the phone made his skin burn. Edwin's number was on the display again. It was his fourth call of the morning. This one he would answer.

"Hi," his voice sounded flat even to himself.

"Oh thank God." The worry was heavily laced with drama. "How are you?"

"I suck." Rolling onto his back, Henry flung an arm across his burning, swollen eyes.

"No, he sucks. You are wonderful and handsome and smart. He is a Class A douche of the highest magnitude and you are lucky to be rid of his lying, deceiving ass." Edwin was getting worked up.

"Why would he do this to me, Edwin?"

"Because he's a narcissistic closet case who only thinks of himself. That selfish fuck wasn't thinking about you or his prom queen wife or those two little children. He doesn't give a rat's ass about other people."

"I really thought he cared," Henry's voice choked up.

"I'm sure he did. In his own sick way. People like that don't truly have emotions for others, at least not in the way that you and I do."

It was good to talk to Edwin. His years of experience helped put things in perspective, something Henry knew he currently didn't have, and might never gain, on this subject.

"Do you think I'll hear from him?" *Please say yes.*

"Of course you'll hear from him. It might not be right away, because he's going to want to make you pay. Make you suffer."

"Well, I am suffering, that's for sure." Henry got out of bed and opened the blinds, shocked to see the sky was blue. *The sky is blue. How could that be?* "But why would he make me want to pay? I didn't do anything wrong. I didn't lie to him. But I did lie for him with that cover-up story to his wife." Henry shook his head, "Ugh, he has a fucking wife."

"Put some clothes on and meet me for a salad at the Crest Café."

"I can't." Henry's throat closed, the lump threatening to choke him.

"Why not?" Edwin wasn't going to let up.

"It was one of our places." Squeezing his eyes shut, hot tears splashed onto his cheeks.

Edwin sighed, "Ok, I'll meet you in twenty minutes at the Hash House, where I will shove a fattening stuffed burger down your throat and have a Banana Latte waiting for you." He hung up the phone before Henry could answer.

Shuffling to his dresser, Henry pulled out a pair of sweats and grabbed a tee-shirt. Right under the shirt he chose was a black tee emblazoned MARINES that Cody had given him. Pulling it from the drawer, he brought it to his face, letting it softly embrace his stubble rough cheek.

"Dickhead," Henry scowled at the shirt, throwing it back into the drawer with a sneer, before heading out of his apartment.

The Banana Latte was sitting on the table by the time Henry reached the Hash House a Go, where Edwin sat with large, sympathetic eyes.

"You really ordered that thing?" He shook his head.

Edwin sneered, "I thought a banana might do you good."

"How thoughtful," Henry shot back with a mock sneer.

"What a fucking weekend." Edwin shook his head and picked up a menu.

"What a fucking weekend is right," Henry concurred. "At least we gave Stephen a great send-off. *Surfer Girl* was an inspired touch, by the way." Henry smiled.

Edwin's shoulders swayed as he preened, "Wasn't it though. A perfect goodbye for our little surfer girl." Putting down his menu, "So, what are you going to do when he calls?"

"Or shows up," Henry said, looking over the top of his menu.

"He has a key?" Edwin's eyebrows were standing at attention.

"Of course he has a key."

Putting the menu down, "Change your locks, sister." Edwin was dead serious.

"I don't think he'd cause a problem." Henry shrugged.

"You also didn't think he was married. The man is a liar. Who knows what else he has lied to you about? Think about it, he lies to everyone. He lies to his wife. He lies to his kids. He lied to you and he lies to himself. The guy is a psychopath, believe me. No one can lead that kind of a double life and be well balanced."

Henry sat listening, in silence. With each sentence, his heart grew heavier as Edwin pulled no punches in laying out the truth. Who was Cody? He really had no clue. A wife and two little girls — that was quite a large package to hide. Did his wife have any inkling of her husband's double life? Was he going back to base when he left Henry's apartment or going home? Did his family live here or in Georgia? There was base housing for families. Did he go to their bed after spending the night wrapped around Henry?

"So is he straight? Gay? Some combination of the two?" Henry looked to his older friend for answers, to help him make sense of the confusion.

Palms in the air, Edwin gave an exaggerated shrug, "I'm not a psychiatrist and I don't know the guy, but my guess is that he's gay and can't come out. Family, military, who knows what his pressures are? So he plays big tough Marine, married the prettiest girl in school and has crafted the perfect facade. Who would ever suspect that? He's from Georgia, you said?"

Henry nodded.

"Military family?"

He nodded again, "His father was in the Corps also."

"Ok, so what do we know? He grew up in the Bible belt, son of a Marine and you know, his father is from a completely different generation. Marines don't have faggot sons. Especially when they are big, good-looking guys like Cody and the family is filled with bible thumpers."

"So, do you think all those comments during sex were some self-loathing thing?"

Nodding, Edwin didn't say a word. Both men sat in silence processing the pieces of the Cody puzzle until after the waiter took their order.

"If he hates himself, can he truly love anyone else?" Henry mused, sipping the Banana Latte, which was actually quite good. Before Edwin had a chance to answer, Henry spat out the question that had been haunting him since the day before. "Do you think he hates me?"

"I think he hates himself because he can't be like you. You are everything he doesn't have the guts to be and he hates that you have the balls to do it and he doesn't."

Sitting back in his chair and looking up at the ceiling to stave off another round of tears, Henry wished with all his heart that he could turn back time, make yesterday disappear – for so many reasons. Ignorance was bliss, that's for sure.

He was finally happy and now he'd never see Cody's Husky-blue eyes across his pillow again. They wouldn't be sharing summer. That thought had occurred to him while walking to the Hash House and seeing spring poppies and day lilies in baskets lining the front of shops along the street. No Sunday BBQ's while dancing at The Hole, no sunsets at the pier.

It was all just gone. Like that. Gone.

"Why am I so sad about all of this when he lied to me about everything?"

Cocking his head to the side, Edwin looked sad for his young friend. "Because it wasn't a lie for you. It was the real thing."

The click in his door lock caused a jolt in his heart. It was Thursday evening and he was sitting at the dining room table filling out call reports for work. Hearing the keys jiggling, he got up to go look through the peephole.

The anger was evident in Cody's jaw as he realized the locks had been changed and he no longer had access to Henry's apartment.

Unlocking the door from the inside, a door they'd stumbled through together so many times, hungry to be wrapped up in one another's embrace, Henry swung it open and stood there, mere inches from the married Marine.

"You changed the locks?" Cody was clearly pissed.

The best defense is an offense, Henry thought. *He's going to throw this on me. He's acting pissed at me for changing the locks on him? Is he fucking kidding?*

With arms crossed over his chest, Henry stood in the threshold, blocking Cody from entering. "What'd you tell Shelby? That you were going out for milk?"

Shaking his head and using his bulk to push past him and enter the apartment, "Don't be a bitch, Henry." He stood with his back to him for a moment, before slowly turning around. "And no, I didn't tell Shelby anything. She and the kids are back in Georgia where they live."

"Right," was all Henry said, nostrils flaring. "I don't remember inviting you in."

"I don't remember needing an invite."

"I don't remember you telling me you had a wife and kids."

"I don't remember you asking."

"So what's your deal, Cody? You straight? You gay? You some kind of closet case."

The Marine was on him so fast, he had no time to defend himself. Shoving him backward by both shoulders, Henry lost footing, knocking into the pointy corner of an end table with his thigh and sending a lamp careening to the floor with a cringe-worthy crash.

He's a Marine. He could kill me with his bare hands, was the thought that made Henry check his own anger, knowing he needed to diffuse the situation and not throw gasoline on the fire.

"Is that what you came here for, Cody? To hurt me? Because you've already hurt me enough. You won. So you can go knowing 'mission accomplished', OK. Just go."

Running a hand over his short hair, the agitation evident in every tight muscle, Cody shook his head. "I didn't come here to hurt you, Henry."

"Then why did you come?"

As Henry rose from the floor, Cody extended a hand, which he ignored.

"I thought we needed to talk."

Ya think? I've been dying for four days while there's been radio silence from you. "I'm listening." Henry winced as he rubbed the spot on his thigh that had been stabbed by the table corner.

"Can we sit?" Cody gave a small smile, a tease of the lone dimple barely making an appearance, as he sat down on the couch.

Henry crossed to an armchair and sat down.

"C'mon Henry, I'm not going to hurt you. I'm sorry about what just happened. Come sit here."

Sitting down next to him on the couch, Henry still kept his distance.

Reaching out, Cody put a hand on Henry's cheek. "I've missed you and I'm sorry about your friend and sorry I wasn't there for you."

Henry longed to let his face rest in Cody's big hand, but the past four days had been hell.

"Why didn't you tell me?"

"Because it was never supposed to be this, we were never supposed to be this. It was supposed to be what it had always been for me, a fling. And by the time it wasn't, I didn't know how to go back and tell you without it totally blowing us up."

"Running into you was a sure way to blow things up."

"That was just one of those things. I never thought that was going to happen. We've been separated for over a year. She's been living in Georgia, and both her parents and my parents were pushing to see if we could work it out. I didn't know she and the girls were coming out until the last minute."

"Did you fuck her?"

Cody remained silent, the muscles in his jaw telling Henry the full story minus a few choice details, like his brutal and humiliating assault on his wife's ass, tears streaming down his face as he pounded into her as hard as he could, trying to convince himself it didn't matter who he unleashed in, a tight ass was a tight ass.

"It didn't mean anything, Henry."

"Well, maybe it meant something to me." As he verbalized it, Henry realized that he wanted so much more than Cody could give him living this double life. He wanted what he thought they had been building towards. He wanted that illusion to be reality. His reality. Their reality.

The dimple appeared, "I'm glad it meant something to you." Looking down at his hands, he shook his head, "I'm sorry that this went down the way it did and that you found out in a really shitty way, but I'm glad you know and that it's not between us anymore."

Not between us? Is he kidding? "Does she know?"

"She suspects."

Pulling her ass hard against his cock, he ground as deeply into her as he could, before pumping in his hot load without a condom. He was drunk and fucking her ass was the only way he could get hard with her, even wasted.

When he was done, "Is that what you do to your boyfriend," she spat between clenched teeth.

"At least he knows how to suck dick."

Her hand was across his face slapping him before his drunk reflexes could stop her. She went and slept with the girls that night and every night after until their departure.

"So what is it you want from me, Cody?" Henry was confused.

"Right now," he smiled, "I would love for you to suck my cock."

"And then what?" Henry wanted to scream at him, *you weren't there for me when I needed you. You weren't there for me. I want someone who is there for me. And you didn't even tell her.*

"And then I'll suck yours. Or maybe to show you how sorry I am, I'll suck yours right now." Grabbing Henry's hand, he pulled him on top of his muscular body, finding his mouth for a kiss that was wrought with pain, longing and confusion. "I've missed your ass," he whispered roughly.

With hands on Henry's rear, Cody pressed them together,

lining up their erections so that their cocks touched through their clothing. Rubbing himself along Henry's hardening cock, "You can't tell me you didn't miss this." He undid Henry's pants and started to pull them down.

Henry pulled his head back to look at the big Marine, "Of course I missed it. I missed you. I missed us. But I don't think I can do this."

"Do what?" Cody's brows knit together.

"Be your dirty little secret while someone else gets the dream."

Rolling his eyes, "Henry, I'm in the Marine Corps, losing a paycheck and pension isn't an option and I'm not gay. Just because I like you to suck my cock doesn't mean I'm gay."

"You're serious." Henry's mouth hung open.

"Yeah, I'm serious. I'm not a fag." Cody pushed Henry off him.

"You've been fucking me for months. We've been in a relationship. What is it you think you are, Cody?"

"Certainly not a god-damn fag," he spat with disdain.

"Yeah, whatever. You keep telling yourself that." Henry shook his head. "I think you should leave now."

"I think that's a good idea." Cody stood and took a step toward the door, then turned back to Henry, "You're throwing me out?" There was disbelief in his tone.

"You need to leave. Now."

He was on Henry like a large cat pouncing on its prey, "You don't give me orders, you little faggot. I leave when I want to leave." And in one swift move, he had Henry face down on the floor. With his knee in the middle of Henry's back and his fingers wrapped tightly through his ginger waves, he slammed Henry's face repeatedly into the parquet wood tiles.

The searing pain was immediate. He felt the first slam and heard a deafening cracking sound that he instinctively knew were the bones in his cheek. On the third slam, his nose crushed to the left, cutting off one air supply. By the fifth slam he was unconscious, his struggling body now limp.

"I'm not a fag and I don't take orders from them."

He never felt the pain of Cody's rage on his ass as the big Marine violently took what he wanted one last time, nor did he feel the thud of keys being thrown onto his back before Cody calmly walked out of his apartment for the very last time.

Sometime after 2 A.M. he regained consciousness. Disoriented, it took him a few minutes to recognize his surroundings and remember the details of the assault. Immediately gripped by fear that Cody was still there, waiting to finish what he had started, he lay there very still until he was certain that he was all alone. Staying in one position to mentally gather the strength to bear the pain, he slowly crawled across the apartment.

When he reached the kitchen, he pulled the phone by its cord until it came crashing down onto the floor next to him. Just the sound of the phone smashing to the floor caused pain in his multiple injuries. Lifting the receiver, he hit the redial button, because it was easier than dialing 911. Listening to the series of rings, Henry prayed the call didn't go to an answering machine.

"Hello," Edwin's voice was filled with sleep.

"I need an ambulance," he thought he said, but wasn't really sure, as he once again lost consciousness.

EDWIN DIDN'T RECOGNIZE HENRY WHEN he stepped behind the curtain in the Emergency Room. Swollen into a grotesque, bruised mask, it was only the shock of wavy ginger hair that assured him that this was his sweet, beautiful friend. The IV with painkillers had knocked him out and he was resting, although Edwin doubted that it was comfortably.

Sighing deeply, he took Henry's hand and held it tightly, "Oh sweet boy, how could that animal have done this to you?"

A nurse walked in, "Are you Edwin?"

He nodded.

"Henry was able to write this down, before they gave him the sedatives and pain medication."

She handed him a piece of paper from a pharmaceutical pad. In scratchy, barely legible handwriting, "Call Schooner. 714-555-3012. Bring wedding pictures."

Edwin looked up at the nurse, "Was he delirious? It says to bring wedding pictures."

The nurse shook her head, "No, he wasn't delirious. The surgeon is going to need photos to help in the reconstruction of the bones in his face so that he ends up looking somewhat like he did before the attack."

Somewhat like he did before the attack? Closing his eyes, Edwin tried to process the information. Facial reconstruction. Surgery.

Sweet, sweet Henry, the boy who had paid for a friend's funeral, when his own family wouldn't, was the victim of such violent hatred just for being who he was. And his attacker, Edwin was certain without actually knowing, was a man whom he had trusted with his heart and body. And now what had that very same man stolen from his soul. This was too steep a price to pay for loving the wrong person.

As he headed down the hall in search of a phone, he thought, *well, I'm finally going to get to meet Boat Boy,* the nickname he had given to Henry's odd-named friend. *Not exactly the way I wanted to meet him.*

Henry had just been moved into an actual room when his old friend, Schooner Moore, arrived. Lightly dozing in a chair next to the bed, Edwin opened his eyes to the pained look on his handsome friend's face. The man had grabbed the heavy plastic footboard at the end of the bed as if to stop himself from swaying and closed his eyes as he slowly exhaled a lungful of air.

Edwin sat there silently watching the pain on his face turn to seething anger. *Lion King,* Edwin thought, *this man is the king and no one hurts a member of his pride and gets away with it.* He looked like he was ready to pounce. Henry had described Schooner as 'larger-than-life' and Edwin agreed with the assessment.

The man was big, several inches over six feet with a strong athletic build. *I'll bet he could give that Marine a run for his money,* was Edwin's immediate thought. With his thick blonde hair, sky blue eyes, and beautifully photogenic features, Edwin couldn't think of a single actor working in Hollywood better looking than this man.

Schooner finally noticed he was being watched and looked over at Edwin. "The Marine?"

"I think so," Edwin sighed deeply.

Nodding, Schooner's eyes focused back in on his friend. "Don't worry. He won't get away with it."

Alarmed that Schooner would go after him and be hurt,

Edwin opened his mouth to protest.

As if sensing that, he shook his head, "Don't worry, it won't be anything physical, even though I would like to kill him, he deserves something much worse."

"Oh you're evil, I like you."

And it was then that Edwin saw the beautiful All-American boy smile for the first time. A smile that almost made him gasp at its sheer beauty. The man was magnificent.

"He really loves you." Edwin looked solemnly at their sleeping friend.

"I'm an only child and he's the closest thing I've ever had to a brother. He was there to pick me up in my lowest moments and he knows things about me other people don't. That's how much I trust him." Schooner sat down in the chair next to Edwin and crossed his long legs.

"You know it's an odd thing for a straight guy to be close friends with a gay man."

Schooner shrugged. "It's not really something I think about. We've been friends for a long time. A mutual friend introduced us and Henry and I just hit it off." He thought for a moment before speaking again, "We love who we love. It may not make sense to anyone else. It doesn't need to. It may not even make sense to you," he paused, shrugging again. "It doesn't need to."

Edwin had the sense that Schooner wasn't just talking about his relationship with Henry, but also of someone else. He knew that he was married, yet he'd bet his last dollar that the love he was talking about wasn't with his wife.

The unlikely pair held a bedside vigil, Schooner taking on the role of primary contact with the doctors, meeting with the plastic surgeon and leaving the room to make phone calls that Edwin got the feeling had something to do with retribution for the Marine. The doctors wanted Henry stabilized prior to putting him under anesthesia for surgery, but didn't want to miss a fine window to operate.

With his jaw already wired and swelling still significant, Henry's ability to communicate was limited when he awoke.

"Squeeze my hand once for yes and twice for no," Edwin spoke slowly to him as if he were talking to a small child. "Do you understand that?"

His strength was limited, but both men could distinctly see the single squeeze.

"Did Cody do this to you?" Edwin asked in a hushed tone.

Again, a single squeeze.

"Son of a bitch," Schooner muttered.

"Do you want to press charges?"

Two squeezes came in rapid succession.

"Are you afraid that he might come back and hurt you if you do, H?" Schooner asked, moving closer to where Edwin was seated.

A single squeeze.

"Hey, buddy, don't worry about that. That motherfucker is going to be spending a good long time in a hell hole in the Middle East and that's a promise. And if he does get back stateside, he will not be stepping foot in California, I can guarantee you that."

Edwin looked up at Schooner, "Is that what you've been doing on that cute little cellular phone of yours?" Edwin loved the new little StarTac phone Henry's friend seemed to have attached to his ear.

Smiling, "My mom and dad send you their love, H."

Inwardly smiling, it was immediately clear to Edwin that Schooner Moore's parents had some very influential connections and that he had called upon them to gain some justice for his friend.

Watching Henry close his eyes and drift back to sleep, both men hoped that they had given him some solace in knowing he wouldn't fall prey to another attack.

"I need to go make a call," Schooner began to move away.

"You needed corroboration?"

He nodded, "Obviously we needed to confirm, but it's exactly as we thought it was.

"Will he really be shipped off?"

There was a look of satisfaction on the handsome blonde's face and he nodded. "Yeah, he's a huge liability to them."

Smiling, Edwin pointed a finger at Schooner, "I knew I liked you."

Laughing, "Well, I think you are going to like me even more. There's a little part two to this that I think you're going to like and I'm going to need your help to pull off. Are you in?" Schooner gave Edwin an irresistible, conspiratorial smile.

Dipping his head and looking up at Schooner through his lashes, "I'm all in."

Edwin wondered if anyone could ever say no to this beautiful White Knight.

Schooner walked into Henry's apartment with a small soft cooler bag and put it down on the coffee table. "Hey, look at you," he smiled at his friend sitting on the couch. "You really look amazing."

Home for several days, Henry's bruising from both the attack and the subsequent surgeries had improved significantly, as had his swelling. Handsome prior to the beating, a team of Southern California's very talented surgeons reconstructed the bones in Henry's cheeks, nose, jaw and eye orbits, resulting in Henry not only looking like his former self, but with a finer, more refined elegance to his bone structure. A one and a half inch scar below his eye on his left cheekbone would add a slightly rugged dimension to his impressive looks.

"I feel a lot better," he said through clenched teeth.

Unzipping the cooler bag, Schooner began to unpack

Tupperware containers filled with colored purees. "CJ has been making this homemade, organic baby food for Zac, so she's made a whole set for you, too. They're labeled, so that you know what they are. And there's some adult flavored food in there in addition to the peas and carrots mush." Schooner smiled.

"CJ made that for me?" His face was still too swollen to register shock.

Nodding, "Yeah, she did. She was really upset by what happened to you. She's genuinely worried."

Using the word genuine in connection with anything concerning CJ Moore felt like an oxymoron to Henry. He and his friend's wife had never been fans of one another and he doubted they ever would be.

Henry had first been introduced to Schooner in January of their freshman year in college. His close friend and dorm mate, Mia Silver, had gotten to know the big blonde tennis player during freshman orientation at the beginning of the school year. The month of January at their school was known as Interim. During that period, many students were off-campus, traveling abroad, and taking classes overseas for the month, while other students remained on campus where they would engage in one very intense workshop class four days a week.

Schooner, Henry, Mia and their friend, Rosie, remained on campus that January, and together became a project-partner team in a workshop on music in American popular culture. The four became inseparable, working, studying, eating and hanging out together seven days a week. During what felt like a magical month, deep bonds were formed, and two very significant relationships emerged.

Schooner and Henry became close and unlikely friends – a tennis star from the all-guys jock dorm and a gay guy from the freak and stoner dorm. Each had never felt more comfortable with another male friend, shedding masks they thought they had to wear for the world, abandoning deep secrets, while learning about who they were to become as men through lessons learned via their friendship.

The other relationship that formed during Interim was between Schooner and Mia. Schooner had a girlfriend right from the start of freshman year, and they were immediately considered a power couple on campus. Even though they were freshmen, there wasn't a soul on campus who didn't know who CJ and Schooner were. CJ MacAllister looked like she belonged with Schooner Moore. Blonde and beautiful, the former prom queen was like a royal at court, always surrounded by her mean-girl minions that often did her bidding. That January, CJ was in Europe studying abroad.

As unlikely a pairing as Schooner and Henry, Schooner and Mia couldn't have seemed like an odder coupling on their small, Southern California campus filled with golden boys and flaxen-haired beauties. Schooner was the quintessential California golden boy. A child model from age four, the tall blonde, blue-eyed athlete seemed like an unlikely love for the little, curly- haired brunette intellectual from New York City. Mia was a quirky, free-spirit, while Schooner fell captive to everyone's expectations of him.

But this love that formed burned with an incandescent intensity, as each experienced that all-consuming first love. There was no doubt in either of their minds that the other was their one and only true love, the person they wanted to share an entire lifetime, their twin flame.

But fate would deal Schooner a blow so powerful that while he appeared whole and unscathed after a period of time, nothing could have been further from the truth.

Schooner Moore died on the last day of their freshman year in college. But only someone as close to him as Henry Clark would actually know his friend's soul had vacated his handsome shell, as he slipped on a mask for all the world to see, pretending he was the same and had gone on living.

But he had not.

Coming back to Henry and Mia's dorm after his final exam on the last day of school, Schooner's plan had been to spend some time with Mia before she left for the airport to fly back home to New York for the summer. Greeted by an empty dorm room with no Mia, and no note from Mia saying goodbye, the handsome blonde was crushed, knowing deep in his soul that all his dreams had been ripped from him in an instant. She was gone. Just gone.

In a moment of frustration, Schooner slammed his fist into a concrete block wall in the dorm's hallway, smashing several bones and ending his bright tennis career. Every part of what he loved died that day.

Heartbroken and not knowing why the love of his life left him, never returning to school, Schooner closed himself off to situations he couldn't control, situations that could hurt him. Love was never going to be his focus, but building a business empire of high-end, state of the art fitness and entertainment complexes would become his life's passion. That, and his children, became the laser focal points in Schooner Moore's life.

Knowing Mia the way he did, Henry knew something very significant had happened on that last night of freshman year to make Mia run and never return. Schooner was so deeply entrenched in Mia's soul that walking away and never turning back had to have been born of a deep, shattering pain. Henry knew that. And he also knew the only one with any leverage to inflict that kind of pain upon Mia, was Schooner's ex-girlfriend, CJ.

He didn't know what she had done. But he knew she had done something to turn fate on its axis and invoke an alternate ending to what should have been written. Although he never verbalized it to CJ, she knew that Henry thought she was involved in Mia leaving Schooner. It was an unspoken, but very clear mistrust, and because of that, Henry was a liability to her.

Minimizing her husband's contact with him would only help to ensure the safety of her treacherous secrets. So CJ MacAllister Moore generally made no bones about her distaste of her husband's relationship with the ginger-haired gay man.

"I watched her make them and feed them to Zac, so I can vouch that there is no poison in any of them," Schooner joked, but both men knew that the thought went through each of their heads.

"Don't make me laugh with a wired jaw, Moore." *CJ Moore being nice to me? Thoughtful? Quick, turn on the TV, Hell must've frozen over.*

Edwin arrived a few minutes later, and he and Schooner left shortly after to do some shopping for Henry. Or so they told him.

"I hope he shows." Edwin was gearing up for drama.

"Me too," Schooner nodded, as he negotiated his Porsche 911 eastward through the streets of San Diego, "I don't want any doubt in this scumbag's mind exactly what happened, who did it to him and why. And our window of opportunity, before they ship him out, is almost up."

Pulling up in front of The Hole, Schooner killed the engine and he and Edwin sat silently like two pumas in wait. After about twenty minutes of watching hot men, not so hot men, bears and biker boys descend the steep wooden staircase into their tropical patio mecca, Edwin whispered loudly, "That's him, I'm sure of it."

"Ok, look down, I don't want him recognizing you." Schooner slid on his Ray-Bans. "I'm looking at the tall, built guy, faded jeans, black V-neck tee and aviator glasses."

"Yes, that's him." Edwin took a quick peek up. "I'm positive." Quickly ducking his head back down, as if getting something from between their low bucket seats.

"I'm going to let him get settled for a few minutes." Schooner reached over in front of Edwin and opened the glove compartment, pulling something out.

"What are you going to do with that?" Edwin asked.

"Insurance." Schooner hit him with his beautiful catalogue cover smile.

Shaking his head, "They are going to swarm you in there."

Schooner laughed, "I'm looking for Ryan, right? He's the bartender with the Merlin tattoo on his arm."

"Yes, that's how Henry once described him to me."

"Ok, I'm going in." Schooner swung his long legs out of the low car.

"Good luck." Edwin appeared nervous.

Pointing a finger at the older man, "Stay here. Do not come in until after he leaves. I don't want him near you."

With a reassuring smile, Schooner was off, heading down the steep wooden staircase toward the patio. As he got to the bottom of the stairs, he whispered, "Showtime," to himself.

Moving through the crowd with a slow grace, the athletic blonde was getting his fair share of double-takes as he scanned the crowd looking for his target. Out of his pants pocket, he pulled a small disposable camera and took a few random shots of the packed club.

With the bar straight ahead, he continued to move in that direction, and as his eyes slowly adjusted to the dark indoor space, he was pleased to find the Marine bellied up to the bar. Snapping a few more shots, this time clearly of Cody as he approached, he put the camera back into his pocket and made his way up to the bar, where he stood right next to his target.

"Is that a bottle of Glenfiddich 18 year old I see on the back shelf?" Schooner asked the blue-eyed bartender with the Merlin tattoo.

"It sure is." The bartender was impressed.

"I'll take a double. Straight up."

"Now, that's a man's drink," the Husky-eyed guy standing next to him commented.

Schooner turned, making eye contact, "Yeah, well, it's my

drink," and tossed back the single malt scotch.

"I haven't seen you here before," Cody commented.

"It's not a place that I usually come. But it happens to be a favorite spot of a friend of mine," he paused. "Although he hasn't been here in a few weeks."

"Too bad your friend didn't bring you here before," Cody was starting to flirt.

Just on the other side of the bar, Ryan was watching Cody flirt with the incredibly handsome blonde and wondered if he and Henry had broken up. With the way the big Marine was eyeing the equally built guy, Ryan assumed the two were no longer together and wondered if that was why he hadn't seen Henry all month.

Ignoring the Marine, Schooner turned to Ryan, "Do you guys have interaction with the management and staff of other clubs around town?"

"Gay clubs?" Ryan clarified.

"Yeah."

"Yeah, we do. We kind of have a reciprocal policy as far as no cover charges for staff and usually the bar managers stay in touch, especially if there's been problems around town."

"Oh interesting. So if there were someone that they wanted to warn their staff to keep an eye out for, that info would get shared?"

Leaning with his elbows on the bar, chin in hand, Ryan corroborated Schooner's supposition. "Oh absolutely, that's totally critical in keeping both our patrons and community safe.

Nodding his head, Schooner reached into his pants pocket and pulled out a disposable camera, handing it across the bar to Ryan. "Good. Then you'll probably want this."

"What's on there?" The Marine was suddenly interested in their conversation.

Ignoring him and focusing on Ryan, "You may want to share the photos on there with the other bars."

The bartender looked at him quizzically and Schooner

continued, "Dude's a closet-case fucking homophobe who landed a buddy of mine in the hospital seriously injured after he beat the shit out of him for being, as he put it, a 'fucking fag'." Schooner turned to the Marine, his voice dripping with venom, "Sound familiar, asshole?"

Caught off-guard, it took but only a second for Cody to recover, his face hardening, shoulders falling back, taking him to his full height, "I don't know what you're talking about."

"Yeah, just like you didn't know you had a wife and kids." Inches from him, Schooner's chest was nearly grazing his opponent's. "Henry's mistake was trusting you."

"Henry?" Ryan's voice was filled with shock. He stood paralyzed for a moment and then looked down the bar, signaling something to one of the other bartenders.

"He sent you to fight his battles?"

"Listen, you douchebag coward, I don't need to lay a hand on you to fuck you up."

"You think you can fuck me up?" with a raised voice he chest-bumped Schooner who didn't budge.

"I already have, you moron," laughing, Schooner just smiled calmly in his face.

Inches from his target, Cody's eyes narrowed, taking in Schooner and making a final assessment on the best way to take down the other man who held his eye contact steadfastly. This was going to be exactly the kind of fight Cody loved, knowing his training would give him the edge to do some serious damage to his opponent.

Security at The Hole could easily be mistaken for either Hell's Angels or members of ZZ Top. Schooner watched as they descended upon the Marine from behind, each grabbing an arm, the element of surprise immediately registering on Cody's face.

"Time for you to leave, scumbag," a raspy-voiced bouncer yanked Cody away from the bar as they started to drag him toward the patio and the establishment's exit.

"Hey Asshole," Schooner yelled out and the security detail stopped.

Sneering, Cody looked back at Schooner, vendetta raging from his intense blue eyes.

Lifting his scotch glass, which he was thrilled to find Ryan had wisely refilled, he tipped it to Cody, "Enjoy your new hell hole in Baghdad, douchebag," and with a smile, he threw back his scotch and turned back to the bar.

"Grab a glass for yourself," Schooner offered and Ryan quickly filled a second glass. Clinking glasses, "To banishing scum."

"How is Henry?" Ryan was concerned.

"Healing. At least externally." Schooner's concern matched the bartenders.

"I guess I should let the other bars know." Ryan lifted the disposable camera.

"I don't think he'll be around long enough. That fucker has no clue how quickly he's about to be deployed."

"You weren't kidding about Baghdad?" Ryan's voice registered shock as he poured himself and Schooner another drink.

With a slow handsome smile, Schooner shook his head, "No. I took the pictures just to fuck with him. Extra insurance. My family is very fond of Henry. They've known him a long time and couldn't believe what that animal did to him. My dad has some pretty influential contacts and he made some well-placed calls."

"He peeled out of here like a bat out of hell," Edwin was upon them. "He was pissed."

"Edwin, this is Ryan. Ryan, Edwin is a good friend of Henry's."

Pulling out another rocks glass, "So nice to meet you."

"Put that thing away," Edwin gestured to the glass. "I want a pitcher of something yummy and I want a pink straw."

Laughing, "Of course you get a pink straw, handsome. I

julie richman

wouldn't dream of anything else." Ryan smiled at Henry's older friend.

H
E COULD FEEL HIM SLIP into the cool crisp sheets and spoon him, his long, muscled body fitting perfectly to his length, but he was too tired to roll over and even acknowledge his presence. He hadn't had a good night's sleep in so long and his entire body ached with fatigue.

The soft kiss on his shoulder brought a smile to his face. He loved how tender he could be.

"How are you feeling," his voice a seductive breath.

"I'm ok. Tired, but ok."

"I worry about you. You know that, don't you?"

He just shrugged.

"I worried about you the whole time I was away. Worried you wouldn't love me anymore when I got back. Worried I'd die in the middle of that squalid war zone and no one would tell you that I was dead. Really, I worried about that. I was so afraid if that happened that you would think it was my choice not to come back to you."

"I didn't think you were coming back."

"All I thought about over there was coming back to you. This. Right now. Feeling you next to me. What it feels like to be inside you. That's what kept me going when I was on missions and nights when it got really bad."

He felt his hand snake around to the front of him. His flat

palm sliding smoothly over his hip bone toward his groin.

"You got so thin while I was away. You really need to take better care of yourself."

His hand was now encircling his cock and as much as he didn't want to get hard for him, his damn penis had a mind of its own. As he started to stroke him, he hardened, saluting the captain.

"Yes, this is how I know how much you missed me, how much you still want me. You never could resist my touch and I love how you are a slave to it. No matter what. A slave to me. You've been my slave since that day we met. Do you know how much I love that?"

Love that? Is he serious?

His grasp tightened on his cock.

"Ouch. That hurts."

"You didn't answer my question." His grip remained firm.

"Yes. I know how much you love that I'm a slave to you."

"Good." He continued to squeeze.

"You're hurting me." The pleasurable pain had crossed the threshold to agony.

"Oh, don't be such a fag, Henry. You know what it's like when I *really* hurt you."

"Please stop. I'm so tired. Please just let me sleep. I need to sleep."

"You'll sleep when I let you," he hissed.

He could hear himself scream as his hair was yanked by the roots and his head slammed into the wooden headboard. One time. Two times. Three times.

It was the same every night.

Drenched in sweat, he shivered as his tee-shirt clung to cold, clammy skin. With his stomach cramping and that God awful headache, he put his head in his hands and pressed the sides of his skull with the heels of his palms, silently begging for the pain to stop.

With a sigh, Henry turned on the light and reached for the bottle of painkillers. He sat there for a moment, after swallowing the acrid tasting pill, trying to slow his breathing. Opening the drawer of his nightstand, he withdrew his PalmPilot and scrolled down to the calendar function.

Putting an X on the date, he added the consecutive number. 127. Tonight was 127. No wonder he was so exhausted. Night 127 of the nightmare. It altered a little, but generally remained the same. And the aftereffects never wavered.

The dream was like a prophecy.

"You'll sleep when I let you sleep."

Henry was quickly losing hope that he'd ever let him sleep again.

chapter
nine

I T HAD BEEN ALMOST SIX months since the attack and with Edwin's help, he was getting out of his apartment every day and finally driving again. At first, it had been a walk up the block for basic necessities and then the five block trek to his therapist's office. Eventually they began including coffee shops and book stores in their journeys, places where Henry could relax without constantly looking over his shoulder.

"I told Schooner about the nightmares," Edwin blew out the smoke from his Galoises, as he picked up his latte.

Shaking his head, an "ugh" sound escaped. "Is that why he wants me to come meet him at his Carlsbad facility? Is it some kind of intervention?" Henry's friend had opened one of his Level Nine, or L9 as they had become known, fitness and entertainment complexes in Carlsbad the year before. It was his most southern location and people were actually driving up from San Diego to join the famed facility and say they were L9 members.

Rolling his eyes, "No, I don't think so. Maybe he just wants to get your tight little ass in the steam room and have his way with you, with what I imagine, and I imagine nightly," his smile bordered on sinister, "to be one formidable cock."

"Why'd you tell him about the nightmares?" Henry was picking at the crumbs of his cranberry-orange scone.

"Because I'm worried about you and I know he is, too. We

want you to get your life back on track, the way it was before." Henry was still on medical leave from his very understanding company, "And I just wanted to hear his voice and touch myself." Edwin puckered his lips and blew Henry a kiss.

"You are a lecherous old thing," Henry laughed, his face relaxing, and the handsome boy Edwin once knew, a boy he no longer saw often enough, was again sitting across the table from him.

"It'll do me good to take the drive," Henry acquiesced, "and I guess work out. It's going to be painful. I haven't been on a treadmill in over six months."

"Well I'll let you see your friend alone this time," Edwin pointed his cigarette at Henry, "but next time I'm coming with you, and if I'm really lucky, coming with him," he finished with a shimmy of his shoulders.

Only Schooner, Henry was smiling as he walked into L9/Carlsbad. He'd been to two other L9 locations, but this was his first visit to this one. Just walking through the parking lot toward the entrance he could already envision the space into which he was about to walk. And his first step through the door did not disappoint.

The two-plus story ultra-modern glass and steel structure resided on a cliff overlooking the ocean. The unobstructed 180° view was breathtaking and inspiring. Halting a foot within the entrance, Henry stood mesmerized. Beyond the main fitness facility with its SkyTrack, was an infinity pool that rivaled the landscape of a five-star resort. Beyond it, ocean and sky stretched to true infinity.

Only Schooner. Henry realized he was smiling, feeling a pride for his friend that one can only feel for those they love deeply. A man that half of southern California thought they knew, yet who was truly known by very few, camouflaged by the perfect mask.

"Can I help you," the perky blonde behind the desk asked, sharing a warm smile.

"Yeah, hi," Henry was brought out of his reverie. "I'm Henry Clark, I'm here to see Schooner."

Her smile brightened even more, "Yes, he's expecting you. Let me page him."

He appeared out of nowhere, and as Henry watched the big blonde cross the facility toward him with a lithe grace that used to dominate southern California tennis courts, he knew that his smile matched his friend's. They enveloped one another in a warm hug that caused staff to turn to see who their boss was greeting so intensely.

It had been nearly a month since they had seen one another, the longest they'd gone since the attack. Henry felt an immediate purge of stress, just seeing Schooner.

"You're looking great, except for those circles under your eyes, but I think those surgeons might have made you too pretty," Schooner kidded.

"Afraid of the competition?"

Laughing, "Bring it on." He slung a muscled arm over Henry's shoulder.

"So I understand Edwin had a little chat with you." Henry broached the subject first, so as not to be blindsided by his friend.

"Yeah," Schooner nodded his head, "that's pretty alarming, H."

"Tell me about it. My nights are hell."

Stopping in front of the glass wall overlooking the ocean at the far end of the club, Schooner turned to Henry, his face serious, his blue eyes almost stormy, "You are letting him continue to steal your life and that is what I don't like, H. Stop giving him the power. The asshole is in a shithole in the Gulf and he's never coming back to sunny, warm southern California. I can guarantee you that. So, take the power back." He gave Henry's shoulder a squeeze.

"I wish I knew how. I'm in therapy twice a week. I never miss a session. I take the anti-anxiety stuff when I need it."

"I've been thinking about this and I just want you to hear me out, OK. Come with me."

They exited the back of the facility out onto the pool deck.

Stopping for a second, Henry took in the view, breathing the sea air deep into his lungs. It felt good, evoking memories of bicycle rides along the water. He hadn't ridden his bike since before it all happened.

He followed Schooner off the left side of the deck down flag stone steps onto a lusciously landscaped path that led to a small building that had been obscured by the trees. Unlike the main facility, the wood structure had an earthy feel to it.

Before they entered, Schooner turned to Henry, "There's someone I want you to meet."

Crossing the threshold, Schooner stopped and removed his shoes and Henry followed suit. From a side room a woman emerged, greeting them with a warm smile.

"Ivy, this is my very good friend, Henry Clark and H, this is Ivy Mattheson, our lead Hatha Yoga instructor."

"So nice to meet you, Henry." She took his hand in both of hers, shaking it warmly.

The jolt of energy from her hands that transferred to Henry took him by surprise.

"I was hoping the two of you could spend a little time together so that you could give Henry kind of an overview of the healing properties of yoga and what medical studies have found." Turning to Henry, "I'll be in my office in the main building when you're done. Take your time." With a touch to Henry's shoulder he was gone.

Shaking his head, "I knew he had something up his sleeve." Henry's smile was warm as he said it, knowing his friend had his best interests at heart.

"Come, grab a mat, we'll sit."

Facing Ivy, "So how much did he tell you?"

The petite brunette shook her head, her long braid swishing like a tail, "He didn't tell me anything, just to clear my schedule. That he had a friend he wanted me to meet who he thought could really get a lot from the benefits of yoga."

Smiling, Henry shrugged, palms in the air, "OK, sell me."

Ivy laughed, a warm throaty sound that matched the warmth in her doe-like brown eyes, "Henry, I couldn't sell hot soup to an Eskimo, so I'm not going to try to sell you on Yoga being the greatest healer on the planet. Although I think it is. But if you have stress issues, relaxation issues, focus issues, blood pressure issues, sleep issues, back pain, depression, PTSD – then I might be able to help you."

"OK, you've got my attention." Henry was already relaxing from the calm atmosphere and Ivy's centered demeanor.

"What do you know about Yoga?"

"Very little," he admitted. "I'm here to be enlightened."

"Aren't we all," she volleyed back playfully.

The next forty-five minutes were spent introducing Henry to some simple stretches and poses, with Ivy explaining yoga's connecting of the mind, body and breath.

Holding the poses was more challenging than Henry anticipated, even though his long, lean limbs were able to adapt to the positions fairly easily. He smiled inwardly thinking, stilling my mind is going to be what I'm going to have to work my ass off to achieve, but knew the benefits of that were probably worth more than his twice a week therapy sessions.

"So, what is the ultimate goal?" Henry felt invigorated, as if he'd opened up a new energy channel that was coursing through him, pulsing life back into cells that had been in hiding for over six months.

"That's a great question. I don't think there are any two

answers that will be exactly the same. This is the personal snowflake for people. Unique goals based on your unique needs." She paused, obviously still considering Henry's question, "I think on a larger scale, as a discipline, the goal is to achieve Moksha."

Unknowingly, the petite instructor had said the magic word. Moksha. Liberation. And Henry Clark knew in that moment that working toward mastering Yoga would become a life's passion as important to his well-being as breathing.

I need to be liberated. I don't want to be a slave anymore.

Strolling into Schooner's office, his friend looked every inch 'The Boss'. With a smug smile, Schooner looked up from his laptop as Henry took a seat across the desk.

"I knew you were setting me up, Moore. I just didn't know what for."

"So what do you think?" Schooner flipped the laptop shut.

"I think it's interesting and I like that it integrates mind, body and spirit in a restorative way."

Schooner remained silent and Henry continued.

"If it can help with the fear and anxiety and the nightmares," he took a deep breath, "I want it to. I really do. I want to fight back, Schooner. What you said to me before about him stealing my power was really true. I want it back."

Schooner's handsome smile reached his clear blue eyes, "Good. Because that scumbag doesn't deserve anything from you. Not your life. Not your thoughts. And certainly not another minute of your present or your future." Sitting back in his chair, he looked very pleased with himself. "So, how many days a week can you commit to this?"

"Well, I have therapy twice a week."

Schooner wasn't waiting for an answer, "Great, so we'll make you a standing three day per week client with Ivy. And since you'll be here, you and I can do some working out, too. And maybe get on that SkyTrack and run through this."

Henry just nodded. Words would have caused his eyes to well up.

"We'll run through this, we will. You're going to be ok." Henry had promised his despondent friend as they ran the empty track behind the dorms.

"I don't know that I'll ever really be OK, H." Schooner looked up at the stars shining down on them and pulled his black knit cap further down on his brow. *"Not until I know why she left me."*

"You will be OK. We'll run through this," and Henry took off in a sprint knowing the competitive athlete in Schooner would have him following suit.

As if sharing the same moment in his mind's eye, Schooner locked eyes with Henry and softly repeated, "We'll run through this."

Bang. Bang. Bang.

He sat up in bed, drenched in sweat. Reaching over to the nightstand, he grabbed the PalmPilot and started to scroll.

X. 206.

Placing the device back on the nightstand, Henry reached over his head, and with his right hand grabbed the neckline of his tank top and hauled it off in a quick, sweeping motion.

On his knees facing the end of the bed, he slowly slid forward with his arms outstretched until his forehead touched the cool sheets. Mindful that his bottom still held contact with the heels of his feet, Henry was satisfied that his form was good as he stretched into the Balasana, or the Child's Pose.

Focusing on his breathing and stilling his mind, the stress relieving position was accomplishing exactly what it was designed to do, as Henry's mind and body calmed.

On the nightstand stood two bottles, one filled with highly-addictive painkillers, the other with equally addictive anti-anxiety medicine.

Henry hadn't touched either since he began working with Ivy.

G ETTING BACK TO WORK WAS the next major stride Henry made, realizing that having a schedule in his life was exactly what he needed to keep progressing in his recovery and keep his mind from wandering off. The first day was difficult as he looked at his navy suit laid out on the bed, thinking *I can't do this. I can't have them all see me.*

Forcing himself to put on the pale blue shirt, then his slacks, he stood before the full-length mirror to knot his favorite tie. And then he just stood there, staring at his reflection. *I look whole,* he thought. Grabbing his suit jacket, he slipped into it and walked back to the mirror. He could see the difference in his face and wondered would others notice it. It was subtle and the shock of ginger hair setting off his violet-blue eyes would probably distract people from the distinct changes to his bone structure. There only one telltale giveaway and that was the scar.

Coworkers and clients alike greeted him warmly, showing genuine concern. Even his straight male colleagues were welcoming. By lunch the first day, being surrounded by people he had known for so many years, felt comforting, not stress inducing. *I should have done this sooner,* he thought, but knew he had not been ready and that things were falling into place again as they should.

The one thing he hadn't quite gotten back to yet was his bicycle deliveries for the Fold and Fluff. At Edwin's insistence,

Henry was back helping out, but his mode of delivery had changed to his car, where he could lock the doors, giving him a feeling of safety on his drop-off route. Looking over his shoulder was something he hadn't let go of yet and wasn't sure he ever would.

So much had changed since he'd first gotten to San Diego, and he knew he'd never be the same person he was when he'd arrived. The innocence of those first months felt as if he were watching a video recording of another person. A very naïve, trusting person. Those early days living in Hillcrest felt wild and innocent, as the world lay before him, begging to be licked, tasted and savored. And he had been all too happy to be the glutton. Gone now, were the carefree free-wheeling days, replaced by structure needed as a scaffold he could tightly grasp onto to keep moving forward. *Just keep moving forward*, he kept telling himself.

The discipline of three days a week at L9, and its clear results, provided a level of confidence Henry was shocked he was seeing so soon as he reclaimed the different facets of his molested world.

Ivy was pushing him, as she always did, forcing him to do just a little more and to do it a little better. Today was no different. As he counted breaths in the Peacock Position, two, three, four, five, his mind was still and focused.

"Into a Low Push-Up for a count of five breaths next and then take that into a Cobra and hold before we call it a day."

As they walked out of the studio together, Ivy asked, "So have you had any more nightmare free nights?"

After they had been working together for several weeks, the trust had been built enough for Henry to share an abbreviated version of the attack and tell Ivy of his recurring nightmare. Smiling, he nodded, "Yes, quite a few."

"That is excellent. This has worked so well for you. I am really pleased."

"You and me both," Henry laughed.

Entering the main building, he immediately noticed Schooner

over at the free weights with three seriously built guys.

I haven't seen them before, Henry mused. *I wouldn't have forgotten that trio.*

As he got closer to the group, the men appeared even better looking than he originally thought. *These guys could be a calendar,* he mused and what struck him hardest was that he had noticed, he had actually noticed. And it had piqued his interest.

As if sensing his arrival, Schooner turned, "H, great timing. These guys need a fourth. Are you available?"

Henry knew the look on Schooner's face. Knew it well. Mr. Moore was proud of himself. Quite proud.

"Guys, this is my friend, Henry," he began.

The three looked over as Henry approached. He was greeted by the warm smile of a Denzel Washington look-a-like and a nod from a handsome Hispanic guy with one of the tightest builds he had ever seen. It was the third guy whose reaction made him tense, yet caused a stir in a place he never thought would stir again. As Henry approached, the dark haired man's pale blue eyes took a walk all over him.

"Henry, this is Derek, Willie and Quinn."

As he shook hands with each, the eye contact confirmed what he had hoped. This was a trio of gorgeous gay men. *Well done, Schooner.*

"Quinn Callahan." The man had a powerful shake. "Spot for me?" he asked, quickly staking his claim.

"Yeah, sure." Henry followed him toward a bench, impressed by his tight ass and muscular calves. With thick hair, a near black, Henry thought his mother would have described Quinn as "Black Irish".

"Are you all friends?"

"Yeah," his smile revealed even white teeth, "and we work together, too." Loading the bumper plates onto the barbell, Quinn sealed them on with the muscle clamp collars and took his place on the bench.

Watching the man's muscles as he pumped the heavy iron, Henry couldn't help but admire his sculptured arms as the planes and shadows began to glisten. He didn't realize at first that he was licking his lips as he watched Quinn's muscles work. There was some kind of primal call in the man's grunts, Henry thought, something so distinctly masculine, yet beautiful. *I could watch him do this for days.*

Quinn finished his reps and Henry secured the bar.

"Are you lifting today?" Quinn was ready to return the favor.

"No, but I'm happy to help."

"Well, thanks." The man looked puzzled. "Run? I usually hit the SkyTrack next."

"Sure." Henry felt immediate relief at Quinn's suggestion. He didn't want to say goodbye just yet, but hadn't figured out how to make the situation continue. *Damn, I'm rusty,* he thought.

Getting into the elevator up to the SkyTrack, Henry could feel the energy, or so he thought, immediately deciding it was all in his head, though he didn't want it to be. Quinn was the first person he'd been attracted to in months. *And how could he not be,* thought Henry, the man was just beautiful with that black hair and pale baby-blue eyes.

The elevator door opened and they were at the top of the structure, the noise from the conversations on the facility's main floor below them just a mere din. Quinn gestured to Henry to step out of the car in front of him. They walked to the railing of the SkyTrack and began stretching side-by-side.

"So where do you guys work?" Henry wondered about the hot trio, half expecting Quinn to answer Chippendale's.

As he pressed off the railing stretching his hamstring, Quinn glanced at Henry, his pale blue eyes doing a quick assessment of the information's recipient.

"We're PD," was all he said.

"You guys are cops?" Henry's look of astonishment could not be hidden.

With a slight nod of his head and a smile, Quinn was off, his first lap on the track underway.

Cops. Hot cops. Hot gay cops. Damn you, Schooner Moore. You're just going to drag me back into this world by whatever means you see fit.

Thank you.

It didn't elude Henry as he began to run, trailing Quinn by thirty feet that he was chasing a hot cop's ass. When he realized that, the thought made him smile, and his smile grew even brighter as he quickened his pace to close the gap between them.

Without breaking stride, Quinn turned around, his pale blue eyes crinkling from his smile as Henry caught up. Checking out Henry's long legs, "You were made to run," he observed.

Henry loved the man's attention to the details of his body. It was a little scary, but he wanted Quinn to notice him. "Schooner and I actually ran track together in college."

"Is that how you met? On the track team?

Henry smiled at the memory, "No, we were friends long before that and we used to run together every night. Finally, we decided to try out for the team."

"I wouldn't have taken Schooner for a runner."

"He wasn't. He was a tennis player, but had to give it up after an injury. That's when we started running."

"Is that what you usually come here for? The track and treadmills?" his breath was not even taxed as he spoke.

"No, not usually." Henry smiled, wondering what the cop would think of his admission. "I do work with the Yoga instructor here."

"Yoga." He took it in stride. "I don't know much about it, but it's a great body and mind tool, right?"

"Very good for that."

"I should try it sometime." Again, that gorgeous white-toothed smile. "But I totally get that. My mind/body thing is cycling."

Henry smiled, "Yeah?"

"Yeah," Quinn confirmed as they finished their second lap on the SkyTrack and began the third. "You too?"

"I haven't ridden in a few months, but cycling is definitely my thing."

"Well, you need to get your ass back in shape," he paused and looked down at Henry's ass with a smile, "and ride with me on the Long Beach/San Diego AIDS Ride."

"Wow. I'd forgotten about the AIDS Ride." *I've been so focused on me, the world has just passed me by.* "I could probably get the Fold and Fluff I volunteer at to sponsor me."

"It's so much better when you have someone to do it with." Quinn was looking straight ahead as he ran.

"Are you serious about doing it together?" Henry was intrigued by this guy, and the thought of wanting to see him again was something he thought he'd never feel with anyone and certainly not this soon. He needed to talk to Schooner. See how much he knew about this guy. Psycho cop after psycho Marine would be the end of him.

"Yeah, I've done it alone the past two years. Those two pussies downstairs don't even own bicycles, so it would be great to have a friend to train with and then do the event together."

"I'm really out of shape," Henry confessed.

Once again the pale blue eyes took a walk all over him, "I beg to differ."

Henry suddenly needed water for his dry mouth.

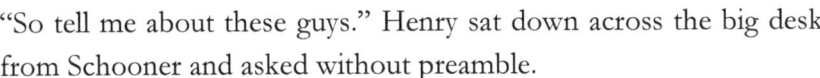

"So tell me about these guys." Henry sat down across the big desk from Schooner and asked without preamble.

Sitting back in his black leather chair, Schooner crossed his muscular arms across his chest and smiled.

"Get that shit-eating grin off your face, Moore, and tell me about these guys."

"Well, they're cops." Schooner's grin continued to expand.

"Yes, I know that."

"And you like cops."

"You're a dog." Henry narrowed his violet-blue eyes.

And both men broke into laughter.

Finally, "No, seriously. I'm afraid of psychos. You can understand that."

"Cops protect people, H."

"Marines protect a whole country, Schooner."

"You have a point there."

"Yeah, and if any of these guys are psycho cops, I want to stay as far away as possible. How long have you known them? How'd you know they were gay?"

"So you and Quinn seemed to hit it off," Schooner noted, shaking his head with a self-satisfied look.

"Answer my questions."

"I've known the three of them for a while. I knew Derek first, when he was on the force in Laguna Niguel. He started working out at the L9 facility there about four years ago. It was probably a couple of months later, that I met Willie. After they moved down to this area, they still drove up on weekends to use that facility."

"What about Quinn?" Henry needed to know more about the Irishman with the black hair and pale baby-blue eyes.

Schooner smiled. "I first met Quinn," he thought for a

second, "I'd say about a year ago. Maybe a little longer."

"And how do you know they are not psychos?" Henry was dead serious.

"I guess you never really know, but these are guys that are active in the community, have good reputations, are respected by colleagues, they do sports camps and stuff. If there were any red flags at all, H, I never would've introduced you." Schooner paused, "Besides I've had some really great conversations with Quinn about what he wants in life and what his goals are, and I think they are similar to what you want." Pausing for effect, "And you like cops."

"What did he tell you?" *Come on, Schooner, spill. You've woken the beast. Now feed it.*

"He wants a loving relationship with a partner, living openly as gay men. Which for a cop, takes a lot of guts. Something this guy is not short on, unlike Psycho Marine. And he'd even like a family someday. He's one of the good guys. I know it in my gut, H."

Henry sat back in his chair and took a deep breath.

"So you liked him?" Schooner seemed proud of himself as a matchmaker.

"I may be damaged, Moore, but I'm not dead. The guy is gorgeous. And seems really nice. I think we have stuff in common. I don't know that he's into me though."

"He seemed pretty into you to me. But hey, what do I know? I'm just the straight guy here." He laughed.

"You really thought he was into me?" Henry needed the reassurance.

"Well, how did he leave it?"

"We're going to meet back here on Wednesday, and we're going to ride together in the Long Beach/San Diego AIDS Ride."

"I didn't know you were doing that."

"Neither did I," Henry smiled.

Schooner just shook his head, his All-American boy smile beaming, "So, let me see if I've got this straight. No pun intended.

He made short-term plans with you. He's meeting you here on Wednesday and he made long-term plans with you. You guys are riding in a charity event together."

Henry nodded, "Yeah and we're going to do some training together since I haven't ridden in over six months."

"He's seeing you this week, he's made long-term plans to keep you in his life and figured out a way to be part of your life between now and then. Yeah, H, I'd say he likes you. Damn he's good, that was a pretty swift move on his part. I like it." Schooner seemed impressed.

Henry just looked at his old friend, feeling hopeful beyond belief. He wanted to get to know this guy, he was excited to get to know this guy. Never did he think that he'd get to this point again, to be trusting enough to open the door even a crack. And Quinn had made it so easy to do. There was none of that crazy testosterone filled danger surrounding the guy, even though he could be brandishing a weapon at any time.

Henry smiled at Schooner. Just as he had done for his emotionally flailing friend years ago, this time Schooner took the reins, steering Henry back onto the right path, but making him do the hard work to free himself from the darkness.

And as Schooner had promised him, once again, the two friends had run through it.

I T WAS THE THIRD WEEKEND that Henry and Quinn had loaded mountain bikes onto the back of Quinn's jeep and driven west to Mission Trails Regional Park to train in the Fortuna Mountains. The first week they stayed on the eastern half of the park with its rolling grasslands and easy trails, working on building stamina for distance to complete the 100 plus mile charity event. The following Saturday they met again, tackling a combination of the eastern and rugged western halves of the park.

Today they had decided to take on more challenging trails and as they struggled up a brutal climb known at The Alley, Quinn turned back to a trailing Henry, flashing his beautiful white smile and yelled, "You ride like a pussy."

"A pussy?" Henry screamed back with a smile. "Fuck you."

"You should get so lucky," Quinn was nearly out of breath as they reached the Fortuna saddle, giving them a quick reprieve as they rode through the notch between the North and South Fortuna Mountains. Turning right, they began their ascent up the trail to North Fortuna's summit.

"You ride behind me because you like to watch my ass," Quinn yelled back, having regained his breath.

"Damn right I do, you've got a great ass." Henry was smiling as he struggled up the trail, the burn in his thighs almost overwhelming. *I'm flirting.* The thought took him by surprise.

"So do you," Quinn called back.

Reaching the summit, they stood there alongside their bikes, silently taking in the spectacular view to the west. Quinn had been right, Henry thought. It was nice to have someone to do this with, share both the experience and the rigors of training. Cycling had become a lone endeavor for him for so many years that he thought it might be hard to share the experience with someone else. But standing alongside Quinn Callahan on a mountaintop, with the bright sun making his impossibly blue eyes appear even bluer, Henry felt a sense of peace and happiness he'd never shared with another person before.

Bumping Quinn's shoulder, "A pussy, huh?"

Quinn laughed, "That got your thighs pumping those pedals."

"Pussy," Henry grumbled and quickly got on his bike, speeding out ahead of Quinn. "Let's see who's the pussy now," he called the taunt over his shoulder.

"I'll gladly be the pussy to see your ass," Quinn called after him laughing.

What Quinn couldn't see as they descended the mountain was Henry's smile as the combination of wind, sun and speed greeted him that Saturday morning. And the cherry on this sundae was knowing Quinn Callahan was watching his ass.

"That scar looks pretty fresh," Quinn observed the white line under Henry's left eye as they sat drinking coffee after the ride. "Good story behind it?" He smiled, clearly looking for some more insight into his new friend.

"No. Bad story behind it." Henry could feel the muscles along his spine contract and it felt like he'd just grown two inches taller in his chair.

"Sorry," Quinn put down his latte, his eyes immediately filled with concern.

Henry recognized the moment with a clarity he often felt when deep into a Yoga session. He could hang onto it and keep himself imprisoned within his own walls, while shutting Quinn out, or he could purge by telling the truth and not letting Cody's actions have power over him or cause him shame. It was the moment of truth, open the door and have the chance to move forward together. Or keep it locked and remain Cody's prisoner.

"I got the shit beaten out of me by a psycho Marine I was dating who was a self-loathing closet case." Henry flung the door wide open with abandon.

"Holy crap." Quinn grew two inches in his chair as his spine stiffened. "Did you press charges?"

Henry shook his head.

"You need to press charges. Do not let this guy get away with it. That's a hate crime." Quinn was getting worked up at the injustice suffered by his new friend, his cop instincts kicking into high gear.

"He was taken care of. The guy is in a hellhole in Baghdad and he's not coming back. His commanding officers know what happened and dealt with it pretty swiftly." Henry played with his coffee cup, nervous energy getting the best of him.

"And you? Have you been taken care of?" The look in Quinn's eyes was something Henry had rarely seen before. What was it? Empathy? Concern? The need to protect and make things right?

"I'm getting there. I'm not going to lie to you, it's been a long haul back."

"I'll bet." Quinn reached across the table, taking Henry's hand in his.

"First was the physical. And that may actually have been the easiest part." Henry was silent for a moment and Quinn didn't try to fill the space with noise. "Emotionally, it's a battle every day. But it's gotten a lot better. The Yoga and getting back to work have provided a structure that I really needed. It's like grabbing the next rung on a ladder."

Quinn looked at Henry's hand in his on the table. "I apologize if I've made you feel uncomfortable," he alluded to their flirtation.

As he went to remove his hand, Henry tightened his grip, holding Quinn's larger hand in place.

Shaking his head no, "You haven't made me uncomfortable. You've made me excited that I'm still alive," and he squeezed Quinn's hand tighter. "Thank you."

Quinn went to speak, a sound escaping, and immediately waved it off with his free hand, too choked up to speak. Closing his eyes, Henry could see that he was processing what happened.

Finally, "Were you in the hospital?"

Henry nodded, "A little over three weeks. A lot of the bones in my face were fractured and with the help of photos, they put me back together."

With an intensity that told the story of what was churning deep within the man, Quinn's eyes bored into Henry's. "You know he's lucky he's in Baghdad, don't you." This time it was Quinn who was squeezing Henry's hand.

"He's the past." And Henry really believed it as he vocalized the words.

"You're right, he is." Quinn smiled, as that attitude sat well with him. "So," he began and stalled.

"So, us?" Henry picked up.

"Yeah, so us. What do you need from me? Are you even interested?"

Henry was nodding, "Yes, I'm interested. Quinn, I'm very interested," he paused, collecting his thoughts. "What do I need from you?" he repeated the question. "I need you to know if I freak out or pull away or I'm kind of slow with things, it's because of what happened and not because I'm not interested in you, because

I'm very interested in you."

"OK."

"I'm scared. For so many reasons. But most of it's my own shit and you need to know that."

"Just talk to me, OK? When something scares you or if I do something to scare you, please talk to me. I want to get to know you, Henry. You set the terms and I will respect them."

They were quiet for a few minutes, both using their coffee cups as props to fill the time and space. Quinn broke the silence.

"I'm so sorry this happened to you and I'm also sorry that I'm the guy that gets to come next. But, at the same time, I'm glad that I'm the guy that gets to come next, because I know you'll be protected and safe. And that's important to me."

Quinn had just said what Henry wanted to hear, *you'll be safe and protected*. Henry so wanted to believe him. And he hated both himself and Cody for not yet having that faith.

And as if reading his mind, "I know saying you're safe with me are just empty words to you right now, even though I know how true they are, you don't. And that has to come with trust. Which, I know, is something I have to earn."

Unloading Henry's bike off the back of the Jeep in front of his apartment, the two men stood in what was their first uncomfortable silence.

"I'll see you at L9," Henry finally filled the space and turned to walk away.

"Henry."

Turning to Quinn, he saw the man approaching him. Quinn's muscular arms swiftly wrapped around him, pulling him tightly to his chest. It was a warm, full-on embrace coming from a place of deep, honest emotion. Not wrought with any sexual overtones, the caring hug allowed Henry, without hesitation, to immediately feel the tension recede from his body as he let himself momentarily melt into Quinn, accepting what the man was offering. Even if only just for a moment.

Pulling away, "I'll see you Monday." Henry forced a smile.

Nodding, Quinn remained silent, his arms crossing over his muscular chest. Leaning back against the Jeep, he stayed there until Henry was safely in the building.

chapter twelve

EREK PULLED HENRY ASIDE WHEN Quinn was in the men's room, and in a hushed tone with his lips barely moving, "Hey, did Quinn mention to you that his birthday is next weekend?"

"No, that dog didn't say a word."

"We're going to throw him a little surprise party at the house. Nothing elaborate, just a few friends and some guys we know on the force. Quinn's partner, Terry, will be there."

For a split-second, Henry felt his stomach knot at the mention of Quinn's partner, until he realized Derek was probably referring to his partner on the police force. "Oh, his partner from work?" Henry tried to be nonchalant.

"Yeah, they've been together for six years. Really good guy and his wife, Patty, is a doll."

As Quinn made his way across the club toward them, Derek quickly ended the conversation, "I'll email you the details."

"Ready to hit the track?" Quinn smiled at Henry.

The sight of his smile made Henry feel like his insides were shimmering. "Yeah, let's do it."

As they walked to the elevator, Henry couldn't shake the flash of despondence he felt when Derek had said Quinn had a partner, and he mistook it to mean that Quinn had a life partner. For just that jarring split second, it felt as if his heart was being sliced from his chest, as he got a quick glimpse at how unbearable the pain would be if he lost this man he had only known a few short months, or lost the hope that they could be something more than friends.

It was in that very moment that he knew, without any doubt or reservation, that he could not bear to be without Quinn Callahan, and it was time to make sure that Quinn knew that.

Derek and Willie owned a mid-century ranch-style house on a block where investors bought and tore down the houses to build modern monstrosities with quadruple the square footage.

"We're hanging onto it for the land value and then we're going to retire someplace tropical."

Henry followed Willie into the living room where a dozen people were standing around, drinks in hand. Putting his present on the gift table, Henry surveyed the surroundings and found the beer cooler. Extracting an icy Corona, he made his way over to Derek just as another half dozen people arrived.

"So how are you getting him over here?"

"Tonight's our monthly poker game, so he thinks he's coming to lose his shirt. He should be here in about five minutes."

At exactly 8 P.M., with a six-pack of Corona in hand, Quinn arrived dressed casually for his poker game with the boys, wearing ripped jeans molded to his gorgeous ass, a V-neck white tee, beat-up sneakers and a backwards Dodgers cap.

Baby blue eyes widened and his jaw literally dropped as he scanned his environs. Henry watched with delight as Quinn took in all the people that were important to his world. And then his eyes landed on Henry, and there wasn't another soul in the room, as the edges of his smile twitched and Henry melted. Henry's reaction mirrored Quinn's and the look that passed between the two men spoke volumes.

I'm here. I'm here with the rest of the people you love.

"He was really surprised," a petite blonde standing next to Henry looked up at him.

"He really was. The look on his face was priceless." *The look on his face was heart-meltingly gorgeous.*

"I don't think we've met before. I'm Patty, Terry's wife. Terry's Quinn's partner," she explained.

Extending his hand, "Hi, I'm Henry."

"Oh." She was surprised and called out to her husband, "Terry, come over here and meet Henry."

Just in the way she said his name, Henry knew he'd been discussed and was now under very close scrutiny.

Early 40's and barrel-chested, he made his way over and with a crushing handshake, "Terry McGowan, Quinn's partner."

"It's so great to meet you." Henry was amused. What had Quinn told them about him? "I'm Quinn's, umm, I guess, bike riding partner."

As Henry worked his way around the room, talking to people and trying to be social amongst a group of strangers, he'd catch glimpses of Quinn, and without fail, his breath would hitch every time. It was the black hair and the white-toothed smile, the pale baby blues and the ripped jeans hugging his ass. *He is so beautiful* and Henry realized he was both in awe of the man and in awe of the feelings that he had been able to stir in him, quelling Henry's fear that Cody had damaged him beyond repair.

Watching him greet and talk to all the guests, Henry wanted to be by his side, talking with friends as if they were a couple, the way Derek and Willie were, the way Terry and Patty were, and the other couples that were scattered around the room.

"Now there must be some Irish blood in you somewhere with that gorgeous strawberry-blonde hair."

Henry smiled at the woman, "I know of Scottish and English

blood, maybe even a little Welsh, but I don't know of any Irish ancestry."

"Don't kid yourself, there's an Irishman in there." She elbowed him. "I'm Jeanne," the middle-aged woman extended a small hand.

"Henry," he smiled down at her.

"Oh, you're Henry." Her eyes widened and she gave him a once over.

"Don't torture the guy, Ma." She was a beautiful brunette with fair skin and black-lashed eyes, the color of Quinn's.

With a jolt to the stomach, it occurred to Henry that he was meeting Quinn's family. And that everyone knew who he was.

"Hi, I'm Quinn's sister, Katelyn." Her smile was as beautiful as her brother's.

"So nice to meet you. You two have the same eyes," Henry observed.

"We got them from our dad."

"He was a wonderful man. God rest his soul," Jeanne chimed in.

"Quinn tells us you're training to do the Long Beach/San Diego ride."

"We are and I'm pretty out of shape."

"Don't listen to him." Quinn came up on them. "He's in great shape," blatantly checking out Henry's ass with a shit-eating grin. "So have you told him any embarrassing stories about me yet, Ma?"

"I don't need to." Jeanne smiled at her son. "I have no doubt that you'll do plenty on your own to embarrass yourself without my help."

Laughing, he hugged his mom to him. "So now you've met my girls." His eyes held Henry's, letting Henry know the importance of the moment, for Quinn Callahan was now the patriarch of the family, and these two women were his world.

"I have and I'm not leaving here tonight without at least one good Quinn story." He looked at Jeanne conspiratorially. "Don't let me down, Mrs. Callahan."

"So polite." She nodded to her son approvingly. Turning to Henry and touching his arm. "Call me Jeanne. I like this one, Quinny."

"Me too." He winked at his mom and was off to another conversation.

Throughout the night, as they locked eyes with one another, Henry felt this terrible longing. Being across the room from Quinn felt like an interminable distance, a gap he somehow needed to close. He wanted to feel the heat from his body, be close enough for him to whisper in his ear.

Wandering into the kitchen, Henry saw a cake that was an exact replica of Quinn's badge laid out on the counter. As he stood there marveling at the craftsmanship of the baker and the intricate details worked into the delicacy, he felt him come up behind him, and stand close enough to feel his breath on the back of his neck.

"That's pretty cool, isn't it," Quinn remarked.

Turning his face to see Quinn's, "It really is," he agreed, "I can't believe the amount of detail. It's so realistic."

"I'm really glad you're here."

"Me too." Henry locked eyes with him, their lips just inches apart, but still miles away from their first kiss.

Derek poked his head into the kitchen, bringing their moment to an abrupt, and unwanted, end. "Come on out and open presents and then we'll cut the cake."

"Presents. This night is just getting better and better." Quinn grabbed Henry by the hand and pulled him out of the kitchen, his grip still tight as they moved through the living room, hand-in-hand, to the couch where the presents were stacked up in a pile on the floor. Only one spot remained on the couch, designated for the guest of honor. Quinn gave Henry's hand a final squeeze before letting go and taking his spot on the couch.

The moment Quinn released his hand, Henry felt alone in the crowded room. Torn away too soon, too abruptly. The loss staggering. His need to feel Quinn overwhelming.

As Quinn worked his way through the stack of elaborately wrapped boxes, the laughter became more and more raucous as he opened each one.

"Seriously people, how many pairs of handcuffs do I need?" He looked around the room, as he held up yet another pair.

Unwrapping a tubular-shaped package, "Oh, it's root beer flavored, huh." He pulled a tube out of a box, "Somebody knows me well. Oh shit, this is from my mom," a blushing Quinn kidded, "Seriously Ma, flavored lube?"

"It was that or WD-40. What was I supposed to do?" she shot back, inciting yet another round of laughter from the room.

Opening the card to the next box, Quinn silently read the message.

> *Quinn – This present is actually for me. There's advantages to being a pussy. —Henry*

Quinn looked at Henry, slightly tipping his head as if silently asking, what's in there? "This is from Henry," he announced.

Opening the box, he pulled out a pair of white second skin cycling shorts.

"What's that? A giant condom? You're not that big, Quinn," someone yelled out, as the ribbing continued.

As Quinn set aside the last package and thanked his guests, Willie announced, "Cake time." Carrying out the badge cake with a 3 and a 2 candle blazing atop, Derek set the cake before Quinn.

Again, Henry found himself across the room, way too far from Quinn's side, as they sang 'Happy Birthday' to him.

As Quinn lowered his face to blow out the candles, his eyes, sparkling in the candlelight, locked in on Henry's, as he made his silent wish.

Wish for me. Wish for me. Henry found himself silently chanting as Quinn extinguished the flame in one sweeping blow.

"Nice blow job," someone yelled, inciting more laughter.

"He's had good practice," the teasing continued.

As guests began to bid their goodnights after the cake had been served, Quinn whispered in Henry's ear, "Hang out, OK."

Henry nodded and started to help with the clean-up as the partygoers said their goodbyes to the birthday boy.

"Bring this one over for a Sunday dinner," Jeanne told her son when Henry gave her a warm hug and a kiss on the cheek. "I like him."

"Don't scare him away, Ma." Quinn teased.

"I'm not scaring him, you rotten thing," she said lovingly.

As they later bagged up the trash, "My mother loved you."

"She's pretty awesome," Henry was smiling just thinking of her, so supportive and an active part of her son's life. He hadn't seen his own mother or sister in over three years, since they had moved to Montana. His mother hadn't even come down when he was in the hospital. *There's no way she'd ever attend one of my birthday parties,* he thought.

"You had quite a haul tonight," Henry gestured to the stack of presents.

"Yeah, but I didn't get everything I wanted."

"What was it that you wanted?" Henry thought Quinn had gotten amazing gifts.

"I want to cook you breakfast tomorrow morning." He paused, "Spend the night with me."

"You know we haven't even kissed yet."

Nodding his head, Quinn stepped to Henry, "We need to fix that. Right now." Reaching out, he stroked Henry's cheek gently with his middle and forefinger. "Thanks for the great gift." He chuckled, "They're white. You're going to see everything."

"I told you the present was actually for me."

And they both laughed.

"You have to know how I feel about you. Are you feeling that for me?" Quinn asked. Without waiting for a response, Quinn hurriedly acknowledged, "I know you're scared. It's understandable."

"You want to know what I was feeling tonight. I was feeling lost, Quinn. I was feeling lost because I wasn't by your side. I wanted to be by your side all night."

A blaze crossed Quinn's eyes as he took in Henry's words. Slipping his fingers into Henry's hair, he pulled him closer. "I want you there, Henry." He brushed his lips softly against Henry's. "You have no idea how much I want you there."

With his hand tightening in Henry's hair and the other flat on his lower back, Quinn pressed himself against Henry's long frame. A low guttural moan escaped as Henry opened his mouth to his first taste of this beautiful man. Slowly, Quinn swiped his tongue along the length of Henry's with a sensuous languid rhythm, sucking the tip of Henry's tongue deep into his mouth.

Henry could feel Quinn's hardness, and the matching response of his own to his partner's excitement. Arching into him, that desire to be close to this man was something he needed to satisfy.

"I think Derek and Willie want to kick us out," Quinn laughed, pulling away to get some air. He smiled at Henry. "So now we've kissed." And he planted another soft kiss on Henry's smiling lips, "Spend the night with me."

Henry nodded and leaned forward to kiss Quinn back, seizing the opportunity to bite his lower lip. "I'd love to."

Nervously tapping his fist on the steering wheel as he followed Quinn's Jeep back to his condo, Henry was not worried about what might happen between them, or getting naked in front of him for the first time. Henry was scared shitless of falling asleep and having one of his sweat-drenching, heart-palpitating, Psycho Marine induced nightmares in Quinn's bed.

I could just turn around and go home. Call him and say I was really beat. Let's do it when we're not so tired. But it's his birthday and he really wants me there. And his lips were so soft. And Oh God when he got hard and pressed into me. And I just want to be close to him. I want to feel him again.

Henry parked in the spot next to Quinn and gathered all his courage. *I can do this. I can still my mind. Ivy has taught me how to do it. And asshole Cody is not going to ruin Quinn's birthday. I can't do that to Quinn.*

Quinn's smile was huge, "I'm bringing a boy home," he kidded, pulling Henry against him to steal another kiss. "I'm so happy you're here." He stroked the side of Henry's face with his fore and middle finger again.

As they entered the condo, Henry remarked, "You are really neat."

"Did you think I'd be an Oscar Madison?" Quinn was amused. "Can I get you something to drink?"

Henry followed him into the kitchen. "No, not Oscar, but I didn't expect spotless. I'll take some water." Henry's mouth was getting dry as his nervous energy surfaced.

Opening the refrigerator and tossing him a bottle, "The truth is, my cleaning lady comes twice a week or I wouldn't have clean underwear or uniforms and you'd see a trail of dirty socks and tee-shirts."

Grabbing his hand, Quinn pulled Henry over to a brown leather couch, situated across from a large TV.

"I'm so glad you came to the party and really happy you're here tonight." Quinn faced him on the couch.

"I almost turned my car around and went home," Henry admitted.

Quinn laughed, "I kept checking my rearview mirror for your headlights because I was afraid you were going to do just that." Quinn took a sip of his water, "But you didn't. What made you keep following?"

"Well, for one thing, it's your birthday. But I also kept thinking about how all night I just wanted to be next to you." Henry watched Quinn's eyes crinkle at the corners at his admission.

Putting his water bottle aside, Quinn reached out a hand to Henry. "Come here," pulling him against him, Henry's head nestled back on Quinn's shoulder.

Kicking off his shoes, Henry lifted his long legs to the couch. "This is nice. Really nice." He looked up at Quinn who was smiling down at him.

"Perfect end to a great night." Quinn tenderly stroked the ginger strands back from Henry's forehead. "There's so much I want to know about you, Henry Clark. And I want to know it all now." Joking he put his hand over Henry's eyes, "Vulcan Mind Meld."

Both men laughed.

"So, you know what recently happened to me," Henry began, "but I don't know anything at all yet about your love life."

"How much do you want to know?"

"Everything you are comfortable telling me." Henry smiled up at him.

Laughing, "Ok, you asked for it. My first kiss was Jennifer Costa. She had really pretty long brown hair and brown eyes. We were seven. I got sent to the Principal's office," he laughed.

"School yard Lothario I see," Henry kidded.

"Totally, I just wanted to kiss all the girls," he paused, "and probably some of the boys, too."

Quinn continued stroking Henry's hair, his eyes shining with the smiles of ancient memories. "My first real guy kiss was senior year in high school, one of my track teammates. His family was as

Catholic as mine so we were both sure we were going to burn in Hell."

"Did you do more than kiss?" Henry shifted on Quinn's shoulder.

"Yeah, but not much. We'd give each other hard-ons, kissing and rubbing each other through our clothes. We'd both go home sticky messes."

They both laughed.

"My first real relationships were in college and there were a few that lasted a couple of months, but nothing earth shattering."

"Any big long-term relationships?" Henry wanted to get this over with, knowing he'd feel unjustifiably jealous.

"There were two. One lasted two years, the other almost four."

Henry sat up to face Quinn. He wanted to see the look on his face and in his eyes when he spoke of his former lovers. Would there still be a hint of his heart with one of them? He needed to know.

"What happened with them?"

"Well, the first one I was in my early twenties. I'd just entered the police academy, so I was getting serious about my life and my career and he wasn't. He was still in his stoner phase and wasn't going to be out of it any time soon. We were just going in two very separate directions."

"And the other one?" Henry asked, relieved somewhat by the first answer.

Quinn looked up at the ceiling, the corners of his mouth twitching as he was formulating what to say. "That one broke my heart."

"What did he do?" Henry wanted to reach out and stroke Quinn's arm, but suddenly felt like touching him was off-limits in the presence of this other person's ghost.

"He cheated," Quinn's beautiful eyes still filled with the hurt just from the memory of his lover's betrayal. "A lot."

"That's kind of a dangerous thing to do," Henry remarked, stating the obvious.

"Yes," he agreed, "it is. I guess I suspected it on some level even though I consciously didn't want to admit it. We always used protection and I guess that was because I didn't fully trust him."

"But you loved him?" Henry could hear it in his voice even before Quinn answered his question.

"I did," Quinn nodded, looking deep into Henry's eyes as if asking him, *And you? Will you be true?*

This time Henry reached out, letting his fingers trail lightly on Quinn's forearm. "I hate that he hurt you. But I'm glad that he's gone." He smiled. "How long ago was this?"

"It ended about a year and a half ago."

"Are you over him?" The fear was creeping in that this guy would come back after he'd given his heart to Quinn. Did he need to get out now?

Threading his fingers with Henry's, Quinn smiled. "I like what you're thinking. You want to know why?"

"How do you know what I'm thinking? And yeah, I want to know why."

Quinn laughed, his beautiful white smile beaming. "Henry, I'm a cop, I read people. And I can't wait to play poker with you. I'm going to rob you blind." His eyebrows went up, "Or maybe we just make it strip poker. You were thinking, if Quinn isn't over this guy, I need to back off and protect myself, right?"

Caught, Henry knew he was blushing.

"And I like it because it means you want to move forward with me emotionally and I know that's got to be tough as heck for you right now."

He just nodded and Quinn tightened his grasp.

"So, I didn't answer your question. Yes. I'm over him. There's nothing he can offer me that I want. And right now. I only want one thing. And he's sitting right here in front of me."

Pulling Henry on top of him, Quinn buried his fingers in Henry's thick hair. "You bit my lip before."

"I did," Henry laughed.

"Do it again."

"You don't have to ask twice, birthday boy." Henry took Quinn's full lower lip between his teeth, biting down gently at first and then sinking his teeth in a little deeper.

Quinn's groan was a beautiful turn-on. Feeling like a teen with uncontrollable erections, Henry heard his own sounds as he felt Quinn hardening against him.

"Now look what you did to me." Quinn's eyes were smiling. "I'm going to need a cold shower."

Laughing, "Me too."

It was somehow unspoken between the two of them that they would take this really slow with the endgame being the long haul. Henry had never taken it slow before and wondered if Quinn had and his gut told him no. They were heading into uncharted territory, both knowing they'd found that someone who could change the course of their lives, forever.

It just felt right.

As Henry explored Quinn's mouth, learning what he could do with his tongue to make the handsome cop moan and get harder, he kept thinking about the feeling he had all night. He had just wanted to be by Quinn's side, be his partner.

"Quinn, I really want you in my life."

Smiling, the strong cop flipped Henry onto his back, covering him with his body. As he pressed his erect cock against the bulge in Henry's jeans, he tipped his head to the side. "I am in your life, Henry, and I'm not going anywhere." Continuing to grind his hips into Henry's, both men stared into one another's eyes, grinning like teens.

With a quick kiss on the lips, "Let me go get us some more

water. I might need to pour it on myself." Quinn laughed and got off the couch, leaving Henry breathless and gasping for air.

Coming back from the kitchen with two water bottles in hand, Quinn stood by the couch, staring down with a smile, as he was greeted by soft snores. Looking at his watch, it was nearly 2 A.M. From a battered wooden chest, he removed an afghan his Grandmother Rose had crocheted and softly draped it over a sleeping Henry.

Grabbing his water bottle, Quinn Callahan headed to the bathroom to end his thirty-second birthday with a very cold shower.

chapter
thirteen

WAKING IN THE PRE-DAWN DARKNESS, Henry blinked a few times fast, acclimating his dry eyes to the unfamiliar surroundings. Feeling the soft blanket, he smiled, picturing Quinn covering him. A shrouded light emerged from behind a door that was slightly cracked open, and Henry hoped that was the bathroom. Getting up, he walked down the hall and peered inside. Silently, he thanked Quinn for being so thoughtful.

Down the hall were two more doors, one slightly ajar. Peeking into the first room, he stood still until his eyes again adjusted, picking up the white from the bed sheet. At the far end of the bed, facing the center as he slept on his left side, was Quinn, his face looking so young and beautiful in repose. Henry held his breath as he watched him sleep. This man's beauty was not just in the way he looked. It was in everything about who he was, and in his heart and in how he treated people. That was evident watching him at his party. This was a man people loved and respected and Henry knew those were things earned through reciprocation.

Pulling off his tee-shirt, he dropped it to the floor and did the same with his jeans, kicking them away. With a few deep, cleansing breaths he psyched himself up. Wanting so desperately to feel Quinn molded against him, the irony didn't evade him that based on where Quinn was sleeping, he would be the front spoon, with Quinn behind him – the same position Cody always appeared in the nightmare. Wishing Quinn was on the other end of the bed or facing the other direction, Henry had hoped to spoon him – not the other way around.

He's not Cody. Don't put that on him.

Sliding under the duvet into the cool sheets, Henry inched his way backward, grabbing a pillow along the way, until he could feel the heat from Quinn's body. He stilled, so that he wouldn't wake him and listened to his steady breathing for a few minutes. When he was certain that he had not disturbed him, he moved back the last length so that he could feel Quinn's warm skin against him.

"Mmmm," Quinn wrapped an arm around his waist, pulling him tightly against his naked body as he inserted a leg between Henry's, tangling their feet as if they'd slept that way for a thousand nights. "You found me," Quinn's voice was full of sleep.

Yes I did and I don't think I'll ever let you go, was Henry's last thought as he let himself relax and fall back to sleep wrapped in Quinn.

His slumber was so deep and relaxed that he never felt Quinn slowly run his hand down his arm, softly kiss his neck or get out of bed. What finally woke him was the growl of his hungry stomach responding to the heady aroma of bacon wafting in from the kitchen. Smiling, Henry stretched underneath the blanket marveling at how something so new could feel so comfortable.

Quinn Callahan was a sight to be seen in the morning. Dark hair askew, sexy, bad boy stubble covering the lower half of his handsome face and dark-rimmed glasses that brought out the paleness and clarity of the blue in his eyes. Bare-chested and in his ripped jeans, Henry wondered if he was hallucinating Mr. September from some hot cop calendar.

His beautiful smile erupted the moment he laid eyes on Henry, "Was I too noisy?"

Henry shook his head, no. "My stomach started poking me to wake up the minute it smelled bacon cooking."

Grabbing the Mr. Coffee carafe, Quinn filled up a police department mug and handed it to Henry.

"I slept really well," Henry remarked.

"Do you usually?" Quinn started laying the bacon strips on paper towel to drain.

"No," Henry shook his head. "That was why I started doing Yoga. I was having really awful nightmares."

Quinn stopped and looked up. "After the attack?" His brows were drawn together over serious eyes.

Henry nodded. "Can I help you with something?"

Pointing to the toaster, "Butter the toast. And how do you take your eggs?"

"Over-easy." Henry pulled the butter out of the refrigerator. "Where are the knives?"

Quinn pointed to a drawer and turned back to the eggs. Smirking, "Over-easy. I'll have to remember that about you."

"About me or my eggs?" Henry laughed.

Quinn laughed. "Your eggs. The rest I hope to find out soon enough."

Henry looked at him and smiled. It was just so easy with this guy and everything felt so healthy and balanced.

"What are you looking at?" Quinn plated the eggs and carried them to the table.

"You, birthday boy, and thinking how easy it is to be with you."

Quinn's eyes were his tell and the way he looked at Henry made Henry feel as if he'd better sit down at the table immediately before his knees buckled.

"That's how I feel, too. It's like we've been hanging out for years. But then I think, I hardly know him," he paused, "and Henry, I want to know everything."

I'm not going to stay a prisoner. I won't be anybody's slave.

"I want you to know everything. A lot of it's not pretty and

127

for most of my life, no, make that all of my life, I didn't even know how fucked up it was until everything happened about ten months ago, and then afterwards, I got into therapy. But even then I couldn't see a lot of what my therapist was saying to me, because I had no frame of reference. And now I do. And what I want is so different than where I've come from."

Quinn nodded and remained silent as Henry bared his soul, laying out a vast array of ugly demons and dark moments, from his first encounter with Jimmy to his final showdown with Cody. Recounting his tale, he could feel the eggs coddling in his stomach as he prayed that Quinn would still want to let him into his life. Part of him wanted to hold back, but he knew if he did, it would eventually run him down and he'd wind up losing Quinn anyway, when the loss would be much steeper and more painful.

When Henry finished, Quinn stood up from the table, turning away, his hand cupping his chin and the lower part of his face. Closing his eyes, Henry braced himself for what truly would be a walk of shame, out of Quinn's apartment, and out of his life.

Henry tried to read the look in those pale baby blue eyes behind the dark rimmed glasses when Quinn finally turned around. *Disgust? Pity? Disappointment?* Henry fought hard to keep his breakfast down.

"From the first day we met," Quinn began, his voice gruff, "you were just this incredibly likable guy. Easy-going. Quick to smile. Happy to lend a hand. It's impossible not to be drawn to you, Henry. Your energy is so good. So positive."

Here comes the but. His throat closed.

"So, the fact that you can still smile and have faith in the world after some of the cards you have been dealt, is incredibly admirable. It's amazing that you've been functional and a generally healthy, balanced and successful human being is a testament to the resilience of your strength and goodness. Getting into therapy and what you're doing with Yoga shows your commitment to leaving the shitty and unhealthy stuff behind and really working on moving forward."

Henry held Quinn's gaze. The build-up and then the blow. He held his breath as he waited for the other shoe to drop. Slowly, Quinn walked to his side of the table. Standing right in front of him, Quinn extended his hand. Looking at Quinn's outstretched palm, Henry was momentarily confused by the gesture, before realizing Quinn wanted him to take his hand.

Leading him back to the couch, they sat in the same positions as the night before. *But now everything has changed,* thought Henry. *Everything.*

"So, let me ask you something really personal."

"OK." Henry was still holding his breath.

"Have you ever topped? Or have you only ever bottomed?"

"I've only bottomed." Henry looked down, feeling suddenly self-conscious.

"So you've never been in a reciprocal relationship where your partner has made your pleasure the number one priority?"

"No. Not really."

"This is going to be a mutually reciprocal relationship, Henry. Is that something you actually want?"

Quinn was asking *him* if he wanted in. "Yes. It's something I want. But even more than that, Quinn, I want it with you."

"Are you sure?"

Henry nodded. "The other day," Henry started to blush, "when Derek asked me to the party, he mentioned your partner, Terry, would be there. For a moment, I thought he was talking about a life partner and not a work partner. And just the thought that we would never be, made my insides physically hurt."

The look in Quinn's eyes melted him. No one had ever looked at him like that before. No one. It made him wonder if any lover had ever really seen him, if they'd ever looked past filling their own need with him merely as the vehicle.

"Quinn, this thing between us. I know it hasn't been physical yet, but every other aspect has been totally give-and-take. I haven't felt like there's been any power games or inequity in feelings. It's just like we've been going down this road together, at the same pace." Henry smiled and let out a deep breath. "It's been really..." he paused, searching for the perfect word.

"Right," Quinn filled in the blank. "It's been really right."

Henry nodded. "It's been really right," he repeated.

Grabbing Henry's hand, Quinn pulled him close, "C'mere, you. I hope you're ready for something really different."

"I am." There was a perplexed look on Henry's face, as a thought took hold. "I deserve this. And I hope I deserve you."

"Come on," Quinn stood and again extended a hand to Henry, leading him into the bedroom.

Henry laughed, "So the birthday breakfast was just a ruse."

Laughing, Quinn nodded, as he unbuttoned the top button of Henry's jeans and unzipped them. Slipping his hands under the waistband of his boxer-briefs, his big hands surrounded the cheeks of Henry's ass as he pulled him tightly against his body.

Quinn's arousal poked at Henry's groin and Henry let out a low moan at just the hint of it.

"That's how much I want you," Quinn's breath warmed his ear.

Henry ran his cheek slowly across the sharp stubble of Quinn's jaw, enjoying the rough scratch on his skin, "Consider me your birthday present."

"You know you are what I wished for." Holding Henry's ass firmly, Quinn ground himself against him.

"I was hoping I would be." Henry's lips softly traced a line along Quinn's jaw to his lips. Burying his fingers in his thick, dark hair, Henry found Quinn's tongue, slowly stroking it, his cock growing harder with every stroke of his tongue.

With a quick tug, they fell back onto Quinn's bed, Henry

landing on top. He knew that wasn't an accident and that Quinn was being sensitive to triggers which the feeling of being restrained might have in his first time being intimate again.

"Tell me what you want." Quinn's hands had not left Henry's ass.

"I want to see your gorgeous body naked." Henry smiled down at him.

"Well, then I think you should take my pants off."

Rolling off Quinn, Henry immediately felt a sense of loss as their bodies moved apart. With fumbling fingers, he undid his jeans. "I feel like a teenager, don't you?"

Nodding, "I do." Quinn shimmied out of his jeans.

"Commando." Henry was wide-eyed at the surprise. "Damn, that is one fine looking cock you have."

"Did you expect anything less?" Quinn looked smug, showing off his healthy length.

"No, and I've fantasized about it plenty," Henry looked shy with his admission.

Quinn turned to him and began removing Henry's jeans so that they were both skin to skin, lying very close. "Tell me about your fantasies."

"I'm living one right now, Quinn." Henry reached out, softly touching Quinn's shoulder and running a hand over the muscles he regularly watched pump iron.

"Good. I want you to feel comfortable and secure, Henry. We have forever."

We have forever?

This man wasn't just about living out fantasies. He was about creating dreams.

"Forever? Are you trying to give me blue balls?" Henry joked.

Quinn smiled. His fingers mirroring exactly what Henry's were doing to him. Their soft, tentative discovery of one another's peaks and valleys, hidden coves and sensitive sinews was literally breathtaking.

"I like learning how to touch you. Look what this right here does to you." Quinn softly traced Henry's quadriceps with an almost feather-like touch. As he reached the bottom, Henry's cock twitched, jumping in response. Smiling, he did it again, eliciting the exact same response. Both men laughed.

"Not exactly scientific, but I'm filing that one away under *How to make Henry hard.*"

"Hmm, well, let me find one for my arsenal." Henry slowly ran two fingers along the side of Quinn's pec down to his ribs. Feeling him harden against his thigh, Henry smiled a self-assured smile. "Good to know." He shook his head.

"What about this?" Quinn traced Henry's jawline. Twitch. "Filing that."

"Does that work for you?" Henry stared into his eyes as he softly caressed Quinn's jaw. His cock got rock hard. "Mmm, mmm, mmm. Prepare to have your jaw touched a lot." Henry laughed, then added, "In public." Leaning in, he followed the line his fingers had just traced with his lips, feeling Quinn shiver.

Slinging a leg over Henry's long limbs, Quinn pulled him against him, aligning his hard cock next to Henry's, which had an immediate matching response.

The involuntary groan from deep in Henry's throat made Quinn pull him tighter as they rubbed against one another. "You feel so damn good." Quinn's teeth grazed Henry's neck.

"Quinn."

"Mmm," he responded without raising his lips from Henry's neck.

"Touch me." Henry knew Quinn would hold back every step of the way until given permission. "I need you to touch me."

He first felt Quinn's finger tracing a line up the sensitive perineum between his ass and his balls.

"Oh God," he whimpered as Quinn's hand gently cradled his

balls, his fingernails lightly scratching them. He stayed there for a few minutes familiarizing himself with Henry's body until they'd hardened into tight, large knots.

Henry buried his face in the crook of Quinn's neck as Quinn continued to explore. Finally his hand encircled his cock, traveling its length and back. His forefinger swept over the wet tip and then his hand left Henry's cock altogether.

Removing his face from the sheltered harbor of Quinn's neck, he watched the glistening fingertip come up between their lips. Quinn's eyes were locked in on his, smiling, challenging, daring. Slowly his tongue moved toward his finger, the edges of his lips curved into a smile. Henry took it as a challenge, his tongue slowly moving toward Quinn's finger to meet his tongue. Arriving at the same time, the tips of their tongues both licked the glistening finger, and then Henry sucked it deep into his mouth.

"Fuck, you're killing me." Quinn did not break eye contact as Henry continued to slowly suck in his finger.

Pulling his slickened finger from Henry's mouth, it made a popping sound and they both laughed.

"I wonder how many popping sounds we can make?" Henry was amused.

Quinn's hand reached back down, slowly stroking Henry and cupping his balls. "Want to hear another one?" He smiled and then dipped his head down taking just the tip of Henry's cock in his mouth. Keeping his lips taut, he pulled it out, creating a large popping sound, and both men laughed.

As Quinn began to take Henry deeper, the rhythm of his sucking hastened, making Henry harden in his mouth. Closing his eyes, Henry threaded his fingers through Quinn's hair and let himself go to the pleasure. There was no threat, no red flags. He could feel the pressure building as he was nearing release.

"Quinn, stop."

Looking up at him quizzically, he stopped, wanting to ensure nothing was wrong.

"I don't want this to be just me. I want it to be us." He wanted to give Quinn the reciprocal relationship he desired.

Shifting his body and stretching out alongside Henry, Quinn went back to what he was doing, letting out a deep groan as Henry took him deep. "Damn, Henry. What are you doing to me?" Quinn pressed his hips toward Henry's face, needing to be deeper in his throat.

As Henry settled into a voracious rhythm, taking Quinn as deeply as he could, he realized Quinn was matching his pace and depth, just as he had mirrored his touch earlier. It was Quinn's way of making sure he felt comfortable and safe and not going past what he could handle yet. Not only was he pleasing him, he was taking care of him as well.

What Quinn Callahan could not see from his vantage point, as Henry Clark came in his mouth, were the tears in Henry's eyes. For the first time in his life, Henry understood the potential of real love during a sexual act, and knew that for Quinn it wasn't just sex, but a means of sharing and caring.

It may have been Quinn's birthday, but Henry was the one who received the gift.

chapter fourteen

"LET ME APOLOGIZE IN ADVANCE," Quinn joked nervously. "But she has been relentless about having you join us for Sunday dinner for weeks now."

Henry just laughed as they approached Quinn's mom's house. "I loved your mom when I met her. She's so real." Henry held a bouquet of Stargazer lilies in his lap, Jeanne's favorite flower.

"Yeah, she's real all right." Quinn rolled his eyes as he navigated the car through the streets of an older housing development.

Taking it all in, Henry envisioned a young Quinn riding his bicycle around the winding blocks. "I'm trying to picture you here as a kid."

"It was a great neighborhood to grow up in. Lots of kids to play with, good local sports teams. My dad coached T-Ball." Quinn's eyes were shining.

Feeling a pang of envy for his *normal* childhood, Henry smiled as he looked at Quinn's profile. "You miss him, don't you?"

"Every day." He appeared introspective. "These last few weeks, with you, I've just kept thinking how much I wished that he could have met you." Quinn reached over and gave Henry's hand a squeeze before announcing, "We're here."

As they entered a 1970's style ranch home, Henry's senses were warmly greeted by the heady aroma of Jeanne Callahan's

'Sunday Stew'.

As Henry handed her the lilies, she reached over and pinched her son's solid upper arm, "I really like this boy, Quinny."

"Me too, Ma. A lot."

"So is this serious?" Jeanne Callahan did not have a shy bone in her body.

Henry could feel the heat rise in his face and hoped no one was actually expecting an answer from him. Instantly he was relieved, when Quinn took care of it with an arm around Henry's shoulder, pulling Henry close against his side, his beautiful smile beaming.

Looking from one to the other, Jeanne smiled and turned to the kitchen, calling over her shoulder, "I've got cold beer in the refrigerator for you boys."

Following his mom, Quinn came back a few minutes later, carrying two Coronas with the limes already perched halfway down their longnecks.

Handing the beer to Henry, they clinked bottles, smiling. "You want to see my bedroom?" Quinn had a devilish smirk on his face.

"That's a given." Henry laughed, as he followed him down the hall.

Behind the wooden door was exactly what Henry had expected. Entering a pale blue room, the color of Quinn's eyes, they were greeted by a twin bed neatly covered with a navy blue quilt and sky blue pillows. Lining the cherry wood desk and bookshelf were trophy after trophy for track and swim team wins. As he walked around the room, bending down to see pictures of a young Quinn, it was impossible not to be transported back to the handsome cop's youth. Lining the walls were music posters – Pink Floyd, Peter Frampton, Bruce Springsteen.

The door squeaked as it closed and Henry heard the click of the lock. Coming up from behind, Quinn wrapped his arms around him, pulling him close, so that he could feel his hard-on.

"Your mom's here," Henry protested.

"Yeah, I know," Quinn laughed, grinding his hard cock into Henry's ass.

"What do you want to do?"

"Pretend we're teenagers." Quinn pulled Henry down onto his bed.

Reaching down, Henry gently rubbed the outside of Quinn's faded jeans, making him even harder. Pulling him in by his shirt, Quinn reciprocated by taking Henry's lower lip between his front teeth. The harder Henry rubbed, the harder Quinn bit, until both were in a state of pleasurable agony.

Letting go of Henry's lip, Quinn flipped onto his back, pulling Henry down on top of him, his hands sliding slowly over Henry's ass and pressing his hips onto his sizable erection.

"Is it bad that I want to fuck you in the bed I grew up in?" Quinn asked. They'd been easing into their physical relationship and hadn't gone past hands and mouths.

Henry shook his head. "Not at all. And if your mother wasn't home…" Henry's voice trailed off.

"Yeah?" Quinn's eyes were shining as he cocked his head to the side.

Nodding, "Yeah." Henry knew he was ready. Quinn Callahan had treated him with such care and respect that it would be a gift to give himself to this amazing man. A man who had a lot of power in his grasp and didn't abuse it.

Sometimes in just a moment you know something. Looking back you'll always be able to pinpoint *the* moment that it happened – or that you finally realized that it had already happened. And it was that moment in Quinn's childhood bed, with the heady aroma of Jeanne Callahan's famous Sunday Stew permeating the air, that Henry Clark knew he was deeply in love and wanted to be Quinn's. Forever.

Pulling Henry's head down for a kiss, Henry felt that Quinn sensed his revelation. "I want it, too," he whispered into Henry's ear, giving him the distinct feeling it wasn't just sex to which he was referring.

Looking into his baby blue eyes, Henry just nodded.

"Dinner's almost ready." They heard Jeanne's voice call from down the hall, almost simultaneously with Katelyn's arrival.

Walking into the kitchen, hand in hand, Henry couldn't hide his smile, as Quinn warmly greeted his little sister and they sat down to dinner. Sunday dinner in the Callahan home was not a short eat and run affair. They stayed at the kitchen table talking for hours, drinking Bailey's spiked coffee and enjoying Jeanne's homemade Irish Soda Bread.

"Are you ready for the bike ride?" Katelyn smiled at her brother.

"I am. Not sure about this one, though." He elbowed Henry.

With a dead serious face, Henry turned to Jeanne, "Do you see what I have to put up with?" And they all laughed.

"Yeah, you love it." Quinn pushed his chair close to Henry's and slung an arm over his chest, pulling his back up against him.

Being in a family environment that was so accepting and open was a new experience for Henry, and every time he started to feel tense, he realized he was the only one. Quinn was accepted and loved for who he was. And so was Henry. This was their normal and they were all at ease and comfortable with it. Quinn's happiness was their only concern and right now it appeared that Henry Clark was making Quinn Callahan a very happy man.

"I'll see you two next Sunday." She winked as she turned to hug Henry goodbye. "Take good care of my boy." She rubbed his upper arm.

"If he'll let me," Henry laughed.

"He'll let you." Her eyes were smiling.

As they drove away, Henry sat looking out the window with a

content smile on his face.

"What are you smiling about," Quinn rapped him lightly on the bicep.

"How great that just was. My first Sunday could have been my eightieth Sunday. That's how comfortable your family makes me feel."

"I like hearing that."

"Well, I liked being there." Henry snuck a look at Quinn's handsome profile. He was looking straight ahead as he drove, with a smile firmly planted on his face.

Without taking his eyes off the road, Quinn reached over and grabbed Henry's hand. "I know it's a work night, but why don't you stay over."

"I need to grab clothes and my car."

Quinn nodded, heading toward Henry's apartment.

Pulling up in front, Henry opened his door, "Let me grab my stuff for tomorrow and I'll be over to your place in a few."

Putting a hand on top of Henry's to stop him, Quinn's eyes were serious, as he said, "Bring clothes for the week."

Silently, Henry processed Quinn's words. "OK," he nodded his head, knowing Quinn was asking him to share his home.

Quinn had already cleared a section of his closet, three dresser drawers and a shelf in the bathroom by the time Henry got there. He appeared to be a little nervous, rubbing his hands together, and Henry realized that Quinn was fearful of rejection or pushing Henry too fast.

Hanging his suits, shirts and ties, Henry stood in the middle of the closet. His clothes and Quinn's, hanging side-by-side. There was something so simple, yet symbolic, that Henry needed to take some cleansing breaths to calm himself and to push away any and all thoughts that he didn't deserve this.

Neatly lining up his toiletries on the bathroom shelf that had been emptied for him, he caught Quinn in the mirror watching his every move. As the reflection of their eyes met, Quinn's handsome eyes took on a serious cast.

"You know you can go at any time," he paused, "or you can stay for as long as you'd like."

"What if I want to stay forever?" Henry boldly asked the reflection.

"Then you're going to need this." Quinn reached into his pocket and pulled out a key dangling from a silver disk keychain and held it up for Henry to see. Reaching around Henry, he laid it gently on the vanity. Never once did he break eye contact with the reflection of Henry's eyes.

They stood there for a moment looking at one another in the mirror. Henry hoped that Quinn could read his expression. Finally, he broke eye contact and looked down at the key on the counter. The silver disk keychain was engraved with his initials, *HEC*.

Quinn put his hands on Henry's upper arms and buried his face in the nook of his neck. The rough scratch from Quinn's five o'clock shadow felt exquisite and Henry was immediately aware of the ache in his balls as his cock hardened just from Quinn's slight touch.

"Stay forever," Quinn whispered into his neck.

Closing his eyes, Henry tilted his head, exposing his neck to Quinn and leaned his weight back onto the sturdy cop.

"I'm going to take that as a yes."

Henry nodded.

Quinn's hands slowly moved down Henry's arms as his lips softly trailed from the nook of his neck to his shoulder. When his hands reached Henry's hands, he took them and wrapped them around Henry's chest, hugging them closer together.

Closing his eyes, Henry tried to let the sensation of Quinn's lips carry him away, but he was wracked with sudden anxiety, his muscles contracting with a jolt.

"Hey." Quinn stopped what he was doing and sought Henry's eyes in the mirror. Wrapping his arms around him tighter, "We don't have to do anything you're not ready to do." Quinn assumed Henry's reticence was still based in the fear of becoming intimate and vulnerable.

Shaking his head, "It's not that, it's not what you think."

Quinn cocked his head, but remained silent.

"I'm ready. I'm ready for everything with you. I want everything with you. I was serious with what I told you today at your mom's."

"Then what is it? I felt you stiffen in my arms, Henry. And not the good kind of stiffen," he added, with a warm smile.

Looking down, Henry closed his eyes and took a deep breath. He let it out slowly before reopening his eyes to face Quinn. "I still have those nightmares sometimes. I just don't want you to see me like that."

The flash of sadness was evident in Quinn's eyes. Shaking his head, "That fucker is lucky he's half a world away." Kissing Henry's temple, "If you have one, I'm here. He's not. I am. So try and relax. We'll deal with it if it happens. Just promise me one thing."

"What?"

"Please don't be embarrassed by it. OK?" Quinn leveled a serious glance in the mirror.

Forcing a smile, "I'll try."

"You don't have to go through this alone anymore," his voice was a mere whisper.

Henry longed to tell this beautiful man that he loved him, truly, deeply and irrevocably loved him, and that it was as clear as day in a teen's twin bed under rock 'n roll posters. But the words were having no part of being vocalized. Instead, he reached for one of Quinn's arms that were wrapped around him and lifted his hand to his lips, kissing it tenderly. Taking him by the hand, Henry led Quinn out of the bathroom and into their bedroom.

"I know you want me to top. I know you want me to do that."

Quinn smiled, nodding, "Yeah, I do."

"And I will. I want to. But tonight. Tonight I want you inside me." He bit his lip nervously. "Is that OK with you?"

"C'mere, you." Quinn pulled Henry to him. "OK with it? I've been thinking about it since that first day at L9. You were just coming toward me, like I was dreaming you or something. I didn't know you were Schooner's friend and you made my blood race."

Reaching out, Henry laid a hand on Quinn's cheek. "I think you are the single best thing that has ever happened in my life, Quinn. Seriously. And I want to know what it feels like to have you buried in me."

Quinn moaned at Henry's words, his hands skimming down Henry's back like stones skipping across a pond, until he reached his ass, where he grabbed on tight, molding Henry's body firmly to his own. Grinding into him, Quinn sought Henry's mouth, as if beginning a new exploration.

As they tumbled onto the bed, Quinn pulled away for a second, breathing roughly. With eyes blazing sincerity, lust and something Henry couldn't quite put a name to, "I will never, ever intentionally hurt you. Ever."

Henry reached around and removed one of Quinn's hands from his rear, taking the palm and placing it flat over his wildly beating heart. Quinn's eyes widened and he smiled, feeling the rapid rhythm.

With his hand covering Quinn's, Henry vowed, "I will always be true to you, Quinn. Always."

And there it was, the vows that erased their partner's darkest and most emotionally crippling fear, replacing it with optimistic hope and dreams.

"Now fuck me. Hard." Henry's eyes crinkled as he smiled at

his beautiful lover.

"You don't have to ask twice."

As clothes rapidly were tossed into a pile on the floor, Quinn peered over the edge of the bed, his brows coming together questioningly. "I wonder if she's going to charge me double?"

"Huh?" Henry's brows knit too at Quinn's non-sequitur.

"My cleaning lady," he laughed. "She's now going to have double piles of underwear and dirty socks trailing this entire apartment because we are going to fuck like wild animals in every room."

Opening a drawer, Quinn pulled out a bottle of lubricating liquid and a condom.

"Is it the root beer flavored?" Henry asked.

Laughing, "No. I had to throw that away. Lube from my mom is over the line. Even for my crazy family."

"I love your crazy family."

With what was now becoming his trademark touch, Quinn slowly swiped Henry's cheek with his forefinger and middle finger. "You know you're quickly becoming a member of my crazy family."

"I need you inside me, now, Quinn. Now." Henry was emphatic.

"Get on your back. I want to be looking in your eyes when I come."

Lying on his back, his already hard cock standing at attention, poised and waiting, Quinn spread Henry's legs apart and pulled him to the edge of the bed. Leaning down, he took Henry deep into his mouth.

"Oh God, you feel so good," Henry moaned, feeling Quinn's tongue swirling around him within the tight vacuum of his mouth.

With fingers woven through Quinn's hair, Henry drove his hips deeply into the warmth of Quinn's mouth, getting lost in his own cadence. As his balls tightened, the pressure mounting, Quinn pulled away, not letting him come.

"Not yet," he was breathless, a lock of his dark hair haphazardly obscuring one of his beautiful pale blue eyes.

Panting too and trying to catch his breath, Henry nodded, knowing Quinn wanted to experience this together. Reaching out next to him on the bed, Henry grabbed the condom and the bottle of lube, handing the condom to Quinn.

Ripping it open with his teeth, Quinn discarded the package on the floor. Looking down at it and then back at Henry with his luminous smile, "She's definitely charging me extra." And they laughed.

Flipping up the top to the lube, Henry watched as a few drops rained onto his hard cock. Reaching up, he handed the bottle to Quinn with one hand while stroking himself with the other, rubbing the slick liquid from his balls to the crown.

Quinn just watched with a smile, before squeezing several drops onto Henry's perineum and watching them slowly course down to the opening of his ass. When they arrived at their destination, Quinn slowly massaged them into the area and added a fresh stream to coat his fingers, rubbing them back and forth slowly on the ring of sensitive skin.

Without breaking eye contact he slowly pressed a finger into the tight opening, using enough pressure to get sucked in.

Henry gasped and Quinn smiled, his own cock twitching with anticipation at his lover's reaction. "Feel good?" he asked, slowly pumping his forefinger into Henry.

"Oh yeah," he smiled, lost to the sensation in his ass, his pumping of his own cock becoming merely background music.

"And how about this?" Quinn's middle finger was now inserted deeply next to its mate, moving in tandem as it stroked the sensitive gland that was bringing Henry close to a frenzied state.

It didn't elude him for a second that these were the two fingers he had come to love Quinn trailing down his cheek and he heard a whimper coming from somewhere so much deeper than his throat.

"Are you ready for me?" Quinn's eyes shone in the semi-dark room as he pulled his fingers out and pressed the tip of his condom-sheathed cock at Henry's opening.

Henry nodded.

Grabbing onto Henry's thighs, Quinn pulled him onto him as he thrust through the small opening.

"Oh God," this time it was Quinn who was moaning as he began, slowly at first, driving into Henry's ass.

"Yes," Henry closed his eyes for a moment, concentrating wholly on the connection he and Quinn had formed. "Yes."

"You feel so fucking great. You are so damn tight."

"Harder Quinn. I want you all the way in," Henry begged, picking up the pace on jerking his own cock.

Grabbing Henry's thighs harder for leverage, Quinn plowed as deeply as he could into him, his balls slapping Henry's ass.

"Yes, just like that. Oh God, you feel so good." Henry stroked himself harder, needing to come.

"You like it like this?" Quinn was fucking him at a feverish pace, lost to his own sensations.

"Oh God, yes," his voice choked, as he exploded all over his stomach and chest.

As Quinn watched the arc of Henry's come, he ground himself as deeply as he could into the depths of Henry's ass. "Squeeze me. Hard," he demanded. "Harder."

As Henry's muscles beared down around his cock, Quinn unleashed with a deep moan, his eyes squeezing shut with his release. He stilled, holding onto Henry's thighs for support, not moving for several minutes. Slowly, he pulled out, causing both men to involuntarily shiver. Peeling off the condom, he tossed it to the floor and grabbed his tee-shirt out of the pile. Lying down next to Henry, he used his shirt to gently wipe up Henry's stomach and chest.

"I think her price just quadrupled," Henry smiled as Quinn tossed the shirt back to the floor. Leaning over, he kissed him warmly, unable to stop smiling.

With a smile matching his lover's, Quinn put a hand behind Henry's neck, pulling him close. Pressing their foreheads together, Quinn breathed in deeply and they both remained silent for a few moments before his lips moved to Henry's ear, softly grazing the lobe with his front teeth.

"Stay forever," was all he whispered.

chapter
fifteen

"**A** cop? Seriously, Henry? Heh." It was a mocking sound.

Turning his head to face him, he tried to speak, but he was so angry, nothing came out.

"He's not going to protect you. I hope you know that." He smiled, that gorgeous one dimple smile.

… And Henry hated himself for thinking it was beautiful.

"If I want to kill you, there's no way he can stop me. I'm trained for this, you know. What's he trained for? Pulling over stoned teenagers for speeding? If something even mildly dangerous happened," he laughed, "he'd be totally fucked."

"Go away," Henry choked out.

"You know you don't mean that or I'd already be long gone." He pressed his long, hard cock against Henry's ass. "And I'm not." He continued to slowly grind against him. "So what, you got your fag-loving friend to ship me to this hellhole. It didn't get me out of your head, did it? I'm not going anywhere, Henry. When are you finally going to figure that out? You're mine. You'll always be mine."

"You're wrong. I'm his," Henry hissed.

"His? Yeah, right," he mocked. "Have you even told him you love him? No. And you know why? Because you love me. He's going to watch me fuck you, watch you take every last inch and see how much you love it, because you know you do. And after I make him watch me fuck you until your ass bleeds, just like I did that last night on the floor, maybe I'll kill him and let you watch that."

Wrapping his fingers through Henry's hair, he slammed his head into the oak posts of the Mission-style headboard. "I love fucking you when you're unconscious and all bloody." He slammed his head again.

"No! No! Get off of me, you sick motherfucker." He fought back, throwing his head in the other direction, away from the headboard.

He was now being restrained and couldn't move out of his grasp. He twisted left, then right, then left again, fighting to break free.

"Let me go," he screamed and the grasp was gone, white light filling the darkness as he gasped for air.

"It's OK. Henry, you're OK. You're here with me. He's not here. It's just us. Only you and me," Quinn's voice was calm and even.

Without even opening his eyes, Henry got to his knees and dragged his wet tee-shirt over his head. Stretching to the sheets, he assumed the Balasana pose and concentrated on his breathing, fighting hard to push from his mind how strange and disturbing this must all seem to Quinn.

Feeling Quinn get off the bed, he heard him leave the room and a heaviness descended, incarcerating his heart. Embarrassed didn't even begin to describe what he was feeling. He'd made it three and a half weeks sleeping every night in Quinn's bed, their bed, before the demons found his new locale. What could have set this off? He wracked his brain, but came up empty-handed. And that was the scariest part. That's how he let Cody hold him hostage, never knowing when he'd break out of his subconscious, angered from being repressed.

Henry longed for his PalmPilot. He needed to record the

number on his nightmare chart, satisfying some OCD ritual, completing what needed to be done. But his PalmPilot was in his laptop case in the other room.

With a big sports bottle filled with water and two towels, one wet with cool water and the other dry, Quinn re-entered the room.

Sitting up on his side of the bed, Henry looked forlorn. "I'm really sorry," he began.

"Shhh." Quinn handed him the water bottle and pressed the cool, wet cloth against his sweat-soaked hairline. "Turn your back to me." Quinn pressed the cloth against the back of his neck and with strong hands kneaded the knots from his shoulders.

"I made it almost a month," Henry's voice was soft.

"Yup and now it's happened and you don't have to stress about the first time anymore."

Peering over his shoulder, Henry looked into Quinn's eyes, "Did you know I was stressed about it?"

Running his index and middle fingers softly down Henry's cheek, Quinn silently nodded.

Henry leaned his face into Quinn's hand, closing his eyes and sighing. "I didn't want that to happen."

"I know. But it was this thing between us – waiting for it to happen. And now it has. So it's not between us anymore. And we're both still here," Quinn smiled, "and he's not."

Turning his face into Quinn's hand, Henry kissed his palm. "It's just us."

"It is just us. That wall had to come down. It did and we're still standing. Nothing left separating us."

Quinn was right. Henry could see it plain as day. Tonight's nightmare was actually a godsend, eradicating unspoken fears and removing boundaries that had been deeply rooted in place.

With a hand on each of Quinn's cheeks, Henry longed to tell him that he loved him, but the words, "Thank you," came out instead.

"For what?"

"Being so good to me tonight. So understanding."

"Pffft." Quinn shrugged his shoulders.

Henry shook his head, not understanding Quinn's intent.

"Henry, this is what you do for people you love."

Searching Quinn's eyes, there was no mocking. Only sincerity.

"Did you just say the "L" word to me?"

"Does that surprise you?" Quinn asked.

"Yes and no."

"Does it make you happy?"

"Very definitely, yes." He brought Quinn's face very close to his. "I'm ready for the rest of our relationship. More than you can imagine. It's all I think about."

"And how do we do that?" Quinn was confused by Henry's response.

Crawling over Quinn, Henry opened the nightstand drawer on Quinn's side of the bed and pulled out a condom and the bottle of lubricating liquid.

"No more barriers. No more fears. Just us. You're right, I needed that to happen tonight. I lived through it. It didn't kill me. I was letting that fear control me." He shook his head.

Quinn's expression was blank as he was processing what was going on.

Taking Quinn's hand, he wrapped it around his cock, and with his hand over Quinn's, they stroked him to hardness. Tearing open the condom packet, Henry tossed the wrapper to the floor, and began to unroll the latex sheath over himself as Quinn watched.

Cocking his head to the side, "Are you going to fuck me?"

"Damn right." Henry smiled, squirting liquid in his palm and wrapping a fist around Quinn's semi-erect cock. "I'm not letting anything or anyone come between us anymore. You. You're my only priority. Making you happy. That's all that matters."

Quinn hardened to a combination of Henry's words and

strokes.

Leaning forward, he gave Quinn a quick, hard kiss. "Now turn around."

Turning on his knees, Quinn faced away from Henry who softly pushed him down by the shoulder so that his face was on his pillow. Pouring some lube onto his fingers, he quickly massaged it into Quinn. There was an urgency in his motions, they weren't slow and gentle, but rather rapid and rushed, as if he needed to get someplace quickly, racing to erase everything that had come before.

Briefly he explored Quinn with his finger, hardening at his sounds of pleasure. Pulling out his finger, he stretched his body along Quinn's, laying on top of his back, his arms wrapped around him. Lifting his cheek off Quinn's shoulder, he gave it a quick kiss and ran his hands down his back as he sat back on his knees behind him again.

Positioning the head of his cock at Quinn's opening, Henry grabbed Quinn's hips, pressing past the tight sphincter ring and was sucked deeply into his ass.

"Oh God," he wasn't sure who said it as he started relentlessly plowing into his lover, lost to the sublime feeling.

"Fuck, I've been missing out," Henry was shocked at how good it felt. Pulling Quinn up by the shoulder into a near seated position, he reached around him to stroke his erection with one hand and wrapped his other arm around Quinn's muscular stomach to control their movement.

"Oh God, Henry. I don't want this to ever end. You feel so good."

"I'll fuck you as often as you want me to," he groaned, buried as deeply as was physically possible.

Taking his arm from Quinn's midsection, they continued to move in rhythm as he reached for Quinn's chin, pulling his face around.

Seeking Quinn's lips, he wanted his tongue in his mouth,

needing yet another point of connection between the two of them.

"Quinn," he cried into his mouth.

"I know, babe. I know."

"Quinn, look at me." Henry stopped moving.

Craning his neck around to see him, he waited for Henry to speak.

"I love you so much."

Smiling, Quinn's eyes said it all. "I know."

"I love you so, so much…" He buried his face in the nook of his neck as he rammed his last powerful thrusts deep into his lover.

chapter
sixteen

THE DOORBELL RANG AND HENRY put the chef's knife down onto the cutting board. Wiping off his hands, he glanced at his watch and headed toward the front door. Shaking his head, he could not contain his smile.

"Did you forget your keys again," he opened the door to a smiling Quinn.

It had become a running joke between the two men. Henry had even bought Quinn a new keychain with a detachable segment for his house keys only to find the detachable section never got reattached and didn't fix the problem.

"Nope," Quinn leaned in, pressing a hard kiss to Henry's lips. "I just need a third hand. It's a design flaw," and he handed Henry the large basket he was carrying.

"What's this," Henry took the basket, leaning his face into it and inhaling deeply. "Oh my God, they smell beautiful. Are they lilacs?" He walked back to the kitchen and put the basket down on the counter.

"Yup. Lilacs and ivy." Quinn watched Henry's reaction as he unpacked the plants.

Feeling the soil, Henry grabbed a cup of water and fed the plants, "Let's get a pot and some potting soil this weekend, we can put them out on the deck. Maybe get a little trellis thing for the ivy." Then he looked up at Quinn, "What a nice surprise. Did you just see them on your way home?"

"Nope." Quinn smiled, his eyes shining with delight.

"So, what's the story behind them?"

"It's more the meaning behind them." Quinn pulled a beer from the refrigerator, "Want one?"

Henry shook his head no, and picked up the chef's knife, poised to slice a tomato. "So, what's the meaning?"

Popping the top off his bottle, Quinn took a long swig of the cold beer, "Ahh, that's good." He looked at the bottle and then back at Henry. "Lilacs signify first love and ivy signifies fidelity," he explained, ending with a shit-eating grin.

"Well I'm not your first love," Henry countered, giving him a hard time.

Looking at him with a hard stare, Quinn pointed the neck of his beer bottle at Henry, "You're wrong."

"Bullshit," Henry laughed. "You loved the dude before me."

"No." Quinn shook his head. "It was nothing like this. This is a whole new level of everything. I had no idea what love was."

Putting down the knife, Henry quickly got serious. "And you do now?"

"God, you're a dick," Quinn laughed. "You know I do now."

Smiling, "I love giving you a hard time."

"I love when you give me a hard time."

"I kinda like it myself." Henry's smile was wolfish.

"What a monster I've created. You're like a little addict." Quinn took another swig of his beer.

Henry shook his head, "No, I'm a big addict. I'm totally addicted and there ain't no rehab for this."

"Oh yeah?" Quinn spurred him on.

"I'm addicted to your smile. I'm addicted to your laugh. I'm addicted to the way you tangle your legs with mine when we sleep. I'm addicted to fucking you. I'm addicted to you fucking me. I'm even addicted to falling asleep in front of the TV on the couch with you."

"Sounds like you might love me," Quinn's piercing eyes were smoldering.

"Sounds like I might." As Henry bent down to take in the fragrant scent of the lilacs, the perfect gift of first love from his first love, he never once took his eyes off Quinn's.

"Come on, pussy." Quinn looked back with a smile.

"I'm very happy just where I am. Nice view from back here," Henry sassed back, referring to Quinn's birthday present that he was wearing on this cool beautiful morning, as they made their way down the Pacific Coast Highway, passing through Sunset Beach. "And we have a long way to go."

Eight months of training had led to this day, participating in the Long Beach/San Diego Challenge, benefitting the Lesbian and Gay Centers of both Long Beach and San Diego. Eight months, countless hours training, a friendship, a love affair, a life partnership and two brand new Cannondale EVO Hi-Mod street bikes.

"What is this?" Quinn had walked into the apartment to find two identical bikes parked in front of the television set.

With a coy grin, Henry said, "I found something useful to do with my last quarterly bonus."

"I can't," Quinn started to protest.

"Shut up. Yes you can. I'm keeping mine and you're going to want to look good if you're riding next to me."

"Seriously, Henry, you need to return it."

Shaking his head, Henry wasn't taking no for an answer. "Don't force me to key it and put a big gaping scratch down the frame, so that they won't take it back." Henry reached into his pocket for his keys and dangled them in front of Quinn, tauntingly.

Suddenly serious, Quinn pointed a finger at him, "Don't you

dare scratch my bike."

Smiling, he flipped the keys back into his palm and returned them to his jean's pocket.

With eyes that bored into his soul, Quinn slowly approached him, knowing his leisurely swagger was killing Henry. His fore and middle fingers trailed down Henry's cheek at an equally languid pace. "You're spoiling me for all other men, you know that, don't you?"

"There will be no other men," Henry held his intense gaze, all the while wanting to melt as Quinn's fingers trailed his check.

"Look at my little bottom being so possessive."

Reaching around Quinn and pulling him in by his ass against his already throbbing shaft, "Does this feel like a bottom cock to you?"

"Feels like my very generous lover's cock to me, who went overboard, and bought me a really expensive gift."

Henry smiled. "I bought us gifts. We've worked really hard for this and we're going to be on those bikes for probably close to eight hours. We're going to need some fine equipment for our fine equipment." He brought his hand around to Quinn's groin and gave him a squeeze. "Plus this gives us about three weeks to get used to them, make any mods if we need to."

Walking over to one of the bikes, Quinn ran his fingers gently over the outstanding equipment. "Henry, a Cannondale like this has always been my dream." He crouched down, looking closely at the parts, and then looked up with a smile, "Actually, sharing this with someone I love who enjoys it as much as I do, has always been my dream."

"Three more weeks, babe, and we'll be living the dream."

As they entered Huntington Beach, a crowd awaited them along the sidewalk. Beachgoers, surfers, gays and straights, all cheered on the 300 plus riders who had undertaken the challenge. The cyclists waved to the passersby, many of whom waved small rainbow flags back at them.

Quinn turned around, "I don't think all the towns will be this friendly."

"Probably not," Henry agreed, knowing that next up was the more conservative and moneyed Newport Beach.

As they hit the causeway over Lower Newport Bay, Henry pulled up alongside Quinn, "See that island over there on the other side?"

"Nice houses and nice boats," Quinn checked it out.

"That's Linda Isle. That's where Schooner lives."

Quinn laughed, shaking his head, "Why am I not surprised?"

It was less than two minutes later when they reached land again on the other side of the causeway, and were met with one awesome surprise. Standing on the sidewalk, with bougainvillea and boats behind them, was their lone cheering section consisting of Schooner Moore, his little girl, Holly, and his son, Zac, who was perched high on his shoulders.

"Holly," Henry screamed out, blowing her a kiss.

The excited little girl danced as she waved, thrilled to see the rider that she knew. "Henreeeeeee," her voice carried on the breeze.

Henry and Quinn waved to Schooner and his small son.

"That is awesome that he brought the kids out to see you." Quinn was impressed.

"Well, that just made my day," and with a new burst of energy, Henry pulled ahead as they cycled along the beautiful beaches of the Newport coast en route to Laguna Beach. "Catch up, pussy." Henry yelled back.

"Not a chance in Hell," Quinn returned. "It's a beautiful day to enjoy this view."

At San Clemente, they hit the halfway mark of their 107 mile journey and took a pit stop.

Getting off their bikes, they stretched out their backs and legs, shook their shoulders and wrists free, and removed their helmets to roll their necks.

Downing cold water and Gatorade that had been set up, their bodies still felt the sensation of riding. Tilting his face up to the relentless blue of the sky, Henry closed his eyes, deeply breathing in the sea-scented air.

He opened his eyes to Quinn's two fingers tracing a path down his cheek. Leaning in for a kiss, Quinn uttered, "Thank you," against his lips.

"For what?" Henry's light brows merged, questioningly.

"The bicycle. It would have been hell on the old one. I can't tell you how much easier it is on this one than it was last year. The difference is incredibly significant."

"Glad you're enjoying it." Henry's grin spoke volumes.

Snaking an arm around his waist and pulling him close, "And thank you for being here with me. When I asked you to come train with me," Quinn closed his eyes and shook his head, "I could not have imagined how amazing my life was about to become."

"You're thanking me?" Henry's eyes were wide, astonished. His hand went around the back of Quinn's neck, as he searched his lover's baby blue eyes. "Quinn Callahan, I'm alive, and I mean that on so many levels, because of you. Because of us. There aren't enough bikes in the world to thank you for what your love has given me." Pulling Quinn's lips to his, Henry got lost in their kiss, allowing himself to feel a sense of total and complete happiness. "I love you, thanks for asking me to train with you," he was smiling as their lips parted.

"Why did we agree to that party tonight?" Derek and Willie were hosting a post-race fundraiser at their home with Henry and Quinn as the guests of honor.

"I don't know. You, the hot tub and food delivered would have been Heaven."

"Too late to get out of it now," Quinn lamented as they got back onto their bikes and merged into the pack of riders, reenergized to head into the uphill climb and cycle the bluffs above San Onofre State Beach and away from the shoreline through, what felt like an interminable ride to Henry, Camp Pendleton.

Finally exiting the base, and heading west toward the ocean with the afternoon's sun glinting off the waves, Henry shoulders loosened, letting go of the tension he hadn't anticipated joining him on this ride. Quinn had ridden behind him the entire time they were on base and Henry knew it was not by accident. His handsome cop was letting him know that he had his back as they cycled through the Marine encampment.

Oceanside was beginning to feel like the homestretch, even though they had another forty miles to go. Behind Quinn again, Henry observed the rhythm of his lover's legs and back muscles, and there was something very Zen about watching this beautiful man, his beautiful man. Just thinking about his dark hair and pale eyes, his full lips and scruffy jaw made Henry twitch. He laughed out loud, knowing the seat of his bike was not the place to get excited.

Quinn. This ride. His new life. Second chances and dreams. An openly gay cop living an openly gay life. As Henry watched him, he realized what a hero Quinn truly was. Not only to him, but what an amazing role model to any little girl or boy who felt different, who didn't fit in. This man maintained who he was in the most conservative and mainstream of professions.

Henry wanted to scream, *He's mine!* With the utmost of pride.

Carlsbad. (Henry blew a discreet, silent kiss up to the cliff that housed L9 as a thank you for everything wonderful it meant in his life – Schooner, Ivy, Yoga, Quinn, the Bike Challenge).

Encinitas.

Solana Beach.

Del Mar.

Torrey Pines.

La Jolla.

Cycling side by side, every muscle screaming as they approached San Diego, Henry could feel the lump in his throat as people waited along the route to greet them. A rainbow colored archway of balloons stretched across the road as they approached the finish line. He and Quinn reached out for one another's hands at the same moment and passed under the arch with their fingers entwined.

Parking their bikes, they turned to one another, falling into a tight embrace, steadying one another as their bodies still felt the motion from hours of cycling. Henry realized there were tears streaming down his face and he could feel small sharp jolts between Quinn's shoulder blades, letting him know his handsome cop too had been moved to tears.

Exhausted. Depleted. Proud. Aching. Satisfied. Overjoyed. Overwhelmed. They stood there holding one another, neither prepared to let go. What began on a SkyTrack some eight months before was now part of a shared tapestry already rich with memories and moments. Arriving at this moment had been a cornerstone of their relationship and when they laid it in the soil, neither could have envisioned the beautiful skyscraper that would grow floor by floor.

"I know I said this was so much better when you do it with someone else, but that's not really the truth. The truth is, it was totally amazing because I shared it with you." Quinn's eyes beamed with love as his two fingers softly trailed down Henry's cheek.

"Thank you for asking me."

"Just sit there," Edwin was having a fine time pampering Henry.

"I can absolutely do that." Henry was too tired to move. Both he and Quinn sat there on the couch being tended to by the other guests like rock royalty.

"I can't even imagine what your body feels like." Edwin sat down next to him, handing him a plate filled with food.

"There isn't any part of me that doesn't hurt. Even my hair hurts from my helmet. My ass hurts. My balls hurt. My thighs are burning." He stopped and looked at Edwin and laughed, "And I'm just a whiny little bitch, aren't I."

"Tonight you get to whine and be as bitchy as you want, cupcake."

Putting his head on Edwin's shoulder, "You're so good to me."

"So how much money did you two raise from all this torture?" Edwin was primping the pillows behind Henry's lower back.

"Good question. I think we're going to do a tally in a little while. Derek's been gathering a lot of it." Quinn looked like it was painful just raising the fork to his mouth.

"You two deserve a vacation after this. You've been training every weekend since you met. It's time to plan a trip, a real trip." Willie suggested, sitting down on a chair next to Quinn.

Quinn turned to Henry, "Imagine just waking up and relaxing. Lying around, reading, swimming, worrying about what's for dinner."

"Now that's what I'm talking about," Willie agreed. "A tropical getaway."

"Someplace exotic like Bali," Quinn reached for Henry's hand and gave it a squeeze, "or the Seychelles."

"Yes, the Seychelles," Edwin closed his eyes at the fantasy, "I hear the people are beautiful in the Seychelles."

"Where are these places?" asked Willie.

"I think they're off the coast of Africa, but that's all I can tell you. I don't know exactly where." Henry looked around for corroboration. "Ok, we've clearly got a group that did well in geography."

They all laughed.

Henry felt Quinn's thumb rubbing along the back of his hand, "We need to look into this vacation," he smiled, the look in his eyes incendiary.

"Yes. We do." He leaned over to kiss Quinn.

Holding a box, Derek came and sat down with everyone. "Ready to find out how much you two bitches raised for the Lesbian and Gay Center?"

Lots of excitement and hooting from the room, "In all seriousness," Derek began, "thank you to the two of you for making this monumental ride. You both have been so dedicated, weekend after weekend, training for today. And we all really appreciate it. And we really, really appreciated being able to sit on our asses while you two nuts went out there and did all the work."

His last statement brought on a round of applause and then he went on, "But now we're going to ask all of you lazy people," he looked around the room, "to dig deep, pull out your checkbooks and do our boys here proud."

Henry handed Derek a manila envelope, "These are the donations from some of the people I work with."

"Wow." Derek's eyes widened as he pulled out the tally sheet from inside the envelope. "That's very generous. Add that to what was donated from the precinct and you boys made a serious impact."

Henry found Quinn's hand on the couch and squeezed it without looking at him, but he absolutely knew the look on Quinn's face, the pride in being supported as an openly gay man by the members of his precinct. It wasn't all that many years before, in 1990, when San Diego police officer John Graham came out to the local press to show gays and lesbians that they could be police officers and good ones at that. With the support of then Chief of Police, Bob Burgreen, Graham paved the way for men like Quinn, Derek and Willie to pursue careers they were passionate about and live their lives openly as true partners with their heterosexual counterparts on the force.

"Oh, I almost forgot." Derek pulled an envelope out of his folder and handed it to Henry, "Here Henry, you should do the honors on this one."

Taking the anonymous white envelope, Henry stuck his finger under the flap to rip it open, as excited as everyone else to see its contents. At first he thought his eyes were not focusing properly on the check, as he stared in disbelief. Shaking his head and smiling, he muttered, "He didn't."

Peering over his shoulder, Quinn let out a low whistle, "Nice," was all he said.

It took Henry a moment to gather himself and let the rest of the room in on the gift, "This is a very generous donation from one of my oldest friends. Actually the person responsible for bringing this guy into my life." He slung an arm over Quinn's shoulder and pulled him in tight, kissing his cheek.

"Enough with you two," Edwin snarked, snatching the check from Henry's hands. "Oh, that is very nice. And notice he did this from his personal account and not business. I love him even more." Edwin continued to stare at the check.

"Where is Schooner tonight? Why isn't he here?" Willie asked

"He was out along the route today with his kids cheering us on." Henry did not directly answer the question.

So Edwin answered for him, "CJ, his wife, doesn't like our boy here." He hit Henry in the biceps. "It appears he wasn't Team CJ when they were all in college and she still hasn't forgiven him."

"What team were you on?" Terry's wife, Patty, asked.

"I was Team Mia. Mia was a close friend of mine and she is the person who actually introduced me and Schooner."

"Well, it appears you were on the losing team," Terry laughed.

"Only because Team CJ didn't play fair and she knows that I know the score."

"Why? What happened?" Everyone loved the gossip, even

though it was a decade old.

"Schooner was really in love with Mia and she left, without a trace. Back then there was no internet, no search engines, no cell phones. And she just went back to New York and disappeared. Never even said goodbye to him. Totally broke his heart. But you see the thing was, Mia loved him just as much as he loved her. So, for her to run like that, something really bad happened, something that totally devastated her. The only person that could have been responsible was CJ. And she's always denied it, but she knows I don't buy that for a minute."

"So, she doesn't like your friendship with Schooner?" Patty asked.

Henry shook his head. "She's never been a big fan of mine. But I do have to say, when my jaw was broken last year, she was very kind in making me all this organic pureed food. She certainly didn't have to do that and it was really sweet of her."

"I'm still not over this check." Edwin was clutching it tightly. "Just thinking about that man gives me a semi and then holding this much money, his money, mmm, better than taking a blue pill."

Laughing, Quinn looked at Derek, "Get that check out of his hands before it gets all sticky."

It was another few hours before Henry and Quinn were able to slip into the empty hot tub in their complex. Sitting side by side, steam curling up into the night air, dissipating in the darkness, they watched the stars shimmer against the black sky.

"What next?" Henry finally broke the silence.

Quinn smiled, "I was just thinking that."

"And?"

"And this is next. This. We're living it."

Henry was satisfied with the answer.

chapter seventeen

"I STILL CAN'T GET OVER that check," Quinn commented as they drove up to Newport Beach.

"That's just who he is. It's not about being showy or anything, it's just about doing the right thing. That's really big with him."

"I've never been to the L9/Newport Beach facility. I'm looking forward to seeing it."

"This was the first," Henry explained. "To me this one feels like a yacht club/fitness club hybrid."

"What?" Quinn's face scrunched.

"Wait, you'll see. You'll have to tell me if you agree."

Pulling into the parking lot, Quinn turned to Henry, astonished, "They have valet?"

Laughing, Henry nodded, "It's quite the concept. He really is a brilliant businessman."

"That I figured out a long time ago." Quinn looked around at the facility perched on the edge of a private marina. "Do people come in by boat to work out?"

Again, Henry nodded, "He's got the whole SoCal scene worked out."

"Amazing," was all Quinn could say as they entered the facility. "It's so different than the two L9's I've been to."

"Good morning," a peppy blonde was behind the desk to

greet them.

"Good morning." Henry smiled at the cute girl. "We're here to see Schooner Moore."

Looking at a computer monitor, she glanced back at the handsome duo, "Henry and Quinn?"

"Yes."

"I'll need some ID. Do you have a membership?" she looked at them apologetically. "Sorry, club rules for everyone's safety."

As they dug for their wallets, they heard a voice they'd just heard a week before, "Henreeeeee."

Running toward them was Holly Moore, ponytail tied up in a pink ribbon and a pink and blue flowered pinafore flouncing around her as she ran.

"Holly." Henry crouched down to catch her, abandoning his ID search. Scooping her up with a twirl, "How's my girl? What happened to your teeth?"

"I got new ones." She smiled, showing off teeth into which her pretty face had yet to grow. Putting her down, she ran to take the empty seat behind the receptionist's station.

"I've got this, Robin." Schooner held up a hand to the receptionist, letting her know the ID's weren't necessary. In his other arm, Schooner held a miniature version of himself, toddler-sized.

"Zac, this is Henry and Quinn."

His pale blue eyes, near the color of his father's, looked as if a storm were brewing within them. Shifting in Schooner's arms, he gave Quinn a hard look, "Stop looking at me," and then hauled off and punched him in the arm.

"Zac!" Schooner admonished the toddler. "That is bad. We don't hit people."

"It probably hurt him more than it hurt me." Quinn smiled.

"Tell Quinn you are sorry," Schooner's voice was firm.

"No. Not sowwy." Zac shook his head.

"Zac." There was no mistaking Schooner was the disciplinarian as he held the little boy up and looked him in the eyes. "You are going to apologize to Quinn and tell him you are sorry. *NOW,"* and he turned the little boy to face Quinn.

With his lower lip quivering, but refusing to cry, Zac managed, "I sowwy."

"Apology accepted." The big cop smiled at the little boy, his eyes revealing a melting heart. "How would you like to go lift some weights with me?"

The quivering lip immediately disappeared, replaced by an engaging smile and head nod.

"C'mon." He reached for Zac who willingly left his father's arms and put the little boy on the ground. Together they walked, hand in hand, toward the free weights.

Henry watched Quinn leading Zac away, his comfort level with the toddler so complete.

"Makes you almost want one," Schooner laughed.

Henry looked at him with a terrified look, "Well, I don't quite know about that. But he seems quite comfortable with the whole thing."

"Hmm," Schooner smiled, nodding his head.

Shaking his head no, "Get that look off your face, Moore."

Sitting down in Schooner's office, Henry just looked at his friend and smiled. "Thank you for that very generous donation to the Lesbian and Gay Center."

"My pleasure. Happy to help."

"I owe you so much," Henry looked deep into his friend's sky blue eyes.

"You don't owe me anything, H. You're family."

"You helped me run through it and gave me the greatest gift of my life. That man."

"You were ready to do the hard work, ready to get healthy on all levels. I'm so proud of you, and I'm just glad I knew him and could make sure you met. I knew from the time I met him that he was just a good guy." He stopped and smiled, "And you two have really built something together. You can't even imagine how much I admire you."

Quinn entered and sat down, a sleeping Zac on his shoulder. "He is really strong for a little guy."

"Strong-willed, too," his father laughed. "I can tell you already, Holly is just going to raise herself. She's smart and focused and has this innate maturity. And this one," he pointed at Zac, "this one is going to give me a run for my money. He's a little hellion."

They all laughed.

"We should take bets now on how many schools he's going to get kicked out of." Schooner smiled at the guys.

"Two," was Henry's guess.

"I'm going with three," Schooner smiled.

"I don't know," Quinn looked down at the sleeping boy on his chest. "Maybe he'll surprise us. But just to hedge my bets, I'll go with one."

And all three men laughed again as Zac Moore burrowed himself into Quinn Callahan's shoulder.

chapter
eighteen

P UTTING THE WATERING CAN DOWN on the wooden deck next to his feet, Henry leaned against the railing, realizing he was looking for support both metaphorically and physically.

"You're not serious, are you?" It wasn't the first time they'd had this disagreement. It was one of the few things that breached the harmony in their relationship. On several occasions, it had gotten pretty bad and Henry thought, this is going to be the thing that eventually breaks us up.

"Yeah, I am. Maybe we just want different things." Quinn's eyes were overwrought with sadness.

"Maybe the timing just isn't right, Quinn," Henry implored, devastated he was hurting his lover but, wanting Quinn to really listen to what he was saying.

"Is it timing, Henry, or is it a dead end?"

Quinn was like a Pitbull and Henry could only imagine what the man was like in an interrogation room. If he wasn't so annoyed with him at the moment, he knew Quinn's tenacity would be making him hard.

"Honestly, I don't really have the answer to that. I just know that the answer isn't, 'No, never'."

Approaching him, Quinn reached out his fingers tracing Henry's check. "It's not that I just want a family. It's that I want a family with you. I know you'd be a great parent. I think we would make great parents."

Henry closed his eyes, leaning his face into Quinn's palm, before taking his hand and leading him over to the two-seater glider.

"I think we would make great parents, too. Our little boy or girl would know just how loved they are and we would raise them with such great values of respect and acceptance. But Quinn, I want you to myself for a bit longer. I know that may sound selfish, but I'm not ready to share you. I like the freedom of just us. The only responsibility we have right now is to each other and these plants." He pointed to the beautiful plantings on their deck that had begun with the lilac bush and ivy.

"Let's travel and save for a house, so that our kids have a backyard to play in," Henry went on.

"Kids? Was that a plural I heard?" Quinn's baby blue eyes sparkled.

Giving the glider a shove off with his feet, Henry looked at Quinn, "A boy and a girl would be nice."

"You're thinking about Holly and Zac, aren't you?"

"Yeah and how good you were with him. That little bugger has got his mother's winning personality," Henry remarked facetiously.

Laughing, Quinn shook his head. "I think he's a pretty cool little guy, but he's definitely going to be a handful."

"So what is it you've been thinking?" This was the deepest they'd ever gotten into the conversation, without one or both of them storming out of the room. "Adopting internationally? Or one or both of us actually fathering a child?" As he said it, a yearning for a baby of Quinn's took root in his soul, appearing literally out of nowhere and firmly planting its seed.

"I'm open." The look on Quinn's face said it all. They may not have an insta-family tomorrow or in six months or a year, but someday, not too far off on the horizon, they would have a family.

They would be a family.

"I'm going to have to keep the PTA bitches off you." Henry shook his head. "You're going to be the hottest daddy in the school. Especially on career day."

With that, Henry abruptly stopped the glider, lurching them both forward and grabbed Quinn by the hand, pulling him toward their bedroom.

The doorbell ringing at 6:15 P.M. could only mean one thing. Quinn was keyless. *So what else is new?* thought Henry, as he saved the work on his laptop to go answer the door.

"What's this?" Henry laughed at the sight of Quinn standing in the doorway with a big box that said *Oregon Scientific.*

Leaning in for a kiss, Quinn smiled his white-toothed beautiful smile and with shining eyes announced, "This is going to educate us on where we're going to travel."

Putting the box down on the kitchen table, he grabbed two beers from the refrigerator and a knife to start cutting away the packing tape on the box.

"Oh yeah? What's in there?" Henry was curious.

"Ah, you shall see." Quinn was enjoying the suspense. Finally, he had the tape removed from the top of the brown box, and opened it. Reaching in, he pulled out a second, slightly smaller box with a picture of a globe and bold letters stating this was the *Oregon Scientific Smart Globe.*

"Check this out." Quinn's excitement was contagious.

Moving closer to read the box, Henry started checking out all the functions. *Facts. World News. Population. Time. Currency. History. Language. Capital. Weather.* The list of the *Smart* Globe's features went on and on.

"What kind of batteries does it take?" Henry got up from the table.

"Looks like four double A's. We should have plenty. I just put some in the corner drawer." He pointed to the far end of the kitchen. Laughing, "It even plays the national anthems from countries all over the world."

Returning with the batteries, Henry sat down next to Quinn and handed them to him. Quinn inserted them and looked around the globe. "How do we make it talk?"

Henry looked it over. No on/off switch. He touched all the little labels on the base, including volume, still nothing.

"Ahh," said Quinn, looking satisfied as he pulled out a little panel in the front, but all it revealed was a map of the fifty states. Looking at Henry, "So, it appears the *Smart Globe* is not for dumb adults."

"Here's a novel thought," Henry laughed, "maybe we should actually read the instructions."

Leveling a dirty look at Henry, Quinn shook his head. "That would be like stopping to ask someone for directions."

Picking up the connected stylus-type pen apparatus, Henry touched it to different spots on the globe. Nothing. He touched it to the labels on the base. Nothing.

"This is why we need a kid." Quinn surmised, sitting back with his beer.

Henry laughed, "We need to get better at this or we are seriously going to embarrass a kid." Henry looked at the stylus in his hand and tried pressing a round area with the Oregon Scientific logo. He tried touching it to the globe again. Nothing. And then he hit this little rectangle on the stylus that he thought might or might not be a button.

Loud music blared from speakers on the base of the globe, "Welcome to Oregon Scientific's Smart Globe." Both men jumped, startled by the sound and quickly descended into laughter.

"Oh my God, you are brilliant. You found the start button."

Quinn was practically in tears, he was laughing so hard at their joint ineptitude.

"How hot am I now?" Henry laughed.

"Seriously fuckable." He reached over, giving Henry's package a squeeze. "But now that we've got it working, let's play with this big ball first." Spinning the globe and smiling, Quinn took the stylus from Henry and stabbed it down onto the globe. "First stop, the Seychelles."

Quinn was spooning him from behind, their legs tangled. "That was really fun learning about all of those countries. I'll definitely pick up the form for my passport next week."

"How long do you think you'll be able to get away for?" Henry snuggled into Quinn a little tighter, feeling the beginnings of Quinn's stirrings.

"I'm going to ask for three weeks, I know I'll definitely be able to get at least two off."

"There are so many places I want to go with you. We need months off."

"Tell me where you want me to take you?" Quinn's lips gently brushed his ear before trailing to his neck. With each kiss, his cock hardened against Henry's ass. "Because I know exactly where I'd like to take you."

"You going to ride me there?" Henry was moaning with every twitch of Quinn's cock.

"I'm going to ride you hard until I'm all done." Quinn's arms were wrapped around Henry's chest.

"It's going to be different this time." Henry turned his face back and Quinn reached for his chin, pulling his mouth to him, his tongue immediately beginning its deep exploration.

Finally letting go of his chin, Quinn let his hand trail down to explore the effects of his kiss. "Mmm," he moaned seductively as his hand wrapped tightly around Henry's erect cock and began stroking him from base to tip.

Henry took Quinn's hand off his cock and brought it up to his mouth. With his face turned so that Quinn could see him, he slowly licked Quinn's palm from heel to fingertips, sucking his fingers into his mouth. He then placed Quinn's now slick hand around his hard cock again and hand over hand set the rhythm of Quinn's strokes.

"It's going to be even better." Quinn nipped at his ear lobe.

With well over two years' worth of clean AIDS tests and a dedicated monogamous relationship, they had finally made the decision to forego protection with a conversation that went, "I thought you wanted to keep using it," "I thought you did," "No, it was just habit more than anything else," "Think you can kick the habit?" "Consider it kicked."

"You have amazing self-control," Henry commented. "If I were in your position, I would have been plowing into you by now."

Laughing, Quinn tightened his grip around Henry, squeezing with his thumb as he stroked him. "Yeah, but you're not in my position." Henry hardened even more with his stroke.

"Oh God, Quinn, do you want to hear me beg you to fuck me. Because I will beg you," he groaned.

"How bad do you want me inside you?" Quinn whispered, clearly enjoying how worked up he'd gotten his lover.

"Oh God, I don't think I can last another minute. Fuck me already, damn it," Henry was whimpering as Quinn continued to relentlessly stroke him.

"You sure you're ready to really let me have you? That's my ass, Henry. Mine."

"Oh God, Quinn."

"Tell me, Henry." He slowed down the pace of his stroking.

"It's yours, Quinn. I'm yours."

Letting go of Henry, he rolled away and grabbed a bottle of KY liquid from his nightstand. Just rubbing it on himself, he thought he'd explode in anticipation. Even after two years, the significance of this night was huge. It was the final level of trust amongst gay men, and although it had been there between him and Henry almost from the moment they met, it was the final vow in a bond that they both knew meant forever.

Squirting some of the liquid into his fingers, he gently massaged it into Henry. "I love you," he whispered.

Turning his head to look into Quinn's eyes, "Show me how much."

Quinn grabbed Henry's thigh, lifting it and with one forceful drive, breached the tight ring of his ass. Both men moaned, synchronized in perfect unison.

"Fuck, you feel good," Quinn's voice was gruff, as he lay still for a moment as if acclimating himself to his new home. And then without warning, he began pounding into Henry's ass, lost in the new sensation. Needing more, greedy for his own release in the warmth that was now forever his. Forever more.

"Oh God, Quinn. God, Quinn." Henry's cries exposed the brink upon which he was teetering, the pleasure of pain eclipsing all other input from his senses. Turning his head, his voice a raspy cry, "Oh God, Quinn. I love you."

With a final thrust, Quinn consummated their bond, holding Henry tightly against him, and staying within him long after they were done.

chapter
nineteen

QUINN WAS OUT ON THE deck doing maintenance on the bikes when he got home from work. Heading to the bedroom to change out of his suit, Henry threw on a tee-shirt and shorts, before grabbing two cold bottles of water and heading out to the deck.

Sitting down on the glider and tossing a bottle to Quinn, he looked at his handsome partner with a smile, "So, I've got some news."

Quinn stopped what he was doing and looked up, "Good news?"

Smiling, Henry nodded. "They announced 4th quarter and year-end sales numbers today."

"And?" Quinn was already smiling in anticipation of the answer.

"You're looking at him. Number one for the quarter and number one for the year."

Quinn got up from where he was sitting on the deck to envelop Henry in a bear hug. "You're a fucking rock star."

"It gets better," Henry was bursting at the seams. "Seventy-five thousand dollar bonus."

"Are you shitting me?" Quinn's mouth was hanging open.

Henry was shaking his head, "No. Seventy-five K. How's that for mind blowing. They based it on earnings and those just came out."

"Holy shit, Henry."

Henry's violet eyes were wide, "I know," he laughed, "and that's not all. Turns out the awards ceremony is out here this year, it's going to be at The Marine Room in La Jolla. So, I am officially asking you to be my date."

"Are you sure?" As much as Quinn wanted to be there to see Henry accepting his accolades, the thought of potentially harming him in a corporate environment was not anything he wanted to do.

"Fuck, yeah, I'm sure. I've never hid my sexuality at work."

"Not hiding it and throwing it in people's faces are two very different things and you know that."

"I'm their top sales guy, Quinn. Trust me, they're not getting rid of me anytime soon. Any other person who was number one for the year would be bringing their significant other without thinking twice and I'm not going to think twice either about bringing you. I want you by my side. Where you belong."

Trailing his fore and middle finger down Henry's cheek, the look in his eyes was a mixture of pride, love and triumph. "I'm so proud of you and I'd be honored to accompany you." When his fingers reached Henry's jaw, his hand slid to the back of his neck and he pulled his lover in for a long, slow kiss. When their lips finally separated, Quinn shook his head, "A seventy-five thousand dollar bonus?" He still couldn't believe it.

"I know, right? I was thinking it will totally pay for the vacation and the rest we should put toward a down payment fund."

"Down payment for what?"

Henry smiled, "At some point we might want to move."

Quinn looked lost.

And Henry's smile grew exponentially. "I don't know, I was thinking a small backyard. Somewhere with enough room for one of those wooden playscapes that looks like a fort. Someplace where the schools are good."

"Mr. Clark, where is this coming from?" Quinn's smile was contagious.

Pointing a finger at Quinn, "Just know this, first we will be filling up pages in those passports with many stamps."

"It sounds like we're now in a position to do that."

"Yes, we are," Henry corroborated, "so let's start working on it this weekend and figure out the details."

"Sounds like a plan."

"And I'll need you home early on the twenty-third, that reception at The Marine Room starts at seven."

"You've got it." Quinn sat back down on the floor next to one of the bicycles and picked up the chain checker.

As Henry walked over to the sliding glass door, he turned around, "Oh and Quinn, one more thing."

Quinn looked up, smiling, "There's more?" he sassed.

"It's black tie."

"Seriously?" He looked pained.

Henry nodded, thinking about how handsome he was going to look. "I can't wait to see you in a tux."

Quinn was silent for a moment, his eyes walking all over Henry just as they did on the day they met. "I can't wait to get you out of your tux."

Standing in the bathroom, Henry struggled to get his cufflinks through the miniscule holes on the starched shirt cuffs and knew he was not going to have an easier time with his bowtie. Finally, he put the cufflinks down, he'd get Quinn to put them in for him and flip the fastening bar. He was definitely going to need Quinn to tie the bowtie that was hanging open around his neck, that was a given.

Running some mousse through his hair to tame it, he stood before the mirror and took some deep, cleansing breaths. Surprised that he was as nervous as he was, the importance of the night was really beginning to hit him. He was making a big statement tonight bringing his gay lover to the company's awards banquet. He hoped in doing this, maybe other gay and lesbian staff members might feel more comfortable sharing joyous work occasions with their significant other at their side.

When the doorbell rang, he laughed and shook his head. Quinn was picking up their matching boutonnieres from the florist and he could just imagine him on the other side of the door balancing the two plastic containers holding the delicate flowers, afraid one would drop and get damaged if he tried to dig out the key in his pocket. It was so Quinn.

In his tux pants and shirt, with his bowtie hanging open, waiting for Quinn to tie it for him, Henry made his way across the apartment, smiling. "Two boutonnieres and a key is too much for you to..." He flung open the door, the rest of his sentence hung in mid-air. Unfinished.

Their faces and their eyes gave the complete story and he knew the answer to the question that he never needed to ask, but reflexively did. "Where's Quinn?" Alarm in his first query. Anguish after that, "Where's Quinn?" his voice reverberated down the hall.

Terry looked down, his shoulders heaving in heavy sobs. "I'm sorry. I'm so sorry."

Henry looked from Derek to Willie, their eyes swollen with anguish. "What happened? Somebody please tell me what happened," he begged, because this could not be happening. Quinn was coming home with boutonnieres, not in a body bag.

"What happened?" Henry was now on his couch surrounded by the officers, although he had no recollection of moving out of the doorway. "Wasn't he wearing his vest?"

"He was," Derek confirmed.

"Oh God, no." Henry fought back the nausea. If he was wearing his vest...

"It was just a DV," Terry began, his voice shell shocked as began to relay the details of what they thought was a routine domestic violence call. "We'd been to this address before, the guy was a hot head but it had never escalated to anything. He and his old lady just usually needed to calm down."

"But what happened this time?" Henry looked from cop to cop wanting the story to change, for someone to give him an alternate ending. Tell him Quinn just didn't want to wear a tux tonight.

"We got up on the porch and rang the bell. The door flew open and there was the guy, gun pointed and cocked. He got off his first," Terry's words choked in his throat, a new stream of tears making their way down his face, "and only, shot before either of us could draw our weapons."

"Point blank?" Henry's breathing was becoming rapid as the air in the room dissipated. He felt like he was on a mountain peak 15,000 feet up and he'd cycled too hard.

Willie got up and went into the kitchen, returning with a cold bottle of water for Henry.

"Yes." Terry's voice was barely a whisper.

"To the head?" He needed to know what happened to his wonderful Quinn.

Terry just nodded, unable to verbalize as he broke down, the vision of what happened clearly ripping his heart out and macerating it, a nightmare that would remain in his soul forever.

Squeezing his eyes shut, Henry envisioned Quinn's last second and was glad he didn't suffer. *His last second. How can any of this be real? Quinn gone? Just like that. How could that even be possible? Tonight we're celebrating. He was going to be standing next to me, my beautiful partner in his classic black tux playing up the beauty of those pale blue eyes that make me melt every time I look into them. I'm not going to look into them again? Quinn can't be dead.*

"I'd give anything…" Terry looked Henry in the eyes.

Nodding, "I know you would. And Quinn knows that, too."

Derek's big arm was around his shoulder and he looked from man to man. Quinn wasn't just a fallen comrade. He was their friend. Their brother.

"The guy? What happened to the guy?"

"Gone." Terry's eyes looked dead.

Henry just nodded, attempting to process. Quinn was not ever going to sit next to him on this couch again. How could that be? How could any of this be? "Jeanne and Katelyn? Do they know? Have they been told?" Henry panicked at the thought of their pain.

"The Captain wanted us to call him after we spoke to you. He and the chaplain are going to meet us there. He thought you'd be more comfortable hearing it from the three of us." Derek explained.

Henry nodded, "I'm going with you."

As he stood, the room spun from the motion and he stilled himself, employing his Yoga techniques to regain his equilibrium.

Reaching the door, he looked back. Everything looked the same. Nothing in the apartment was moved or different, nothing askew or awry. Except that he'd never see Quinn in their home again. He wasn't going to fall asleep with Quinn's legs tangled with his. Ever again. How could that be?

He sat in the row behind Jeanne and Katelyn in the church. The last thing he wanted to do was to make Jeanne feel uncomfortable in her house of worship, surrounded by her relatives and her priest. Knowing the Catholic Church's view on homosexuality, he didn't want to do anything to add to her stress.

Edwin sat on his left, his hand on top of Henry's left hand. Schooner was on his right, his left arm slung over Henry's shoulder. Next to Schooner was his wife, CJ, and beyond her sat Schooner's parents, Dee and Gavin. Henry's mother and sister didn't make it down.

Staring straight ahead, preternaturally calm in an eerie sort of way, Henry was focused on something in the distance, though most likely not the priest's words, as he conducted a High Mass. In Henry's lap sat a small, black day pack, which he held tightly with both hands.

Edwin and Schooner were having an entire conversation around him, mouthing the words to one another as Henry sat oblivious to their exchange.

"What's in the pack?" Edwin mouthed, his eyes darting to Henry's lap.

Schooner shook his head, "I don't know," he mouthed back.

"He's scaring me," Edwin's eyes shifted to Henry.

"I know." Schooner rubbed Henry's shoulder softly.

The ornate church was filled to capacity. Law enforcement from all over the state were in attendance, as were elected officials and far reaching members of the Callahan clan. The turnout to say goodbye to the fallen officer brought an odd comfort, as if hiding in ritual would bring some answers that would never actually come, but as long as the voices droned on, goodbye was still a breath away.

Henry was glad that it had been a closed casket wake because actually seeing Quinn lying in there was more than he knew he could handle. At least this way, he told himself, he could pretend his Quinn, who wrapped around him like the missing puzzle piece that completed a beautiful picture, was not lying there hard and stiff and lifeless in that box. He could pretend this whole surreal thing didn't even involve his Quinn, until the first skirl of the bagpipes soared to the church's vaulted rafters to accompany Quinn's departure from the building. With the unmistakable opening notes of *Amazing Grace*, there was no pretending anymore.

Taking a deep gasping breath, Henry tried unsuccessfully to

fight the tears, holding on tighter to the day pack.

Edwin squeezed his hand firmly, and Schooner looked up at the ceiling in an attempt to fight his own tears and stay strong for his friend, but as the pipes cut to the quick, there was no turning back from emotion or from the reason they were there.

With an honor guard of pallbearers carrying the coffin from the church, Jeanne and Katelyn fell in step behind it. Jeanne looked over at Henry, her eyes shrouded from the swelling of her lids. She appeared to be reaching out for him to join her, when a relative grabbed her hand, flanking her side, and pulling her into the rhythm as they followed the coffin. Edwin was having none of that, as he pulled Henry into the line to ensure he have his rightful place as they escorted Quinn from the building.

Exiting the dark church, the bright morning sunlight was blinding, but Henry's eyes had adjusted enough to see them load the casket into the hearse. A low moan escaped his throat as the bright sun overhead cast harsh shadows on the undeniable truth.

From the steps, Henry could see Jeanne scanning the crowd before being escorted into the limo. She was followed by a rush of relatives Henry had never seen at family events over the last few years, who crushed into the long, black stretch limousine with her. *Who were these people?* He felt as if they were widening a gulf that was becoming impossible for him to get across, pulling Quinn even farther away from him.

Feeling Schooner's arm around his shoulder, he looked at his friend blank-faced, not knowing what to do next as the hearse began to pull away, accompanied by a full police escort, with an impossibly long procession beginning to wind behind it.

"CJ is going back to Jeanne's house with my parents. She's been on the phone with caterers all week. You two will ride with me. Come on."

Traffic was halted throughout the city for Quinn's procession, and the route was lined with citizens waving American flags.

"Quinn would've liked this. He loved when people came out and cheered us on the route for the bike challenge. Except those were rainbow flags," Henry noted.

"What an amazing turnout," Edwin marveled, "and there must've been at least 500 people in the church. He was very well loved."

Henry nodded, "Yeah, he was," and he looked out the window at the line of people who came out to say goodbye to his love. "I hope we don't miss the graveside service," Henry was beginning to show agitation.

"I think we're OK." Schooner looked into the rearview mirror. "There are a load of cars behind us with their lights on and the police escort will wrap up after the last car and radio ahead."

"They are not starting without you, don't worry." Sitting in the back seat, directly behind Henry, Edwin gave his shoulder a squeeze.

Lifting his sunglasses, Schooner peered into the rearview mirror to catch Edwin's gaze. This situation was becoming more heartbreaking by the second for fear that Henry's rightful place would not be recognized.

Parking on a thin lane in the cemetery, they walked up a hill toward where a large crowd was gathered. By the time they reached the back of the pack, they were in a place where Quinn's casket was not even visible. Henry stood there holding onto his black day pack and looked from Edwin to Schooner, his chin trembling slightly.

"Oh no, no, no, no, no." Edwin shook his head and looked at Schooner.

With a nod, the big blonde said, "Let's go," grabbing Henry by the upper arm and using his height and bulk to push through the crowd, "Excuse me, excuse me. Coming through."

On the other side of the throng of people, several rows of white wooden folding chairs were set up for family and those close to the deceased, with row after row of people standing behind.

Next to Jeanne were two empty chairs.

Turning to them, Schooner said, "Take the two up front, I'll be in the row right behind you," and he escorted Henry and Edwin to the front.

"Oh thank God," Jeanne exclaimed when Henry took his seat. "All I could think when all those good for nothing relatives of mine piled into the limo was how mad Quinny would be."

Henry took her hand and squeezed it. "I was afraid we were too far back in the procession and I was going to miss this." Henry's eyes filled with tears.

Jeanne shook her head, unsuccessfully trying to hold back her tears, "I never would have let them start without you."

"Thank you," he choked out between sobs.

While others may not have given credence to his relationship with Quinn, Jeanne Callahan knew exactly what he meant to her son and what her son meant to him.

Quinn Callahan was laid to rest under a sky that rivaled the blue of his eyes. As Henry looked up at the expansive heavens, he wondered if he'd always be able to remember their exact shade of blue and what it felt like the first time he saw them, as Quinn brazenly checked him out. He was pleased that not a cloud marred the sky, as if it were a gift for Quinn's sendoff.

Ending with the Twenty-third Psalm, Henry could feel his anxiety starting to crest. When this ended, he had to leave Quinn here. How was he going to do that? Just walk away? Leave him to be buried?

In lieu of a three gun volley, because neither Jeanne nor he felt that they could handle the gunshots, they had opted for the ringing of twenty-one bells. Henry counted, and with each peal, he willed them as hard as he could to go slower, but he couldn't halt time, just as he couldn't turn it back to his last day with Quinn.

16. *Oh God, this is going too fast.*

17. *Please just stop here.*

18. *I'll do anything. I promise.*
19. *Don't make me leave him here.*
20. *I can't say goodbye.*
21. *I'm not ready.*
I'll never be ready.

The honor guard removed the flag draping his coffin and Henry flinched, as if they had taken Quinn's blanket away on a cold night. Off to the side, a bugler played Taps and he could hear the sobbing of everyone around him.

With precision that was truly a form of art, the triangular flag was now ready for presentation. As the guard turned to face the front row, Henry recognized him from the police softball league. There was a moment's hesitation and a look of panic in his eyes, unsure to whom he should present the flag. Henry met his gaze and shifted his eyes to Jeanne, indicating that it should be presented to her.

As the flag was laid in Jeanne's arms, Edwin squeezed Henry's hand tight. It was apparent people didn't know how to respond to him. He wasn't a spouse. He wasn't recognized as anything by law. In their confusion, and some with the intention of doing the right thing, Henry was left to suffer and he did so, silently, stoically and at times, invisibly.

The crowd lined up, and one by one, they each took a long-stemmed red rose and laid it on the coffin, as they said their final goodbye to Officer Quinn Callahan.

Feeling a squeeze on his shoulder, Henry looked up at Schooner. "We're going to wait down at the car for you. Take whatever time you need."

Henry nodded.

They were finally alone, for the first time since he was told of Quinn's death. Getting out of his chair to approach the coffin was going to take more strength than he thought he could find. And he was digging deep.

So he sat there, "I know I'm supposed to say goodbye to you now, but I don't want to. I don't ever want to say goodbye to you. Ever." He was silent for a few moments, "I still can't believe you were taken from me, and I just don't know how I'm going to go on without you. I don't know if I can. You were the brightest light in my life. You were everybody's sunshine, Quinn, and I look at this coffin before me and I just don't understand how you can put sunshine in a box."

Covering his face with his hands, he finally let the tears flow unabated, crying for all that was lost and all that would never be. There was nowhere to go from here and he'd put off the inevitable for as long as he could.

Approaching the coffin, he took a deep breath as he stood there for a moment thinking how surrealistic everything felt, like he was watching some esoteric foreign film. Moving roses to clear a space, he tried to gauge approximately where on the surface of this box would be right above Quinn's heart. When he was certain that he had cleared away the roses from the right area, he unzipped the day pack. Reaching in, he pulled out a perfect cane of lilacs cut from the bush Quinn had brought home.

Lovingly, he placed it on the coffin, gently running his fore and middle finger along the wood as he leaned forward to leave a final kiss for his first love.

Jeanne Callahan's house was packed with people who'd come to pay their last respects, from members of the force to relatives to every teacher who had ever had Quinn as a student. This well-loved man was being given a glorious send-off.

Walking in with Henry and Edwin, Schooner mumbled, "What did she do?"

This was not your typical, bring a casserole, bake a cake post-funeral gathering. There were carving stations and wok stations and wait staff with silver hors d'oeuvres trays.

"Oh my God, I'm so sorry," he apologized.

"Sorry?" Edwin looked at Schooner as if he were crazy, "Boat Boy, this is fabulous. And Quinn totally deserved a special party because he was one special man."

CJ approached them, looking stunning in head-to-toe designer black. She gave Henry a loose, pat-on-the-back hug and an air-kiss. "I'm really sorry about Quinn." In her eyes was sincerity and this was the only way she knew how to help.

"CJ, thank you. Really. This is incredible. I really appreciate it."

She nodded, "I have staff to clean up later so that Quinn's mom doesn't have to lift a finger and there's going to be trays of food for you to bring back to the condo."

"Really, thank you, for everything."

She nodded and turned to make her way over to correct a waitress who was spending more time fraternizing and flirting with the officers than serving.

A few minutes later, Jeanne made her way over to them. Giving Schooner a hug, "I cannot believe this. Thank you so much for making such a beautiful luncheon."

"It's our pleasure." He leaned down to hug and kiss her.

"I need to borrow you for a second," she touched Henry's arm and he followed her down the hall toward the bedrooms.

Entering her room, she picked up the flag off her bed, the flag that had just draped Quinn's coffin. Pressing it to his chest, "I want you to have this."

"No, Jeanne."

"Yes, Henry."

"He was your boy."

Jeanne looked up at him, tears cascading from her eyes and splashing onto her cheeks. "He was your man."

189

And she pressed the flag to his chest and left the room.

Clutching the flag, he stood there reeling from her words.

He was your man.

He was your man.

He was. He was my man.

There was only one place he needed to be right now. Making his way down the hall, he slipped into Quinn's room and closed the door behind him.

Standing within the blue walls, clutching the flag, this was the room where they made out like teens, the place he told Quinn for the first time that he was ready to have sex with him. The room that held all of Quinn's track trophies. The very spot where he realized he was in love with Quinn Callahan.

And now, here he stood in the middle of the room, without Quinn, clutching the flag from his coffin. Silently, he cried, holding the flag as tightly against his chest as he could.

He heard the door open and close, but couldn't force himself to turn around and hoped the person would just leave. But they didn't. The minute he felt the hand on his shoulder, he knew exactly who it was and he didn't want him to leave. Turning, he sobbed openly against his shoulder and the man let him. Holding him as he wept.

Finally, he pulled his face away and between sobs asked his friend the one question to which he desperately needed an answer, "How are we going to run through this one?"

Tightening his hug, his friend answered honestly, "I don't know," he sighed. "I don't know."

chapter twenty

"MM, YOU FEEL SO GOOD. So warm. I've missed you." He pressed his lips to Henry's shoulder.

Stiffening in his arms, Henry could feel his lips form into a smile. Without turning around he knew exactly what that smile looked like. Right down to the single dimple.

"Get out of here. Now," Henry's demand was forceful.

But he just laughed. "I'm not going anywhere. I'm right where I want to be. Right where you want me to be."

"No, I don't want you here."

"Yeah you do, Henry. Or I wouldn't be."

Was he telling the truth, Henry wondered? Did he really want him there?

"I told you the first little thing that happened, he wouldn't be able to handle it."

"Don't talk about him." He wasn't going to let him disrespect Quinn.

"He was so easy to get rid of." His laugh was hollow.

"Get out of here now." Henry was seething mad.

Spooning him closer. "I'm not going anywhere. It's time you accept that. You're mine. You'll always be mine."

"I'm not." Henry drove his elbow back hard into him.

"Oh, so that's how you want to play." He yanked Henry by the hair so that he would have access to his mouth, his tongue immediately making its way past Henry's teeth, an 'mmm' of pleasure escaping his throat.

"No," Henry protested.

"Come on, Henry, you know it feels good to kiss me." His tongue snaked back into Henry's mouth, boldly claiming what he had come for, what he wanted.

Tasting his own salty tears as they found their way into their mouths, Henry finally rolled over to face him. He felt the one hand that was in his hair pull their heads closer together as his other hand slid down his back molding Henry to his erection.

"You're finally listening," he said against Henry's mouth with a smile. "You'll always be mine."

Henry didn't answer, unable to speak through the onslaught of tears, nor could he separate the disgust from the excitement as he kissed him back.

seth

for me not to be drawn to him, but I didn't get the impression that he wanted to drag me off and fuck my brains out."

"Oh, I don't know about that," Kami disagreed.

"What do you mean? Don't hold out on me, bitch. You know how long it's been since anyone has even made me look twice."

Kami laughed, clearly loving that she was torturing Seth. "You seriously didn't notice the night before the wedding when it was just the gang of us sitting around the table out on the deck drinking champagne?"

"Notice what?" Seth had his puss face on.

"He was hanging on your every word, Seth."

"No, he wasn't." He waved a dismissive hand at her.

"You know me better than that. If he totally wasn't into you, I would say that to you."

"So you thought he was into me?" Seth's big brown eyes were wide, waiting for reassurance.

"I definitely do; but here's the thing, put yourself in his shoes."

"I'd rather put myself in his pants," he muttered.

Kami sat back and laughed. Seth Shapiro was one amusing man. "Seriously Seth, here's a guy who basically knew nobody there. He knew Schooner and Schooner's parents. He hadn't seen Mia in over twenty years. OK, and he probably knows Holly and Zac, too. But that's it. And then there's this extremely loud New York crowd who apparently have this very close and dysfunctional relationship."

Although she'd been a Manhattanite for twenty-five years, Kami was a southern debutante from Birmingham, Alabama, and the sweet drawl had never left her voice. "And have you ever listened to this group? It sounds like a busload of old ladies at a chicken market in the Caribbean."

Seth laughed, "I guess we're not the shyest crowd on the planet." He seemed proud.

"So as I was saying, put yourself in his shoes. He's the total stranger in the crowd, we all have a lot of history. We work together. We socialize with one another. We're all a family. I think he did very well under those circumstances."

"And you think he liked me?" Seth hated how needy that sounded the minute it came out of his mouth.

"Seth, you are like the mayor. You run everything. Everyone knows you. You're at the center of everything and you had us all marching to attention last weekend. You are a force to be reckoned with. And you just don't give a damn what walls are in front of you, you put your head down and charge through them."

"Ugh, you make me sound like a farm animal. Do you think I scared him?"

"No. I think he was just trying to get a read on you."

Seth sighed, looking forlorn.

Shaking her head with a smile, "In over twenty years, I have never seen you react this way."

"I felt like I knew him, Kami, and I couldn't understand why he didn't know me."

"Wow," she was struck by his raw candor.

"And we don't know anything about the guy."

"Oh, but we do," Kami disagreed.

"What? What do we know?"

"We know some really important things," she paused and laughed at the face Seth was giving her. "He's been Schooner's friend all these years. Schooner, a huge control freak, trusts this man to run his vast west coast operations, or maybe I should say, empire. We know he was Mia's friend first in college and she introduced him to Schooner, and from the reaction she had when she saw him again, after all those years, well, the word overjoyed doesn't do it justice. If the two of them love this man so much, then I think we've just met the latest member of our little dysfunctional family."

Seth picked up his phone and looked at the picture again.

"There's something about him, Kami."

She smiled at her friend. "Well, enjoy the opportunity to find out exactly what it is. Why don't you give Yoli a call? Find out if she's transitioned the advertising and marketing over to him yet. She may not have, just because she probably doesn't want to overwhelm him. But just let her know that you'll be available to work with him directly, and get him up to speed, so that it's one less thing she's got on her plate as she picks up Schooner's responsibilities."

"Yeah, but you usually do the day-to-day stuff on the L9 account."

"In the name of love, I am officially sharing it with you."

"OK, I'll call her in the morning and make the offer."

"She'll be thrilled. You just took a headache off her hands."

He snickered, "Well, I'd like to make his head ache in my hands."

There was just something about Henry Clark and Seth Shapiro had to know if he'd felt anything, too.

Almost 8 P.M. on Wednesday night and Seth sat in the quiet of his office, looking at the lights of lower Manhattan and the Freedom Tower. He hadn't spoken to Mia in over a week, arriving at the office one morning just after she'd called in. Schooner had taken her on a honeymoon sailing trip on their boat, headed up the coast to capture fall foliage and the Northern Lights.

"I just hung up with Mia," Kami had told him when he got to the office that morning. "Try her cell, they might still be in port. The signal wasn't great, but she definitely wanted to talk to you, too."

"She knows my cell number." The news did nothing to improve his mood. Sitting down at his desk, he tried her cell, but it went right to voicemail, and his mood became even fouler.

"So what did she have to say?" he asked Kami later that day.

She laughed, "I wondered when you were going to ask. She said they're having a great time, but she misses the kids and she misses us. She sounded like she was ready to come home. You know Mia, she doesn't do well with the whole relaxing thing."

"BBC relaxed is an oxymoron."

Early on in their friendship, when Seth had given Mia the nickname 'BBC', she returned the favor with her pet name for him, 'Princess'. Having survived breathtaking highs and gut wrenching lows, the two had a relationship that was thicker than blood. Oftentimes words were not needed between them, yet the other instinctively knew what was being thought.

As he sat in the quiet office, everyone gone for the evening, Seth thought about how different things felt without Mia around. The energy felt incomplete. And in some ways, he felt incomplete.

He literally jumped in his chair as his thoughts were broken by his desk phone ringing.

"M. Silver and Associates. This is Seth Shapiro."

"I somehow knew you'd still be there and would pick up the phone. I'm sure everyone else has gone for the evening."

"Am I that predictable?" He sat back in his chair, smiling.

The soft laugh on the other end of the line felt like a caress, and he actually felt himself pressing his cheek into the phone, as if it would bring them physically closer.

"Well, I don't know you well enough to really answer that. But my gut tells me there's nothing predictable about you."

Seth smiled into the phone. He had put off calling Yoli to offer help, feeling as if he'd look too transparent, so this call was a surprise. "How are you doing, is everything falling into place for you out there?"

"Oh, so you do know who you're talking to?" he sounded amused.

to set him up. There were a few men in his life, who were just close friends, that he could count on when he needed a 'date' for a function. But there had been no one special, no one that made him look at his phone, and will it to ring, as he'd been doing for days.

It's time to put the word out that I'm looking, he decided. *Finally.* People will be shocked and happy, he mused and most would attribute it to losing his best friend to marriage. The truth was, Mia and Schooner had been back together for a while now, so it wasn't their marriage precipitating this – it was the relationship that made them decide to finally marry. And *that* is what he wanted.

Picking up his cellphone off the small wrought iron table next to him, he looked at his darkened phone. Henry now had his cell number and he knew his phone's silence was going to drive him insane.

Why didn't I get his number? He shook his head. *I'm out of practice.*

He began to loathe his silent phone as the next few days passed, looking at it obsessively, as if it were a mute jailer, refusing to use the key to free him from exile.

It was 4:12 A.M. three nights and three very long, pissy, moody days later, when the sound of a text coming through woke him.

Reaching over to the nightstand, he grabbed his cell and glasses. Area code (619) and a number. No name was attached to the contact record. It wasn't anyone in his address book.

Smiling, he reread the single word message a few times.

Anytime

He now had his number. Sitting up in bed, he smiled at the phone, his wonderful hope-bearing phone. It was 1:12 A.M. in San Diego and Henry Clark was thinking about him. He was awake and thinking of him three days later. That was a damn good sign.

Sleep was Seth's one word response.

H: Sorry. I woke you.

Seth smiled at the message. There was only one answer for that. **Anytime**

H: ☺

Shocked that his heart could actually be soaring over receiving a smiley face, snarky, sarcastic Seth Shapiro was certain he would wake up in a few hours to his alarm, check his horrible, little tease of a phone and find no trace of the conversation. If he'd dreamed this, he was going to be super pissed-off.

H: Seth

S: Yes

H: I'm sorry I woke you

S: I'm not

H: You're not?

S: No.

H: I'm smiling

S: Me too

H: Call tomorrow?

S: Yeah. Night Henry

H: Night Seth

This had better be on my phone in the morning, Seth rolled back over. Smiling to himself as he settled back into his pillows, *who knew this could happen - anytime?*

chapter
twenty-two

HENRY CLARK LIKED TO TEXT. That was Seth's observation and he was OK with it. As long as the communication kept going, he didn't care what medium was used, he felt like the door was finally open – and he wanted to ram through it and knock it down.

> **H: Hey, if you talk to Schooner, can you find out if he can come out during the photoshoot?**

> **S: Oh, please, I have not spoken to either one of them since they left on their Robinson Crusoe adventure.**

> **H: LOL. Well, if you do get a chance, tell him if he comes out, I'd like to throw a birthday party for Edwin.**

Edwin? Who the fuck is Edwin? Seth's mood took an immediate nosedive. And how could I ever be jealous of someone with the unfortunate name of Edwin?

> **S: If I hear from them, I'll ask.**

Figuring Schooner and Mia would eventually hit a port and texts would come through, Seth left Mia a message. **Who the fuck is Edwin?**

Seven hours later, as he was wrapping up for the day, his cell buzzed. **Henry's Edwin?**

His heart sank. Henry's Edwin.

S: Yes.

M: Schooner is laughing. He said it's you in 30 years.

S: Fuck you, both. What the hell does that mean?

M: He says you'll love Edwin and that you are Edwin.

S: BBC, I'm getting pissed off. Who is Edwin? Is it Henry's lover?

The texts went silent and he thought if they sailed out of port without telling him, he was going to go out of his mind. *You are Edwin? What the hell was that supposed to mean? What the fuck was Schooner talking about?*

He jumped when the phone in his hand rang and the avatar with Mia's mischievous smile was shining back at him.

"BBC."

"Oh my God, Princess, I have missed you. We're almost home, we're just north of the Cape," Mia's voice crackled in the poor connection, "and I'm picking up cell signal from there."

"Thank God. Enough of this honeymoon crap. Come home now."

"How are my babies? Have you seen them? They were asleep when I last called."

"I saw them last night on the way home. They are fine. Running your parents ragged."

"That makes me feel better." Mia sounded relieved.

"Now who the hell is Edwin?" Seth had enough of the chit-chat. His heart had been hanging out on a street corner for two weeks.

"Let me put Schooner on."

"Hey Seth," the familiar voice sounded concerned. "What's going on with Edwin? Is everything OK?"

"Yes, Henry wants to make him a birthday party and wants

you to come out for it when we're out there doing a brochure photo shoot."

"Excellent. I'll check my calendar when we get back."

"Schooner, who is Edwin? Is that Henry's partner?"

Through the crackling static, he could hear Schooner's laugh. "Edwin? No. But he is an amazing friend. He's been to Henry what you are to Mia. And I never thought about it before, but you could be Edwin's spawn." He could hear Mia saying she needed to meet him.

"Is he involved with anyone?" These people were pissing him off. He needed answers.

"Edwin?"

"No, not Edwin. Henry."

There was silence on the other end of the line. "No. Not that I know of." Schooner's demeanor immediately changed.

"So, you're just going to leave me hanging there?"

"Seth, it's not my story to tell."

Feeling his throat closing, he knew Schooner was right. If he and Henry Clark were meant to be – as colleagues, friends or lovers – then those stories would be revealed as part of their trust.

"OK, I understand. Just answer me one question."

"I'll try," Schooner promised.

"Will this guy break my heart?" Feeling incredibly vulnerable, his best friend's husband was one of the few people on the planet with whom he could be so honest and now he'd just admitted his interest in his friend.

"I don't know the answer to that, Seth. All I can tell you is that he is a great guy, as are you."

And the line went dead.

"Seth Shapiro, as I live and breathe." Scott Hoover looked up from his camera perched on a tripod in the entranceway of L9/Carlsbad. "Has the island of Manhattan crumbled into the sea?" Scott pulled a lens out of the pocket of his cargo shorts and swapped it out with the lens on the front of the camera body, before walking down the path to greet Seth with a warm hug.

Dressed in a dark gray Dolce & Gabbana suit and claret red tie, Seth looked as if he might be part of the shoot if they'd been doing a piece for corporate investors.

"Just helping out the new guy," Seth tried to make light of showing up for a shoot outside of Manhattan, something he never did.

"Quite magnanimous of you." Scott was quickly catching on to exactly why Seth was in southern California.

"Is he here?" It was still early, but Seth was on east coast time. Even with his flight getting in late, he couldn't sleep and Scott was clearly there trying to catch the early morning golden hour light for the outdoor shots.

"Yeah, I saw him go in a few minutes ago."

Bringing Henry up to speed on the project had actually been quite fun. He was a quick learner and provided a fresh set of eyes. As a way to get him to start understanding what was successful in marketing and advertising materials, Seth had been sending him ads from other companies on a daily basis, and asking Henry to tell him what worked and what didn't work and why.

"Headline is dull. Picture doesn't even give you a hint at what the product is and there is nothing in the copy that makes me want to buy this. And where is their web address? I can't believe they left that off. And the whole thing just feels kind of off-balance to me." Henry was on point and succinct with his analysis.

"You're going to end up a marketing guy, yet." Seth had told him earlier in the week.

"Well, I really do appreciate all your time and help. I'd wish you'd let me at least pick you up at the airport when you get in."

"Not necessary, my flight gets in so late and I need to grab a rental car. I'll meet you at L9 in the morning," he had told him. Truth was, Seth didn't want to see him after a long day of travel, but rather after a good night's sleep and a hot shower.

Arriving in his room at La Costa a little after 1 A.M., Seth went to open the glass door to his balcony to listen to the surf, when he noticed a bottle of wine sitting next to the ice bucket. Picking up the bottle, he was surprised, in a very good way, to find he was holding a bottle of Silver Oak Alexander Valley Cabernet Sauvignon, one of his personal favorite wines. Leaning against the silver bucket, was a small cream-colored card. The note was handwritten.

Seth –

Welcome to the other coast. Enjoy this thank you for all you've done for me. Word on the street is that you're a Cab lover. Look forward to seeing you in the morning.

~ Henry

Holding the card in his hand, he smiled as he reread it. So much had changed in the last few weeks. Gone was that crazy obsession and confusion he felt right after meeting Henry, replaced by a business relationship that was quickly becoming a friendship. There was the layer of tension between the two men, it was still there, but other aspects were beginning to grow and become real.

Now, as he entered the L9 facility, Seth knew he looked damn fine in his D&G suit and looking attractive for Henry Clark was at the top of his agenda. It actually might have been the only thing on his agenda.

The receptionist looked up with a smile, "Good morning, Mr. Shapiro. Henry is expecting you," and she called back to his office to let him know of Seth's arrival.

Seth could feel him and instinctually knew he was approaching from the left. Turning slowly, he had been right on the mark. He watched Henry approach, a broad smile on his face, his long, tan runners' legs, a sight Seth was not ready for, inciting instant dry mouth.

Extending a hand, for a formal business hello, Seth, the king of everything in his business domain, was at a loss. Ignoring the outstretched hand, Henry went in for a warm hug, and Seth wanted to slap himself for stiffening as Henry's arms encircled him.

"It's so good to see you again," Henry greeted.

"It's really good to see you." Seth was immediately taken by the violet in Henry's eyes.

"Have you been to this facility before?"

"No, not this one," taking in the ocean view. "Schooner is really a genius."

"Every facility is so different. It's really quite visionary." Henry appeared proud.

"And the man has a sixth sense about real estate." Seth was lost in the view.

"Let me show you around. I'm sure it will give you some ideas on how you'd like to direct Scott."

Touring the inside first, Henry kept a running dialogue, pointing out the site's unique aspects. As they exited the back to the lushly landscaped patio and infinity pool, he remarked, "I need to get you out of that suit."

Surprised, Seth looked at him wide-eyed, "Oh really?"

Opening his mouth to speak, Henry stammered without actually producing any words, as his cheeks took on a pink glow. Recovering, "Let's go over to the pro-shop and get you a tee-shirt and some shorts, it's going to be close to eighty degrees today." They started to walk and Henry looked at Seth, smiling, "You really do rock a suit."

And it was Seth's turn to blush.

"Thank you for the wine. That was very thoughtful." *Very thoughtful?* Seth wanted to slap himself. *Who says that?* Why was he tripping all over his own dick with this guy?

"Did you have a chance to drink it?" Henry looked pleased.

"No, I got in too late and I'm three hours ahead. And that wine is too good to drink alone." He hoped Henry would take the hint.

Entering the pro-shop, they were immediately met by staff, "Please help Mr. Shapiro with anything he needs and bill it to the house account," he instructed them. "I'm heading back to my office, which is right down that hall, just come find me when you're ready."

Henry was on the phone when Seth sat down across from him, looking like an L9 member (which he was). Smiling at him, he mouthed the words, "You look good."

Seth sneered back at him.

Hanging up, he laughed, "What's the sneer for?"

"I feel half-naked. How do you people do business like this?"

Henry laughed. "I was a suit guy, too. But I'm getting used to this really quick."

Pulling out his laptop, Seth opened it on Henry's desk and turned it so that it would be visible for both of them.

"I'll come around," Henry offered and sat down next to Seth, pulling his chair closer.

You are killing me, Mr. Clark, Seth thought.

"Here's what we've got for the final layouts for each brochure. If you're good with all of these, we'll be ready to pull Scott in and map out all the visuals and let him do his thing."

They spent the next two and a half hours working through the details of each of the pieces and giving Scott their final input for the corresponding images.

"He's good to go," Seth advised Henry. "When he's done, he'll work directly with our art department and the next thing you'll see is a final comp. That's where we catch anything before it goes to press. I want to meet with him tomorrow morning in Newport Beach to make some final decisions on the models for that brochure. They look fine, but I just like to see them live, prior to committing."

"We're going to want to hit the road early." Henry didn't skip a beat and Seth didn't show his surprise at the word "we're".

"So, I'm being a terrible host. Your stomach probably thinks it's mid-afternoon. Let me take you to lunch."

As they passed Scott setting up the lighting for work with two models, he turned to Seth and mouthed, "Lucky bastard."

Smiling, Seth nodded and followed Henry out to the valet where his BMW was brought around.

"Are you ready?" Henry lowered the roof and put on his sunglasses. Reaching across Seth, his arm grazing his thighs, as he opened the glove compartment and pulled out two L9 caps, tossing one onto Seth's lap.

The brush of his arm on his thighs had Seth speechless, until they turned onto the Pacific Coast Highway, "Where are we headed?"

Henry smiled, "One of my favorite places, the Ocean Terrace at George's on the Cove in La Jolla."

"Outdoors, I'm assuming?"

Nodding, Henry laughed, "Yes, and on the ocean."

The sun felt good on his face, as Seth took his seat facing the water. "This is gorgeous," he remarked.

"Hello, Mr. Clark," the cute brunette waitress was flirting with Henry.

She is misinformed, Seth was internally sneering. *Back off, you little bimbo.*

"How are you, Brandy?" he smiled at her. "How about a bottle of Albarino and two glasses of water."

Take charge guy or just playing the good host? Seth wondered.

"A bottle of Albarino? How are we going to work this afternoon?"

With a smile that made Seth want to reach out and grab the man's hand, Henry laughed. "Who said anything about working this afternoon?" He paused for a moment, "Though I have a feeling no matter what subject we start with, we're going to end up back on a work topic. So this is kind of like a working lunch."

When the wine arrived, Seth proposed the first toast, "To Mr. and Mrs. Moore and our working lunches on their behalf."

"Mr. and Mrs. Moore." Henry just shook his head. "Those two together, finally, just shows you that happiness doesn't always have to be an elusive dream."

"Well, it eluded the two of them for a long time."

"Was Mia unhappy?" Henry became very serious.

Seth thought for a moment, sipping his wine as he formulated his response. "Mia is generally a happy person and she can take any situation and find the positive in it."

"That's true," Henry smiled, remembering a rambunctious sixteen year old college freshman who was basically her own traveling party.

"But as you know, she had some bad shit happen to her that she never dealt with."

Henry knew that Seth was referring to a rape that happened during their freshman year.

"And when it finally caught up to her, she hit rock bottom. And it was a long climb out of that hole. But she did it. She worked hard and did it, only to be slammed by another devastating blow when she lost someone really special on 9/11."

Seth watched the violet in Henry's eyes darken, as the muscles in his jaw twitched. He just nodded and put his sunglasses back over his eyes, erecting a barrier between the two of them.

I wish I knew your story, Henry Clark.

"You were there for Mia?" His question was simple when he

finally spoke again.

"Yes, I was."

"I'm glad she's had you, Seth. I'm sure she's made it through all she has because you were there for her." Henry refilled their wine glasses as the waitress dropped off their ceviche appetizers. "So has it just pretty much been you and Mia all these years?" Henry finally asked.

Nodding, "And our partner, Kami. We were building the business and very involved in a lot of charitable things in New York City. It's really kind of been a whirlwind." Seth laughed. "But that might be because Mia is her very own cyclone."

Sitting back, Seth waited for Henry's next question. He appeared to be leading up to asking him if there was anyone or had been anyone special in his life. But he didn't ask the question, and Seth wondered if it was because he didn't want it to lead to questions about his own personal life.

"So tell me about Edwin?" Seth felt adrift and needed to bring Henry back from wherever he'd gone.

Smiling, "You're going to love Edwin and Edwin is going to love you." And just like that, Henry started talking again and Seth was glad to have him back.

"I can't wait to meet him."

"Saturday night. And he has no clue."

"This is going to be fun." Seth loved parties and a surprise party for a wild, old queen was a recipe for a good time even if he didn't know another soul there.

Lifting his sunglasses from his eyes, Henry's tone was sincere, "I'm really glad you're here."

"I'm really glad you wanted me here."

And with that, Seth Shapiro hoped that Henry Clark would let him in, before he started erecting his own unretractable walls, and the chasm between them became too wide to negotiate. Seth knew the window of opportunity was shrinking.

For both of them.

S: Can I help you run errands or set-up for the party? Schooner and Mia are spending the day with his parents and I'm going to go bat shit crazy just staring at the ocean.

H: Are you sure you don't want to just spend your day relaxing?

S: I don't do the relax thing and I'll have you know I am legendary for my party planning prowess.

H: That wedding you put together for Schooner & Mia was pretty spectacular.

S: What's your address? I'm coming over.

"Hey, good morning," Henry opened the door with a smile and pulled Seth into a warm hug.

Stiffening in his arms, yet again, Seth wished he could reciprocate, but this guy was giving him such mixed messages, and there was no way he was going to let go of his emotions until he knew what was going on.

"Nice place." Seth surveyed the spacious condo.

"Why do I get the feeling you are redecorating in your head?"

Laughing, "Busted. I could have a lot of fun with this space."

"Next trip you can take me décor shopping." Henry seemed more relaxed in his own environment.

Next trip? It was hard for Seth to fathom because they were colleagues, that this was going to be a long term relationship. They would see each other. Have contact with one another. Attend events together.

Sitting down on the couch, "Tell me what you've got planned for tonight."

Walking him through the arrangements he'd made for the

caterer, bartenders, the cake, Henry laid out the evening's plan.

"So, what's the theme?" Seth asked when he finished.

"What do you mean?" Henry looked totally perplexed.

"The theme for the party." Seth was looking at him very seriously.

"Umm, birthday." Henry's answer sounded more like a question.

Shaking his head, "What am I going to do with you?"

Henry smirked, "That does seem to be the burning question, doesn't it."

Engaging his beautiful eyes with a no-nonsense stare, Seth nodded, "Yes, it does. But that is a later conversation. Right now, we need to salvage your lame-ass attempt at a party. Tell me about Edwin."

With a smile that spoke volumes of his love for the older man, "Well, he's turning 70, but he could run circles around the two of us. He's kind of old Hollywood matinee idol. I think that's the best way to describe him. He's bold and brash and always tells it like it is. I've always felt like he's everything I'm not, but sort of wish I could be. He does not care what other people think."

"You know when he enters a room?" Seth asked, as he began to Google information on his phone.

Nodding his head, Henry laughed. "Understatement."

Turning his phone to Henry, "Is this near here?"

"Not far."

"Let's go, we have a shitload of work to do if we're going to throw Edwin a party as fabulous as he is."

It wasn't until it was out of his mouth that Seth realized he'd said, "we're" and Henry hadn't corrected him that it was his party and not theirs.

Henry Clark was killing him.

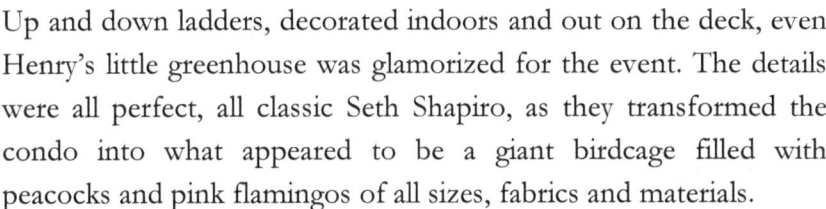

Up and down ladders, decorated indoors and out on the deck, even Henry's little greenhouse was glamorized for the event. The details were all perfect, all classic Seth Shapiro, as they transformed the condo into what appeared to be a giant birdcage filled with peacocks and pink flamingos of all sizes, fabrics and materials.

"You should have been a set designer," Henry noted as they completed the final touches. "Edwin is going to go crazy when he sees this."

Climbing the ladder to tack up the last of the netting, Henry used his full height to reach high up on the wall of the vaulted ceiling. "Is this the right spot?" he asked.

Hour upon hour of working side by side, watching his hot ass and muscular legs climb the ladder over and over again, had Seth seriously distracted. He never wanted to jump another man, they usually came clamoring around him, wanting to be a part of his world, but this man was making him ache – both physically and emotionally. And he wanted to jump his bones, much to his own astonishment.

"Earth to Seth, do I have this in the right spot?" Henry was stretched to his full-length.

"Oh yeah, looks great." He pulled his eyes from the low-hanging waistline of Henry's shorts and the exposed banded top of his underwear.

Coming down off the ladder, he looked at his watch. "Wow, the caterer is going to be here in about thirty minutes. I need to hit the shower." Pausing for a moment, "I should have told you to bring a change of clothes. Why didn't I think of that? It's crazy for you to run all the way to La Costa and back again. I can lend you a fresh shirt."

"No, I'm good. And I've got Edwin's present back there." He

picked his keys up off the coffee table.

"You bought Edwin a present?" Henry's eyes were filled with awe, surprised by Seth's endless generosity.

"Pfft... did you really think I would show up to a birthday party empty-handed?"

Without any forethought or warning, Henry closed the space between them, enveloping Seth into a warm hug, his face in the nook of his neck.

This man is a hugger. Seth stiffened.

Pulling away slightly, "Thank you for everything."

Seth just nodded.

Placing his lips next to Seth's ear, Henry whispered, "And please stop getting so tense every time I hug you. I'm beginning to get the impression you don't want me to touch you."

Seth shook his head.

"What?" Henry whispered.

"I don't want you to stop." And although his body was giving a distinctly different message, Seth knew he would fall apart if Henry were to pull away and not touch him again.

The party was in full swing when Seth came back through the doors. Standing just inside the entrance, he took stock of the six hours of decorating he and Henry had done, and had to admit this was one of his better ones, even with the abbreviated planning and short set-up time. The two of them had made a great team, working in tandem, totally in sync with one another. Seth scanned the room, looking for him, but didn't see him anywhere and felt a void immediately hit his chest.

It didn't take long for him to figure out who the guest of honor was, fully decked out with a peacock feather headband and pink feather boa. Seth approached him, present in hand, "I'm told that I could be your evil spawn."

Edwin openly checked out Seth from head to toe, lingering on his dark curls, his full lips and his crotch. "I've heard a lot about you since his trip to New York."

"Did I scare him that much?" Seth's smile was conspiratorial.

"To the core," Edwin confessed dramatically, and the two men laughed, bonding instantly.

"Now that's a recipe for trouble."

"Boat Boy!" Edwin opened his arms and Schooner wrapped the older man in a bear hug.

What is it with them and the hugging out here? Seth's facial expression bordered on disgust.

"And you must be Minx." Edwin embraced Mia.

"Minx? That's a good one." Snickering, Seth was clearly most amused.

"Shut up, Princess." Mia swatted his upper arm.

"My favorite people all meeting one another," Henry joined the group.

"This looks amazing," Mia was looking around.

Henry pointed to Seth.

Smiling, "I should've known. This definitely has his signature all over it."

"At least someone's a useful gay," commented Edwin.

"I was very useful today," protested Henry. "Tell them, Seth."

"He takes direction very well." Seth rolled his eyes and they all laughed.

Engaged in conversations throughout the night, Seth found himself constantly searching for Mia and Schooner, his comfort zone and for Henry, his distinct zone of discomfort. Seth realized that he was intentionally keeping a physical distance from Henry and he began to get agitated, feeling like a fish out of water versus the usual alpha fish in the tank.

Stepping out onto the deck, he found the outdoor space as

crowded as the indoor and started planning his escape. Not being able to resolve his inner conflict of trying to avoid the man and wanting to be with him – alone with him, intimate with him, was disconcerting and making him anxious.

Re-entering the condo, he slipped down the hall. Opening a door to peek in, possibly finding a place of refuge. He smiled when he realized it was the master bedroom. Closing the door behind him, Seth tried to come to terms with the onslaught of conflicting emotions, feeling at once like a stalker, yet closer to the man in his domain.

He walked over to a bicycle leaning against the wall and gently ran his hand over the sleek frame. A helmet hung from the handle bars. *Henry Clark liked to cycle.* Seth smiled to himself, having just learned something personal he hadn't known about him. He walked over to the dresser. A small knotted driftwood sculpture sat next to a picture frame holding a photo of Henry and another man, a man with a beautiful smile and impossibly blue eyes. They stood alongside their bicycles, wearing racing shirts and numbers. Seth found himself smiling at the picture of Henry and the man. It was impossible not to. They exuded pure happiness.

"His name was Quinn."

Seth hadn't heard Henry come out of the en suite bathroom.

"He's very handsome."

Henry picked up the picture and smiled at it, "Yes, he was."

Seth cocked his head, his eyes imploring Henry for an explanation. *Was?* His first inclination was that he'd been lost to AIDS.

"He was a cop," Henry explained. "He was killed in the line of duty."

Seth immediately felt his eyes fill with tears as his heart stopped beating for a moment, "Oh my God. I'm so sorry." Seth caught his breath. "Was he your partner?"

Henry nodded, smiling at the picture as he placed it back

down on the dresser. "Yeah."

"I didn't know."

"I know," Henry smiled at him and squeezed his shoulder.

"I feel like I should let you hug me." Seth broke the somber mood.

And this time when Henry's arms went around him, Seth hugged him back tightly.

H: Where did you go? When did you leave?

S: I was getting tired and knew I had to drive back to the hotel. I looked for you and didn't see you, so I just slipped out.

Seth looked at his lame text. He knew when the evening ended, he'd want to stay, and not just to help Henry clean up. And then what? Awkwardness. Do I stay? Do I go? Do I get rejected?

H: You didn't even say goodnight...

S: Goodnight

H: Don't do that, Seth.

S: I'm sorry

H: Are you?

S: If I've upset you, then yes, I am sorry.

H: I'm hurt.

S: Then I'm REALLY sorry

H: We really need to talk, you know that

S: Yeah, but not now, Henry. It's almost 3 A.M.

H: Don't blow me off

S: ☺ Great choice of words

H: ⇐ not smiling

S: I'm sorry I didn't say goodnight to you

H: I was just really floored that you were no longer here ?

S: I feel bad. It was really selfish and rude of me to do that. I really am sorry.

H: Tomorrow is your last day out here. We're spending it together.

S: We are?

H: Yes. We are.

H: I can't believe you left.

S: I feel really shitty.

H: You should.

"I do," he said aloud to his phone. "You didn't deserve me making you feel bad. I'm an ass."

Fifteen minutes later.

S: Henry – are you still up?

H: Yes

S: You wanted me there?

H: Yes! You were questioning that? Is that why you left?

S: Yes

H: God, Seth. You are such an ass.

S: I am REALLY sorry

H: Have you eaten breakfast?

S: What time is it?

H: Almost 8. I'll take you to a place Edwin and I always used to meet for breakfast

S: ☺ Do they serve crow? Seagull? Pigeon? (Pink Flamingo, Peacock)?

H: LOL. What's your room number?

The rapping on his door four minutes later took Seth by surprise. Hair askew, wearing only a pair of blue L9 gym shorts, he got out of bed and looked through the peephole, ready to growl at the housekeeping staff.

"Oh shit," was his kneejerk reaction.

"Nice greeting," Henry said from the other side of the door. "After last night, I thought you'd be a slight bit more contrite."

"Where were you texting from?"

"The lobby. Open the freaking door, Seth."

Unlatching the safety chain, Seth flung open the door.

Breaking into an immediate smile, Henry checked him out, ruffled hair to bare toes, "Nice," he concluded.

Grunting at him, Seth closed the door behind him.

They stood there, facing one another, so much to be said. Seth felt truly naked in just his gym shorts, knowing baring his emotions was going to leave him a lot more vulnerable than baring his body to this man and this was just the tip of the nakedness. So to speak.

"I'm sorry about last night." Seth opened his arms and Henry came to him.

"You feel so good." He tightened his hold on Seth as he felt the ornery New Yorker melting into his arms for the first time.

Pulling his face back to look into Henry's eyes, "I am really sorry about last night. Really, really sorry. We haven't talked. This thing between us is confusing the crap out of me and I panicked. That's the truth. I just panicked."

Henry smiled, "Do you actually think anybody would believe that someone made Seth Shapiro panic?"

Seth thought for a moment and then let out a laugh, "Not for a second."

"Get dressed and let's go out for breakfast."

"OK," he began to turn away, but Henry yanked him back by the hand and wrapped his arms around him again.

"You're actually a really good hugger."

"Can we just keep that between us?" Seth smiled at the handsome man standing in his hotel room. "I'll be right back." And he disappeared into the bathroom.

He found Henry on the balcony when he emerged, "We have a bottle of Silver Oak to drink today."

"Take that back to New York with you."

Seth shook his head, "I love Silver Oak and I want to share it with you."

Sitting in the hangar-like darkness of The Menu Restaurant, Seth perused the menu with a scowl on his face.

"What's wrong?" Henry asked.

"I'm just not used to this whole enchilada/taco thing for breakfast. We eat bagels and Eggs Benedict in New York."

Henry sat back and smiled. "You are so not my type."

Seth's look was deadly, "Great. Thanks." He looked back down at his menu.

"Seth, don't."

"Don't what?" there was a pissy edge to his voice.

"Don't think that's bad."

Putting the menu down, Seth sat back in his chair, "You just told me I'm not your type. It wasn't exactly what I wanted to hear. That's not a feel good statement, Henry."

"It doesn't change the way I feel." Henry's eyes held Seth's, as if daring him to blink.

Seth shook his head. "Don't expect me to ask that next question on the heels of what you've just told me."

"How I feel about you?" Henry was not going to back down from the challenge.

Crossing his arms over his chest, Seth did not respond, his jaw solidly set.

"I'm hoping we're in the same boat," Henry began. "There is this undeniable thing between us, Seth, you know that." He paused, and appeared to be grappling with himself about what to say next. If he should say it. "You said something to me at Schooner and Mia's wedding that just rocked my world."

"What did I say?" Seth was surprised by Henry's statement.

"You started talking about wanting a relationship. About reading the Times on Sunday mornings with your lover. About traveling to Bali and the Seychelles."

"Yeah."

"Why Bali and the Seychelles?"

Seth shrugged and just shook his head. "I've always wanted to go there. They're exotic, romantic. I've just always wanted to go to both places."

Henry looked at him, but remained silent.

"So that rocked your world?" Seth was lost.

Nodding, "Yeah."

"I'm not sure I understand, Henry."

"I know. And I'm sorry if I'm not making sense." He took a deep breath before continuing. "Quinn and I were planning a trip to Bali and the Seychelles right before he was killed."

"I'm really sorry. And I'm sorry if what I said to you at Schooner and Mia's wedding was disturbing."

"It was disturbing. But you know what the most disturbing thing about it was?"

Seth shook his head.

"That you made me realize that I still wanted that dream, too.

227

That dream of sharing with someone. Having someone. I had denied that for so long and then you said it. And I just couldn't shake it."

Seth remained silent. Not responding to Henry's admission.

"Talk to me, Seth. I feel this wall rising rapidly and I don't know how to stop it."

When he began to speak, Seth's voice was very low and modulated. "It appears I said something that was a trigger for wonderful memories you had. But what you are responding to is not me, Henry. You've been very clear with me this morning that I am not the person you want."

"Are you shitting me? Is that what you took from this?" Henry's frustration was mounting.

"Yeah."

"OK, you listen to me, Seth Shapiro, and I mean really listen without putting your shit or spin on it. We have talked nearly every day for the last month. It's a really messy situation because we work together, and getting involved with someone you work with, is risky. I don't want to lose my job and you're not going to be leaving yours. So if this thing between us blows up, doesn't work out, whatever, no matter how mature we want to be, it's still going to be funky for us, and everyone around us. I know that. You know that."

Seth held his eye contact, but didn't speak. He appeared to be seething mad and on the edge of a sarcastic retort. But he remained silent.

"We live three thousand miles apart and that is not going to change for either of us anytime soon. You are like no one I've ever met before, and that is why I said you're not my type. I've never been around someone like you. When we were in New York, you were like the star, with everyone buzzing around you. Everyone wanting your approval and attention. And I knew that first night, that you had been Mia's rock until Schooner found her again. I watched her children fall asleep in your arms because they are so comfortable with you and love you so deeply. And I knew then, that there was a lot to you. That you were one really complex man. Probably more complex than anyone I've ever met. And in one brief moment, you opened up to me and you shared your dream with me. You let me see past all that tough, snarky New York bullshit you've got going on, and you told me your dream. And it's haunted me every moment of every day since."

"I'm not him, Henry. And just because I want to travel to the same exotic locales, I'm not him. I'm not that dream you had."

"Did you not listen to a fucking word I said when I was pouring my heart out to you? When I told you that I didn't want you to leave last night? Did we not share the best day yesterday putting that party together? Every phone conversation? Every text? Can you honestly say to me that you have not spent the last month thinking about me?"

"I'm not him." Seth appeared defeated.

"You need to let that go. That is your shit." Reaching across the table, he pulled a hand off Seth's chest and held it tightly. "Tell me you have not spent the last month thinking about me. Tell me."

"You know I have."

Henry smiled and squeezed his hand. "Then let's figure this out."

"I don't want to be somebody else's dream, Henry." The sincerity in Seth's eyes was haunting.

"You're not. Please believe me. It's you I can't get out of my head. And I don't know what to do with it. Admitting that to you scares the living shit out of me because you have me so off-balance."

With his free hand, Seth pulled his phone out of his pocket, swiped it on and passed it across the table to Henry.

Picking up the phone, Henry looked perplexed. "It's a picture of me." He looked at Seth and then slowly smiled. "You have a picture of me?"

With a sheepish grin, Seth nodded.

"That's really kind of stalkerish." He looked back down at the picture. "But I like it." Looking back up at Seth, "You don't do anything to it, do you?"

"No." Seth was adamant. "But now that you've suggested it," he teased, raising his eyebrows. "I showed you that picture because, I don't do that. With anybody. That is just not me. Not who I am. I don't sit and look at some guy's picture and think about him and wonder what he's doing."

"And you've been doing that with me?"

Seth nodded, "And I hate it."

Laughing, "So what are we going to do?"

"I don't know. Try to be honest with each other moving forward. Get to know one another. We talk every day, Henry."

"We need to talk every night, Seth."

Smiling, he gave Henry's hand a little tug. "We can do that."

The waitress set down two plates of breakfast enchiladas on the table and a check and quickly moved away. Pushing it around his plate, Seth looked up, "I'm going to give this a try," as if the first forkful were a symbolic gesture. "Not bad," he quickly followed the food with a big swig of coffee.

They ate in silence for a few minutes, then Seth put down his fork, abandoning his attempt at finishing the enchilada. "Thank you for being so honest, Henry. I really appreciate and admire that. I don't know that I could have put myself out there the way you just did. And I'm really glad you did."

Henry nodded and Seth went on, "And thank you for making me listen. You were right. I was erecting that wall as quickly as I possibly could."

"Why?" Henry's brows knit together.

"Because I care about you. I really, really care about you. And I was just trying to protect myself."

"Is that your usual M.O.?"

"No," Seth shook his head. "My usual M.O. has been work, friends, nothing serious."

"Have you ever been in love?"

"No. Not even remotely. Does that scare you?"

Henry shook his head, no.

"Maybe it should. Maybe I just don't have that gene or the capacity."

Laughing, "Oh, you definitely have that gene. I've seen you with Mia and her kids and you were filled with love. Maybe you just haven't met the right person. Or been ready."

Seth smirked, "Thanks for having that faith in me. Or for being totally delusional."

Grabbing the bill, Henry commented, "I feel like I just went twelve rounds."

When they got up from the table, Seth placed a hand on Henry's arm, stopping him. "Henry," was all he said, before wrapping his arms around the other man.

"How am I going to let you get on a plane?" Henry whispered gruffly in his ear.

Pulling his face away to look into his violet eyes, Seth shook his head, indicating he didn't know. Slowly, Henry ran his fore and middle finger down Seth's cheek and it was in that very moment that Seth Shapiro knew he'd better get his shit together because he would be miserable if he ever lost this man.

chapter twenty-three

H: WHY AM I HERE and you are there on Thanksgiving? We should have planned this better.

S: Honestly, it never occurred to me that it would suck so badly without you.

H: And?

S: It freaking sucks without you.

H: Yeah, it does. Tell everyone I say hello.

S: Call over there later. You'll get to talk to everyone. (And I'll get to hear your voice)

H: You'll get to hear my voice tonight regardless.

S: Not soon enough.

H: Happy Thanksgiving, Seth

S: Happy Thanksgiving, Henry

"BBC, it's time to baste the turkey," Seth reminded Mia.

Opening the oven, she pulled out the rack, "Wow, that is beautiful." She admired her turkey with a smile. "I am totally channeling my 'Inner Martha' today."

"Sweetheart, I am your 'Inner Martha'."

"Do I need to hide the neck for you before Schooner gets it?" Her grin was conspiratorial.

With a sigh, "No, let Pretty Boy have it. He deserves it."

"A kinder, gentler Seth? Who is this man?" she teased her best friend.

"Maybe," he agreed.

"Is this the influence of one Henry Clark?" she nudged him.

Shaking his head with a sigh, "I feel terrible not inviting him. I didn't even think about it, Mia. I'm so used to not having someone and then this day comes along and I feel," he paused, searching to articulate his feelings, "I feel like half of me is missing." Putting his hand to his chest, "It feels half empty."

"Wow. I didn't realize it had gotten this serious." She paused, and in a low voice, "Have you two become lovers?"

"Not physically. The most he and I have done is hugged one another."

"How about emotionally? It sounds to me like you are very emotionally involved. Is he?"

Inadvertently, he reached up and touched his cheek where Henry had run his two fingers, "Yeah, I mean, I don't even know how to describe us or where we're at. We're just trying to get to know each other. But with the specter of work conflict stuff, and being separated by 3,000 miles, and we know I'm not the best relationship guy in the world, it's a challenge."

Putting a hand on Seth's upper arm, Mia became very serious. "Do you miss him?"

"Every minute of every day."

"Then figure it out."

"So, I got the invitation to the joint L9/MS&A Christmas party at L9/NYC. Did you design the invite?"

Stretching out in bed and looking at the Manhattan skyline, "I did. Do you like it?"

"Loved it. Is the party mandatory?"

"Considering you are the Executive VP of Operations, I'd say yes."

"Excellent."

Seth could hear Henry's smile on the other end of the phone.

"They've got a block of hotel rooms at the James Hotel in SoHo. You, Lucas, and the managers from each of the facilities will come in. You'll get a call from a coordinator putting together all the travel and stuff."

"OK."

"So, how do you feel about staying through New Year's?" Seth asked, tentatively.

"Do I have a date?"

"Of course you have a date." Seth closed his eyes, imagining what it would feel like to have Henry next to him, to be seeing those violet eyes across a pillow, and running his fingers through his thick hair.

"Then I'll stay."

Seth didn't respond.

"You're awfully quiet," Henry filled in the pause.

"I'm just smiling. I'm glad we're spending the holidays together and that you'll be here with all of us."

"I miss you, Seth. I really miss you."

Smiling, "I like hearing you say that. I miss you too, Henry. A lot."

"I like hearing you say that."

"What if it's really horrible when I have to leave and come back to California?"

Seth laughed, "That would be a great thing." He stretched across the bed.

"A great thing? How so?" Henry was confused by Seth's

response.

"Because it will have meant that we did well when we were together. That we can be together and be happy."

"Is that a concern of yours?" Henry asked.

"Yes, doesn't it concern you?"

"No. Not at all. I know how I feel when I'm with you."

Smiling into the night, Seth savored Henry's confidence in them. Henry was so sure and Seth knew he needed to hear that, especially in moments when the obstacles seemed so ridiculously huge, that even trying, felt ill-fated. But Henry was there every day with confidence. Confidence in them. Confidence in him, that he could surrender himself to a relationship and allow himself to be vulnerable – and feel.

"I can't wait for you to get here." Seth snuggled around his phone.

Never in his life had he wanted someone to be there with him as much as he wanted Henry Clark by his side. He was still too afraid to get his hopes up about having him in his bed, and the vulnerability of intimacy beyond sex.

The L9 group arrived the day before the Christmas party, with the exception of Henry and Justin, the manager of the Studio City facility.

"I'm booked on a flight tomorrow morning, I'll be there late in the afternoon," he promised Seth.

"You're going to be exhausted."

"I already am."

"Ugh. I can't believe this happened. Are you going to have to fly back after the party?"

"I'm trying to get everything I can done today, so that I don't have to. But if I do, I promise I'll be back for New Year's."

A water-main break adjacent to the L9 facility took out a portion of the first floor of the L9/Studio City club, before they could stop the torrential flow. The day had been spent moving equipment and securing what they could, while the flood restoration people brought in the trucks to suck up the water and the large fans and dehumidifiers to start drying the place out.

"What can I do? Can I do anything?" Seth wanted to make things easier for Henry, relieve his stress.

"Just meet me with a Gin & Tonic at the party."

"I can do that."

Hanging up the phone, Seth walked into Mia's office, dramatically throwing himself down in the chair across her desk.

She just looked at him as if saying, "Ok, tell me…" without actually saying a word.

"He's flying in tomorrow. He'll be here for the party tomorrow night."

"OK, well, that's good."

Making a face, he sighed. "I guess so. Nothing else better happen. No delays. No flight cancellations."

Mia laughed, "Oh Princess, stop pouting. He'll be here. And think about it this way, when he sees you, you are going to look so hot he's going to want to rip that suit right off your tight little bod."

"Well, that's true. I will be looking spectacular. I'm doing Armani with a touch of Valentino."

"See? He won't be able to resist." Mia smiled, "So, you'll be strategically positioned at the top of the marble stairs, looking out over the first floor. He'll arrive and scan the room and then let his eyes drift up to find you."

"Oh, I like that. Keep going," he urged her on.

"Casually leaning on the railing at the top, you nod to him, drink in hand. But you make no move to go greet him."

"That's going to be hell holding myself back." Seth rolled his eyes.

"And with those long, lean legs of his, he bounds up the staircase, two at a time, to close every inch of distance between the two of you." Mia was getting into her own drama.

"Oh my God, BBC, you are giving me a hard-on." Seth adjusted himself.

Mia smiled devilishly, "He reaches the top of the stairs and slowly approaches, his eyes devouring you. It's been way too long."

"BBC, I think it's been way too long since you've had sex. Is Pretty Boy not meeting your horny forty-something year old needs?"

"Bite me," she laughed. "You know better than that."

"Ugh, I haven't had sex in so long. I hope I remember how."

Cocking her head, her eyes filled with emotion, "And when was the last time you made love?"

"I'm really scared, BBC."

The look in his eyes was one Mia had seen only a few times over their twenty-plus year friendship. Getting up, she walked around the desk and stood behind his chair, wrapping her arms around his neck and bending to kiss the top of his head.

"It's going to be great," she whispered into his dark curls.

Looking up at her, "Why does everyone feel the need to hug me?" he snarked.

"Because you're just lovable, Princess." And she hugged him even tighter.

Seth wasn't at the top of the stairs surveying his domain, like he was the king, when Henry arrived. Standing in the main rotunda under a domed ceiling painted with mythical frescoes, he was talking with a financial services company client of M. Silver & Associates as Henry Clark approached and stood next to him.

Holding a cold Gin & Tonic in his hands, Seth took a sip and handed it to Henry with a smile. "You made it."

"Finally." Henry took a sip of the drink, then extended his hand to the other man, "Henry Clark. I'm with L9."

Just looking at him, Seth could feel his blood race. In his black suit and white shirt, he cut a striking presence. His silk tie was a deep holiday crimson. But what was making Seth's heart melt, was the fine silk and cashmere Emporio Armani winter white scarf hanging open down his lapels. Few men could pull off the look and Henry Clark was showing them all how it was done.

L9 and MS&A had left presents in the hotel rooms of their employees. Crystal ornaments. Fine chocolates. Holiday CD's created just for their organizations. But in Henry's room, Seth had instructed the concierge to leave a special bag on the pillow, inside was the Armani scarf with a card that read, *To keep you warm, when I can't. —S*

Seth had hoped he'd wear it, but knew it might be too bold a look.

"This place is amazing?" Henry scanned the rotunda in awe. It was his first time in the L9/NYC facility.

"That's right, you haven't been here. You went straight to the wedding when you were here in September and then right back home."

"Can I borrow you to give me a quick tour?" They excused themselves from Seth's client. "One quick stop at the bar for another one of these." He held up the empty Gin & Tonic glass. "There isn't enough alcohol in this building after the last few days I've had."

Heading up the marble staircase, Seth steered Henry off to the right. "Let me show you Schooner's office." They passed through a reception area and Seth let them in, flipping the light on and closing the door behind them.

Turning to Henry, "I have never wanted a hug so badly."

With a smile that said everything Seth ever wanted to hear,

Henry came to him, enveloping him in his arms and holding him to his chest more tightly than he ever had before.

"Mmm," the sound emanated from deep in Henry's chest. "Don't make me let you go."

"Now, why would I do that?" Seth smiled into his shoulder.

"You can't imagine how much I have missed you."

Looking up at him, "I think I have a pretty good idea." Seth tried to drink in the color of his eyes, needing to commit it as a clear memory for the next time they were apart.

Taking two fingers and trailing them slowly down Seth's cheek, "Good."

Seth could see the exhaustion around Henry's eyes. "When was the last time you ate?"

He thought for a moment. "California."

"As much as I want to keep you to myself and not share you with anyone, starving you is probably not in my best interest." Taking him by the hand, they exited Schooner's office.

"I like the way your hand fits in mine." He smiled at Seth and neither one of them let go as they inserted themselves back into the party.

"Seth. Henry." Mia was waving at them from a table.

"Go have a seat and I'll get you some food," Seth offered and headed toward a carving station and buffet.

Henry and Mia were deep in conversation when he got back to the table.

"The insurance guys were there this afternoon and I met with the general contractor. It's going to take a full seven days to dry out. Obviously the loss of business, and inconvenience to members, is huge. Members all got an email and I was thinking maybe we should do a mailing or something with like a $5 gas card to drive to one of our other LA locations."

Mia looked at Seth, shaking her head. "I think you're rubbing off. He's becoming a marketing guy." Looking at Henry, "We can get on that immediately. We'll grab Yoli and Schooner before the end of the night and have them bless the budget."

"So, what's up for tomorrow?" Seth asked Mia, as he plucked a bacon-wrapped scallop off Henry's plate.

"We have all this kid's stuff. Both Nathaniel and Portia have holiday parties we need to bring them to, so I don't think we'll be able to do anything until at least the evening."

"Looks like we're on our own," Seth advised. "Brunch in Brooklyn?"

Henry laughed, giving Seth the smile of an inside joke, "I don't think you'll be taking me for enchiladas."

"Not likely."

Seth could tell Henry was losing steam as the night wore on. "You OK?"

He nodded and smiled at Seth, rubbing a hand across his upper back as he leaned in to whisper. "I think I've hit the point of beyond exhausted."

"Do you want to leave?"

"Yeah, but I don't want you to have to leave your colleagues and clients. I'm just going to head back to the hotel."

Seth nodded.

"Don't you give me those big brown, sad puppy dog eyes, Seth Shapiro." He continued to rub Seth's back. "I haven't had very much sleep in the last two days. I just need to pass out for seven to eight hours and I'll be ready for a great day tomorrow. I promise."

Putting his forehead against Henry's, "I know. Just having you here and seeing you leave." He didn't finish his sentence.

"I know. If I wasn't this exhausted," he paused, not finishing his sentence either. "Walk me out?"

A cab pulled up to drop someone off as they exited the building. "You're in luck."

But Seth wasn't feeling very lucky.

Standing next to the open cab door, Henry pulled Seth in for a crushing hug. "It's killing me, too," he whispered.

"I miss you already." Seth was too overwrought not to be brutally honest. As they separated, he lovingly smoothed out Henry's scarf.

"Are you zuzhing me?"

Laughing, "Yes, I'm zuzhing you."

Henry smiled, "I'm usually the zuzher."

"Well on this coast, I'm the zuzher."

Closing the door to the cab, Henry quickly lowered the window. Holding up the end of the scarf, "I really love this," and then mouthed the words "thank you," as the cab peeled away from the curb, leaving Seth wanting with all his heart, for the very first time.

chapter twenty-four

H: Getting in the cab. How long will it take? Is Brooklyn like a faraway planet?

S: LOL … you'll be here in 10 minutes

H: That's 9 NY minutes too long

S: ☺ See you in a few

Seth quickly looked around his brownstone duplex. It looked perfect to him, right down to the minutest of details, the artwork, the original ceiling medallions, the throw pillows and area rugs. And he knew that if it looked perfect to him, it was perfect. Stepping into the bathroom he artfully messed up his dark curls and smoothed down his pale grey V-neck cashmere sweater. As his fingertips noted the softness of the Scottish wool, he smiled at the thought that this would be what Henry felt when they hugged. He had literally rubbed a dozen cashmere sweaters across his cheek to see which was the softest, knowing Henry's face would be nestled in it.

Shaking his head he thought, *when do I ever do that for anyone?*

By the time the doorbell rang, his stomach was fully knotted with excitement.

Opening the heavy wood and glass door, a rush of cold winter's air blew in around him, but the warmth of Henry's smile, and his rested eyes, obscured the grey threatening skies.

"Come in, it's freezing." Seth ushered him into the front

hallway.

Henry's hands were full carrying a medium-sized corrugated box, its top flaps nestled into one another, but not sealed. He unzipped his overcoat and eased his arms out one at a time, transferring the box from one hand to the other, but not putting it down. Seth took his coat and hung it on a brass coat rack.

"This is amazing," Henry exclaimed. "This view." He walked through the living room and dining room with its modern, open kitchen to the glass French doors and windows lining the back of the brownstone. "You have an unobstructed harbor view of downtown Manhattan. This is like something out of *Architectural Digest*."

Seth came to stand next to him and take in the majesty of the New York City skyline, trying to see the view through a first-timer's eyes.

Elbowing Seth, Henry smiled at him, "My place must've seemed like a hovel to you."

Seth smiled, still looking at the view, "No. Not at all. It felt very comfortable. I loved being there." Decorating for Edwin's party was one of the happiest days he could remember. Just being with Henry in his home, and feeling the easy camaraderie they shared as they worked side-by-side to create a vision, was what had made it so special.

"What is that down there?" He pointed to a walkway.

"That is the famed Brooklyn Heights Promenade. We'll go take a walk on it later."

Turning back to face the living room, Henry scanned everything appreciatively from the wood parquet floors to the bay window off the living room in the front of the flat, to the exquisite molding on the twelve foot ceilings.

"This should be in *Architectural Digest*."

Seth laughed.

"Has it been?" Henry was wide-eyed.

"No. Not *Architectural Digest*."

"But it's been in magazines?"

"It has," Seth was trying to be humble, but it was hard. "Come sit." He touched Henry's upper arm, guiding him toward the couch. He needed him to put down that damn box so that he could get his hug. He had not gotten his hug yet and he needed to feel Henry's arms around him.

Sitting on the couch, Henry turned to face Seth. "So," he began, "I carried this on the plane with me, because I wanted to make sure it got to you safely."

Seth's eyes widened, "There's not a cat in that box, is there?" Visions of fur balls on his rugs was seriously disturbing.

Henry laughed, "No cat. But it is something you can kill."

There was alarm on Seth's face and Henry laughed even louder.

"This is my holiday gift to you and a house gift. And well it's just something I hope you'll love."

"You carried this box on a plane. I know I will love this."

Handing the box to Seth, Henry looked like he had stopped breathing.

Disengaging the flaps at the top, Seth pulled them open and peered in. Taking a deep breath, he looked up at Henry with an astonished smile, "Wow. What an amazing gift. That is so beautiful. Let me put the box down on the table so that I can get it out without damaging it."

Carefully he lifted it from its box and held it out in front of him, marveling at its delicate intricacy and beauty. "Did you…"

Henry was nodding. "Yes. I grew it. It's from a bush I have and I've been working on it for many years now."

"And you are giving it to me?" Seth's awe was evident.

Henry's eyes misted as he smiled. "You're the person it's meant for."

"I am honored." Seth continued to inspect it from all angles.

"How is it in bloom in December?"

Henry laughed, "That hasn't been an easy feat, but with my greenhouse and grow lights and, well, the right drugs, I played a little trickery on it."

"Promise me you'll teach me how to care for it."

"I will."

Looking up at Henry, "I love this. I don't think anyone has ever given me a more beautiful or thoughtful gift and knowing you created it… I just don't have words." Putting it down on the coffee table, he continued to closely inspect its intricacies. "The windswept shape is just magnificent and the gnarls in the bark."

Henry sat there silently, watching Seth's heartfelt reaction.

Looking up at Henry, "A bonsai lilac tree. It is so elegant. I really, really love it."

"It's going to look good in this space."

"Yes, it will," Seth agreed. Standing, he walked into the dining room and picked up a box lavishly wrapped in blue foil paper with blue and white ribbons. "Well, my holiday gift to you is not even in the same league, Mr. Clark."

"You gave me that beautiful gift I was wearing last night," Henry protested.

"Well, I have a little theme going here." He handed the box to Henry and sat down next to him.

Smiling, Henry ripped off the paper of the flat square box and opened it. "Oh, that is gorgeous. You really don't want me to get cold, do you?" Lifting the elegant, oversized blue and white silk and cashmere scarf from its box, he looked at Seth, lost. "How do you do one like this?"

"C'mere, give me that." Seth took the scarf from Henry and draped it so there was a solid ring around the front of his neck, with the ends falling chicly on the sides.

Henry stood up and walked over to a decorative mirror hanging on the wall. "I like that. I'm totally rocking a New York

City hot guy look now." He admired himself in the mirror.

Coming back to the couch, he sat down next to Seth. "I love it."

"And I really love the bonsai."

Henry's arms went around Seth, pulling him close and Seth laid his head in the soft scarf, taking in Henry's clean scent and the warmth of his arms.

"I'm so glad Schooner and Mia had plans today." Seth burrowed his face in a little more.

"Do we have plans today?"

"We do." He moved out of Henry's embrace, looking at his watch. "And we'd better get a move on it, so we don't miss our reservation."

Grabbing a coat, Seth expertly wrapped his own scarf around his neck in one quick motion that yielded perfection.

"I need to learn to do that." He mimicked the motion of Seth's expert scarf slinging. "I don't have a lot of practice living in San Diego."

Descending the brownstone's steps, Seth took a deep breath, "It smells like snow."

"You can smell snow?"

"I can. Most people can't, but to me, there is a distinct smell in the air right before it starts snowing." They turned left on the sidewalk and began to walk down Seth's street.

Bumping him with his shoulder, Henry looked like a kid stranded in a candy store. "I hope we get snowed in. I've never been in a snow storm."

"Never?" Seth was surprised.

Looking around at the brownstones lining the narrow street, "This looks like the movie, *Moonstruck*," Henry noted.

"This is the *Moonstruck* neighborhood. The external shots were done all over Brooklyn Heights and our two bordering neighborhoods, Cobble Hill and Carroll Gardens."

"I love that movie." Henry continued to take in everything, "How old are these brownstones?"

"They date back to the 1850's or so. Come, we're going to turn here," and Seth reached for Henry's hand as they crossed the street.

"This is Clark Street," Henry turned to Seth, his face beaming. "There's a street named for me."

"There sure is," Seth smiled.

"I love this neighborhood. I feel like I'm in Jack Finney's *Time and Again,*" observed Henry, his eyes darting left to right as he tried to take in the elegant row houses on both sides of the narrow street.

"That's one of my favorite books," Seth's eyes crinkled as he smiled, learning yet another small detail about this man who was making him feel things he never knew he had the capacity to feel.

They walked up Clark Street for another two blocks, "I just want to pop in here for a second." Seth led Henry into a small neighborhood grocer, grabbing a copy of the hefty Sunday New York Times.

Smiling at him, "I'm going to get the whole New York experience here, aren't I?"

Coming out of the store, they continued to the next corner. "OK, we turn here." Seth pointed left.

Looking at the street sign, Henry laughed. "This is Henry Street?"

"Not only is this Henry Street, but you are standing on the corner of Henry and Clark." Pulling out his cell phone, "Go stand in front of the street sign. You definitely need a picture of this."

"This is so wild," He posed under the sign.

"Come on, give me your best hot model look," Seth implored, before joining him in the picture for a selfie.

Looking back at the sign, Henry laughed as they continued down Henry Street. "Are we going someplace on Henry Street?"

"We are. Just a few more blocks."

"I think I belong here, Seth."

"Well, I definitely think you should spend considerably more time here. But that's just my opinion."

As they neared the end of the street, Henry pointed straight ahead, "What bridge is that? Is that the Brooklyn Bridge?"

"No, that one is the Manhattan Bridge. The Brooklyn Bridge is hiding behind these buildings. You can see it from my deck though."

So entranced by his surroundings, Henry hadn't realized that Seth had stopped walking until he was a few steps in front of him.

"We're here."

Turning back to Seth, he cocked his head to the side as he took in the neon script in the restaurant's window that read, *Henry's End.*

"Henry's End? We're eating at a place called Henry's End?"

Smiling as if he'd been holding onto the biggest secret, he nodded. "We are," and opened the door for Henry.

Entering the cozy brick-walled restaurant with its heady aroma of grilled meats and exotic spices, Henry turned back to Seth with a smile, "I love this."

"I thought you might." Seth was pleased seeing Henry's delight at the experience.

"I love the ambience and how warm and cozy it is in here and the way the windows are fogged up from the cold, and we're like in our own little cocoon. I didn't even realize how cold it was out there until we came in here."

Perusing the menu, "Want to share some small plates to start?" Seth asked.

"Sounds good." Henry's smile had not left his face since they'd walked out of Seth's apartment

When the waitress arrived, Seth ordered some house specialties. "And we'll take a bottle of the Silver Oak, Alexander Valley."

"That's becoming our thing, huh?"

"I like that we have things." Seth reached out for Henry's hand.

"Seth, we have more than things. We have something really special." Henry watched Seth's dark eyes widen, as if he were quickly searching for a place to hide. "Don't look so scared."

"I'm not scared." He gulped down a glass of water too quickly.

"Hey, pass me the business section." Henry pointed to the Times. Sitting back, he opened the paper, folding it properly to read the columns.

As they picked at plates of charcuterie and cheese, crab cakes and wild mushroom salad, Seth googled information on how to care for his new baby, his bonsai lilac tree. It was the second link he hit that caused him to sit up straight in his chair.

Sliding his phone across the table to Henry, "Were you aware of this?"

Picking up the phone to read what had caught Seth's attention, he looked up, locked eyes with him and nodded. "Yes," was all he said.

"Was that a part of it? A part of why you gave it to me as a gift?"

Sliding the phone back to Seth, Henry picked up his wine glass.

"It's why I thought it was perfect for you and wanted it to be yours, Seth," he paused. "I want to be your first love."

Seth began to speak and stopped, clearing his throat with a sip of wine to compose himself first. "I think you've already accomplished that."

"Yeah?" Henry's eyes were imploring.

"Yeah," Seth confirmed.

It was three hours and a second bottle of Silver Oak before they got up to leave the warmth of the restaurant and brave the cold.

"Look out the window." Henry was beaming. "You called it. It's snowing."

Wrapping his scarf around his neck perfectly, Henry was out of the restaurant and on the sidewalk, looking up and letting snowflakes fall on his face.

"This is just perfect," he said, as Seth stepped out of *Henry's End.* "C'mere," he pulled Seth to him by his scarf, which was hanging open around Seth's neck. With a swoop of his arm, Henry wrapped it around him perfectly.

"You just zuzhed me," Seth looked at him incredulously.

"Damn right I did. I can't be seen on the streets of Brooklyn with someone that's not zuzhed properly." Henry smiled, pulling Seth in closer by his scarf, "You do realize what just happened this afternoon?"

Seth looked at him, quizzically.

Henry went on, "You spent hours over brunch with your lover, hanging out and reading the New York Times."

"Ah, but you and I are not lovers," Seth protested.

"We're not lovers?" Henry shook his head, "You've got that all wrong." Reaching out, he let his fore and middle fingers slide slowly down Seth's cheek, as Seth melted into his touch. "We're not lovers, yet." And he allowed his hand to slide behind Seth's neck as he pulled him in for a long, soul-binding kiss, acquainting himself intimately with his new lover, and fully capturing the elusive dream he had thought would never be his again.

Pulling his lips away with a final soft kiss, Henry searched Seth's face, enjoying the myriad of wanting and emotion his dark eyes could no longer hide. Slowly, he slid his hand from Seth's neck down his arm, until they were hand-in-hand, fingers intertwined and smiled at him, "Now, let's go home."

Tokyo Tea at The Hole. The bartender thought someone was a hottie!

Sometimes you just need a sign.

T HANK YOU FOR TAKING THE time to read Henry's story.

For those of you new to my work, although HENRY'S END was written as a stand-alone novel, the characters of Henry Clark, Seth Shapiro, Schooner Moore, Mia Silver, CJ MacAllister, Holly Moore, Zac Moore, and Kami Townes first appear in SEARCHING FOR MOORE, the first book in the NEEDING MOORE SERIES trilogy. To learn more about the journeys of these other characters, please check out the series.

To those of you who have read the NEEDING MOORE SERIES and BAD SON RISING, I hope you enjoyed seeing old friends again and learning about different portions of their lives not previously visited.

acknowledgments

S PECIAL THANKS TO THE LAMBDA Archives of San Diego and their detailed recaps of significant events by year. It was truly fascinating to read the history of San Diego's LGBT community and its growth and growing pains, triumphs and losses. The information I was able to source, that became part of the fabric of this book, was truly a godsend.

A special shout-out to Auntie Helen's Fluff and Fold. The organization mentioned in this book that began in Gary Cheatham's garage is a real non-profit and is still in existence today.

Heartfelt thanks and love to …

Kristen and Cleida, thank you for your ongoing love and support, for sharing my work with so many people, for making me snort and laugh and cry, for joining me on the road and teasers and casting and sanity and insanity and helping me fling open the cage to unleash the flying monkeys and Fireball guzzling and for everything you do to make my life more wonderful every single day. Love you, BBCs!

Vi and Penelope, you are my rocks, my sounding boards, my reality check, my blurb queens. You'll tell me when the baby's ugly and I learn so much from the two of you daily. We've chosen a crazy path that makes an E ticket roller coaster ride seem like an emotional walk in the park, and I don't even want to imagine being on that roller coaster without the two of you. My sleep patterns might be slightly better though without joining in on the daybreak chats before I shop and roll back over. But so much good stuff is going on at that hour. Who knew?

Mindy, for always being there ... always ... and for being my first reader when the panic sets in (always) ... and I need you to read it NOW ... Someday I'll write our story (What are the statutes of limitations again... just kidding). Love you, Rosie!

OJG3, you're my Henry and that's why this book is for you. I learned very early on that love is love. Thank you for that. (And thank goodness we didn't have $19).

Mom... I don't have the words. But I don't need them. Because you know.

Mark and Max, thank you for learning to live with this and making it the new norm. I know it's not easy to live with someone who has other people living in their head. I hope it makes life more interesting.

And lastly, to Patricia Nell Warren ... thank you for writing "The Front Runner" (check out this book, people!) You paved the way. Decades later and that book is still in my soul. Highest compliment I can pay.

And to everyone who has had the courage to be themselves ... and to be proud ... no matter how different or unpopular it may have been ... this one is for you.

Till we meet again ...
~Julie A. Richman

A UTHOR JULIE A. RICHMAN IS a native New Yorker living deep in the heart of Texas. A creative writing major in college, reading and writing fiction has always been a passion. Julie began her corporate career in publishing in NYC and writing played a major role throughout her career as she created and wrote marketing, advertising, direct mail and fundraising materials for Fortune 500 corporations, advertising agencies and non-profit organizations. She is an award winning nature photographer plagued with insatiable wanderlust. Julie and her husband have one son and a white German Shepherd named Juneau.

Contact Julie

Twitter @JulieARichman
or
Website www.juliearichman.com
or
Facebook www.facebook.com/AuthorJulieARichman
or
Instagram: AuthorJulieARichman

My website has my signing schedule, links for signed paperbacks,

character profiles and more.
www.juliearichman.com

Join the mailing list to find out about upcoming releases and appearances.
http://eepurl.com/RYac1

Searching For Moore

I LOST THE LOVE OF my life when she disappeared without even a goodbye.

It was the 80's – there was no internet, no Google, no cell phones.

If you wanted to disappear, you could.

And she did.

She crushed my soul.

A friend just told me he saw her on Facebook.

And now I'm a keystroke away from asking her the question that's haunted me for two decades.

"Why did you leave me?"

Two decades after she broke his heart, sexy entrepreneur Schooner Moore uncovers the truth and betrayal his life has been built on when he Facebook friend requests college love, Mia Silver. Determined to win Mia's love once again, Schooner embarks on a life-altering journey that could cost him everything.

This is the first book of the Needing Moore Series trilogy and is not meant to be read as a stand-alone.

julie richman

Moore To Lose

CONTINUING THE FIGHT FOR THEIR happily ever after that began in Searching for Moore, Schooner Moore and Mia Silver struggle to overcome the ghosts and baggage they accumulated during their time apart.

Exploring the missing 24 years when they were separated, Moore to Lose follows Mia's journey from heartbroken teen to kickass businesswoman to her emotional reunion with Schooner and the exploration of the love that was ripped from them.

But is their love really strong enough to overcome the damage of those missing 24 years or will they continue to be ripped apart by pasts that can't be changed?

Moore Than Forever

"YOU HAVE NO IDEA OF what you do to me, Baby Girl."

"It's smoochal."

Is the love they always dreamed of enough?

Continuing the emotional journey of love and betrayal that began on a college campus in Searching for Moore and turned their worlds upside down in Moore to Lose, handsome, California entrepreneur Schooner Moore and sharp and sassy, New York advertising agency owner Mia Silver continue to be confronted with the harsh reality of the remnants from the lives they lived apart for 24 years.

Now, Schooner Moore and Mia Silver face the ultimate challenge — were they really meant to be together or will their pasts continue to tear them apart?

On the heels of the birth of their newborn son, Nathaniel, Schooner and Mia must decide if their love and loyalty to one another is strong enough to learn to grow together as a couple or if the life they always dreamed of sharing was better left as a teenage fantasy.

This is the third and final book in the Needing Moore Series and is not meant to be read as a stand alone. Book 1 — Searching for Moore and Book 2 — Moore to Lose should be read prior to reading Moore than Forever.

Needing Moore Series Box Set

ALL THREE BESTSELLING, TOP-RATED Books from The Needing Moore Series by USA Today Bestseller Julie A. Richman, **PLUS**never before seen **BONUS CHAPTERS** for each book.

"I have read well over 125 books since I received my kindle last February (2013). That being said, this first book in this series is the BEST book I have read. I am so sorry to say but it has to be said that E L James, Sylvia Day, etc. have nothing on Julie Richman."

"I loved this story. I could not put it down. Every girl wants a man like Schooner."

"Did I mention how insanely HOT these two are together? Scorching, fanning myself, hot!!"

"I think this is one of the best series out there, Hookers! It is an amazing story, it is full of emotion, and it is real. The relationships are complex and the characters are unpredictable. Julie will wring you out emotionally and leave you craving Moore!"

"I just finished this book and my heart is pounding! I too am a Facebook friend request away from a past love. This book has you hooked from the first pages! I cried, I laughed and I cheered! Such real characters and a love story that every girl dreams of having."

"OMG need "moore" Schooner now!!!!!! ... I cannot get

julie richman

enough of this story. Every once in a while a book or series comes out that has me salivating at every word and this fits that bill to the tee!"

"This is just writing at its best. It's so witty and the characters are so well written. I could not put this book down!"

"This series is awesome. It just sucks you in and doesn't let you go."

www.ingramcontent.com/pod-product-compliance
Lightning Source LLC
Chambersburg PA
CBHW070851250626
47159CB00003B/1021